Frozen Crimes

by

Chrys Fey

Disaster Crimes, Book 5

Frozen Crimes

Cover Art by *Kim Mendoza*

The Wild Rose Press, Inc.
PO Box 708
Adams Basin, NY 14410-0708
Visit us at www.thewildrosepress.com

Publishing History
First Crimson Rose Edition, 2020
Trade Paperback ISBN 978-1-5092-3291-8
Digital ISBN 978-1-5092-3292-5

Disaster Crimes, Book 5
Published in the United States of America

The crunch of the shovel pounding into the snow and ice filled his ears. It was all he could hear. The rest of the street was silent beneath its wintry blanket. Breathing was difficult with the icy air clogging his lungs. His nose burned. His throat was dry and on fire. But he ignored it, focusing on his task.

Crack, crack, crack.

He jabbed the shovel into a hunk of snow. On the third hit, it shattered into several pieces. He scooped them up and flung them to the side. He surveyed what remained. There was one big ball in the middle of the path that needed to be dealt with next. He moved over to it and struck it. That one impact had it severing in two. He was about to hit it again when something crashed into the back of his head.

Explosions of white light danced over his vision. Pain enveloped his skull. The shovel slipped from his fingers. Blackness cloaked his mind, coaxing him into its depths.

Beth. Her name was a whisper in his head, as if his thoughts were being sucked into a wormhole.

His legs collapsed under his weight.

Cold. It seeped into him, consuming him. And then his consciousness fled down that same void that ate his thoughts.

Praise for Chrys Fey

Get *THE CRIME BEFORE THE STORM*, Donovan's FREE short story and prequel to *HURRICANE CRIMES*, by signing up for Chrys Fey's newsletter: http://bit.ly/2UlZjU0

~*~

"*HURRICANE CRIMES* by Chrys Fey is a pure delight. It is a romance first and a suspense novella second, but both are combined in a perfect formula for a wonderful afternoon's reading."

~Readers' Favorite, silver award 2019

~*~

FLAMING CRIMES: "The natural disaster of wildfires is captured vividly while focusing on the aftermath and devastation caused by such catastrophe. The book is full of action, suspense, and adventure."

~InD'tale Magazine

~*~

WRITE WITH FEY: "A must-read book for those who are serious about writing but are clueless or doubtful of their writing capabilities."

~Readers' Favorite, bronze award 2019

Dedication

To the Space Coast Book Lovers attendees
and ALL readers of the Disaster Crimes series
who have been waiting for this book.
I hope you enjoy it!

And a huge thank you to Lori Graham,
my editor, for being in Beth and Donovan's
corner from the beginning.

Chapter One

Beth shuffled her feet as she entered the kitchen, on the prowl for a late-night snack. Her seven-month pregnant belly led the way, and the little one inside her was craving ice cream, in the middle of November, while Florida was in an unexpected cold snap. She took down the biggest bowl she could find from the cabinet, and then she tugged out the tub of Neapolitan ice cream from the freezer. She scooped out big hunks of the frozen dairy treat. From the pantry, she brought out rainbow sprinkles, a bag of gummy bears, and a jar of cherries. She shook sprinkles on the mounds of ice cream, added a handful of gummy bears, and squirted whipped cream in the shape of the infinity symbol. To the top, she added five cherries. Her cravings knew no limits.

She rubbed her belly through her shirt. "What do you think? Is this enough?" A little squirm made her smile. Taking that for an affirmative, she carried the bowl to the couch where she balanced it on her belly and watched TV. Sighing with pleasure, she scraped the bowl clean with her spoon, making sure to get every sprinkle.

Her cell phone chimed as she set the empty bowl on the coffee table. Seeing Donovan's face on the screen, her heart skipped a beat, and she accepted the video call. "Hey, Daddy."

Donovan grinned on the screen. A beard shadowed his face from one too many nights on the road for monster truck shows. His hair was several inches longer than normal, too. He looked just as sexy, though. More so even. He had been gone for a month, and she missed him a lot.

His violet eyes sparkled. "Hey, gorgeous. How are you?"

"Good. A moment ago, I consumed a giant bowl of ice cream. You're lucky you didn't call then. You would've been horrified by the scene."

Donovan chuckled. It was great to hear that sound. "Do you remember what we did with that ice cream sundae in San Francisco?"

Her cheeks warmed. That warmth spread throughout her body and between her legs. Boy, did she remember. They had drizzled melted ice cream, chocolate syrup, and whipped cream over each other's bodies and had licked, kissed, and sucked it off. "Why did you have to remind me? You know I'm one horny pregnant woman."

He grinned. "Yes, I recall. The night before I left was quite fun."

She shook her head. "You not being here has been complete torture. I'm deprived."

Donovan laughed again. "Baby, I'll be back home to take care of your needs soon. That's a promise. Speaking of…how's our urchin?"

"Quite content. He or she is drunk on dairy and sugar." They had decided to keep the sex of the baby a secret, so it'd be a surprise on January 15th, the baby's due date. They asked their doctor to keep the baby's gender on the down low and only tell them how the baby progressed developmentally. Their little urchin would come into this world shrouded in mystery, like a real Goldwyn, like his or her daddy.

Donovan smiled. Then he shook his head, and his smile faded. "I miss you. I miss touching your belly."

"I miss you, too." Her throat tightened as she looked down and lovingly rubbed her belly for him. "*We* miss you."

He took a deep breath. "I wish I was home."

"I wish you were home, too." She sighed. "How was your day?"

"We arrived in Atlanta yesterday. Tomorrow the two-day event starts."

"Have a blast for me."

"I will. I need to get some shut-eye, baby. I'm exhausted."

"Okay. I love you," she said. "Goodnight."

"Love you, too. Night."

Beth disconnected the video call with a heavy heart. She wanted Donovan home, so she could go up to their bedroom with him, let him pop the horny bubble inside her, and cuddle with him until she dozed off to sleep. Feeling lonelier than before the call, she shut off the TV and walked to the downstairs guest bedroom. Without Donovan, she hated sleeping in their big bed. And because of her belly, she tried not to go upstairs too often. She tripped once on the staircase shortly after Donovan left and that was enough to scare her.

In the guest bedroom, she settled in the twin-sized bed. She thought of Donovan sleeping in the cab of a truck, on a tiny bunk, in a rest stop or parking lot somewhere, and that made her even sadder.

She was drifting off to sleep when a soft tapping

noise on the window beside the bed had her eyelids snapping open. She lay still, listening. The noise couldn't have been from a tree branch or bush, because the fire from April had burned everything within a foot on that side of the house. But it could've been an insect flying into the glass, or some other critter. When the sound didn't return, she closed her eyes, dismissing what woke her.

She had begun to relax when the tapping returned. This time, though, she noticed something she hadn't noticed before...the tapping had a pattern, and the rhythm was "Shave and a Haircut, Two Bits." No insect could create that. Only a human.

Beth gripped the blanket as she held her breath. Someone was outside her window, lurking. Her thoughts ran rampant. Did someone want to break in and steal from her? Were teenagers taunting her for fun? Or was it more sinister? With the things she'd been through, including kidnapping and death threats, nothing was far-fetched. She couldn't stop herself from imagining the worst, although she thought she'd experienced the worse when she was kidnapped and bleeding from a gunshot wound after a tsunami. Now, lying alone in bed, she realized that wasn't true—she hadn't experienced the worse because she was still alive after those incidents, and now she was with child. Anything that happened to her would put their baby at risk.

The tapping resumed. There was no mistaking that rhythm. Unless it was a ghost playing tricks on her, someone was on the other side of her window.

She sat up, drew the comforter away, and set her feet on the floor. Inching down the length of the bed, she shifted away from the window. As far away from the window as she could get, she stood and backed toward the door. Standing in the doorway, she stared at the window. Blinds covered it.

As she crept into the hall, the tapping became knocking. She rotated and hurried down the hall, past the kitchen and dining room to the staircase. Knees shaking, she made her way up the stairs. In the bedroom she shared with Donovan, she went to the window in the east-facing wall. With the tip of her finger, she lowered the slant in the blinds and peeked out, but she couldn't see anything from that angle. At the north-facing window, she scanned the front yard. Still nothing.

She picked up the cordless phone from the nightstand and dialed 9-1-1.

"9-1-1, what's your emergency?'

"There's someone outside my house. Whoever it is keeps knocking on the downstairs bedroom window where I was sleeping. My husband is out of the state for business, and I'm seven months pregnant."

"An officer is being dispatched. Is there someplace upstairs you can hide until the officer arrives?"

"Yes, I'm upstairs now."

"Good. Stay there, and stay on the line. When the officer arrives on the scene, I'll let you know."

"Thank you."

She sat on the edge of the bed, with Donovan's baseball bat lying across her lap. Donovan kept the bat next to their bed for security. She'd never had to use it, never had the need to even move it from its place. With the weight of it on her thighs, she recalled how Donovan had snatched this same bat off the wall rack, where it had been stored, when someone had broken into their apartment years ago. No one had been found then. Ever since, that bat had a place upstairs within easy reach. Beth was skilled with a baseball bat, having played softball in high school, but never had she needed to wield a bat with a belly heavy with child. Or any sort of weapon for that matter.

Her grip was slippery with sweat. Pressing the phone between her ear and her shoulder, she got up and peeked out between the blinds. Silence buzzed in her ears. They picked up every creak and groan of the house. Each noise made her suspicious, jumpy. Her heart thundered in her chest.

Fear was natural. Even being a woman versed in self-defense, she wasn't immune to it. In her line of work, she knew what people were capable of with fists, feet, and more. And in her life, she had experienced more horror than most. Being pregnant and alone, the fear anyone would've felt at that moment was magnified for Beth.

"Ma'am."

Beth gasped and hopped away from the window. It took her a moment to realize the voice had come from the phone pressed to her ear.

"Yes?"

"The officer is searching your property now. He'll knock when he's through and tell you what he saw. I'll let you go now."

Beth whispered into the phone, "Thank you. Goodbye." She put the phone back on the receiver and scanned the front yard for evidence of the police officer. She spotted the beam of a flashlight waving back and forth over the lawn. Several minutes later, the officer cut across the lawn to the front door. A loud knock sounded. Beth made her way downstairs. After checking through the peephole, she opened the door.

"Ma'am, you called about someone sneaking around your property?"

"Yes, I did." She told him what happened, and he told her he didn't see anyone.

"If you suspect the person comes back, call us right away."

"I will. Thank you for checking."

"Take care."

She nodded, and then she bolted and locked the door. She debated whether or not to call Thorn. Their good friend was also a detective, but if she told Thorn, he would pass the news on to Donovan, who'd want to end his tour and rush back home against her wishes and the wishes of his entire team. She couldn't allow that.

Before going back upstairs, she rechecked all the doors and windows and made sure the security system was armed. In her bedroom, she forced herself to lay down on the bed.

Beside her, the bat rested on Donovan's pillow, and her fingers curled around the handle. The handheld phone was also on the pillow. Hours went by as Beth struggled to fall asleep.

Eventually, exhaustion pulled her into a fitful sleep.

****

Morning came too quickly. Yawning, Beth went downstairs to the kitchen, craving caffeine. Luckily, her doctor had said one cup of coffee a day wouldn't hurt the baby, and she really needed one today. Her phone chimed with a video call alert as she stirred sugar into the milk-lightened drink. Despite her night, she summoned a warm smile.

She tapped the green icon. "Hey."

"Hey, beautiful." Donovan's smile vanished when he got a good look at her. "You look tired."

She sighed. The story of what happened last night was on the tip of her tongue, but she held it back. For all she knew, no one had been there. The knocking could've come from a nocturnal animal—a silly raccoon searching for food and warmth.

That's when she thought of the security cameras hidden among the eaves that could provide confirmation. Until she knew her suspicions were true, she'd keep Donovan in the dark, to prevent him from panicking.

She shrugged. "I had a bad night's sleep."

"Was it the baby?"

She nodded. "Our little urchin was having a dance party last night." She pointed the camera toward her belly. "You have to see this thing. It's a monument of its own."

Donovan's laughter helped to banish some of her stress from the night. "That baby is a monument of our love." His face altered, becoming serious. "I hate that I'm not there for this."

"You're not missing much. All my belly has done is grow another inch."

His gaze lowered. "Still, I want to be there for this, for it all."

Her heart wrenched. She wanted him home, too. And not just because of her scare last night, but for the same reasons he wanted to be home. It was a miracle she was pregnant, and she may never be pregnant again.

This could be a once-in-a-lifetime experience for them, and he was miles from home. Throughout her pregnancy, he had to go on the road for weeks at a time. It sucked, but it was his job, his passion.

"I know." She longed to slip her fingers through her cell phone, to touch him. "This home is amazing, but it's too big for me by myself, even if my belly grows another foot." She smiled when Donovan smiled. "What do you have on the schedule for today?"

"Stunts, racing, and then tomorrow, a fan day."

A surge of hope rushed through Beth. He'd be home soon! But then she remembered he wasn't due back home for another week. As if reading her mind, he added, "Meetings with sponsors and the team after that to discuss next year."

Next year. Those two words hit her in the gut. Next year would be full of competitions, shows, and travelling nationally and internationally, if the opportunity was granted to him, as it usually was. In the beginning of their relationship, she had joined him on the road to experience his career up close. It was exciting. She had even gone with him to Japan for a competition where he had a ton of fans. Now, she won't be able to tag along. Not pregnant or with a child in tow. The excitement of his job wasn't meant for her anymore.

"We'll be waiting for you." She knew that was exactly what she'd be doing from now on…waiting for him.

"I love you," he said.

She tried to hide the disappointment inside. "I love you, too."

Feeling so lonely, knowing she'd have days and

weeks in the future of being just as lonely, she ended the video call. She laid her hand on her belly. "Your daddy will be home in a week. Then he'll be all ours." She paused. "Until the next competition."

Thinking about that, she reheated her coffee and drank it at the table. Donovan loved monster truck driving, and she would support that forever, even if it meant being left behind sometimes, because she wouldn't be left behind forever. In the meantime, she had eight days before Donovan returned. She had to be sure she was safe—her and their baby.

After eating a banana muffin, she viewed the security footage from last night. None of the angles provided anything, though. Not so much as a glimpse of an intruder tiptoeing around—only the cop searching the property and darkness. Lots of darkness. Not even the glowing eyes of a critter showed. For all she knew, someone could've known exactly where the cameras were in order to avoid getting caught.

That thought chilled her to the bone. She glanced over her shoulder at the kitchen window. Was the culprit of her fear still out there?

Chapter Two

Donovan stood next to Venom—his monster truck. Other trucks were on display for fans to gawk at and to pose in front of for pictures. He liked to use this time to meet the fans. Currently, he was posed next to his truck with a family of seven while a kind stranger took their picture with a cell phone. The picture taker handed the phone back. The family thanked him and circled his truck to see it from all sides.

"Mom, Dad, look!" A little boy ran up to his truck. Hopping up and down, he pointed at the cobra poised to strike on the neon green paint. "Look. Look. It's Venom!"

Donovan grinned at the boy's enthusiasm. The boy was about half the size of the tire in front of him. He climbed inside the giant tire and stood with his hands touching the top of the tire's inner rim. "It's so big!" The boy squealed with delight.

"Nathan, get out of there." A woman hurried over and extracted her son from the inside of the tire.

"It's okay," Donovan said. "He couldn't hurt it." He smiled and held out his hand to the child's parents. "I'm Donovan, the driver." When he looked down at little Nathan, the boy stared up at him with wide eyes and an unhinged jaw. In that instant, Donovan felt more like a superhero than a monster truck driver. It was funny how a child's admiration could make you feel a thousand feet tall.

"You're his favorite driver," his mother said.

Donovan squatted in front of the boy. "Hi, Nathan."

The boy's cheeks brightened. "Hi," he whispered.

"You like monster trucks?"

Nathan nodded.

"I liked them when I was your age, too. Maybe one day you'll drive one."

"I hope not," his mom said.

Donovan smiled.

"Moooom," Nathan sang out in utter embarrassment.

"Would you like to sit in the driver's seat?" he asked the boy.

Nathan's smile split his face. "Really?"

"If your parents say it's okay." Together, they peered up at the boy's mom expectantly.

The woman glanced at her husband, who nodded. She sighed, and then laughed. "He'd love that. Thank you."

Nathan jumped up and down with glee. "Yes!"

Donovan opened the driver's door and picked up Nathan, so he could clamber into the seat. He looked so tiny sitting where Donovan usually sat. With his hands wrapped around the steering wheel, he perched on the edge of the seat. His feet dangled in the air. He made engine noises with his mouth and swung his legs back and forth. He moved the wheel from side to side as much as it would allow him. Then he examined the dash with all its switches, knobs, and gauges. His eyes were lit with the wonder all children—boys and girls alike—experienced when they saw such a massive vehicle and could explore it. It was as thrilling as going inside a firetruck, which Donovan had loved to do as a child.

"All right, Nathan. Come on," his mom said. "Other kids want to have a turn, too."

Donovan peeked past them to see two other kids eager to sit in the driver's seat. He picked up Nathan and set him on the ground.

"What do you say, Nathan?" his dad prompted.

"Thank you!" Nathan held up his balled fist.

Donovan bumped the little boy's fist with his own. "You're welcome, Nathan. I hope you enjoy the show."

Pretty soon, Donovan had a line of kids waiting for their chance. He enjoyed watching them pretend to drive his truck. He couldn't help but imagine his own child doing what these kids were doing. The thought filled him with joy. His son or daughter would sit on his lap, holding the steering wheel with his help, and he would drive the truck around his personal track. Beth would be in the passenger's seat. They'd look at each other and smile as their child's giggles fluttered around them. He wouldn't do any tricks until his son or daughter was at least eight years old, but boy, he couldn't wait for the day when he could show his child what he loved to do.

His longing for Beth intensified at that moment. He swallowed to push it down and regretted being gone for so long. When he chose this for his career, he had been single and thought he'd always be single, except for a few girls here and there, of course. Before Beth, he hadn't wanted a wife or children. After her, he had wanted it all. His career had been his passion, but now life with Beth was his passion, and his job was taking him away from that. He didn't know what to do. On one hand, he wished he didn't have to leave the life he wanted, but on the other hand, he had built his career over many years. It supported his family, which was always his top priority.

That night, Donovan took his place behind the wheel. If Beth were there, she would've taken his wedding ring and slipped it onto a chain around her neck. Since she wasn't, he tucked the ring into his front pocket. Then he tugged on the straps of his harness, something Beth usually did.

He drove onto the arena to the rumble of engines and the roar of the crowd. Six old school buses were lined up behind a ramp, the ramp Donovan drove toward. He pushed down on the gas pedal, accelerating. The truck zoomed up the ramp. At the top, the shocks sprang as the truck lifted into the air. The feel of the truck rising up and up and up filled him with the rush he always got from performing stunts. Through the windshield, he saw the yellow school buses, the stands packed with people, and above that, a black sky speckled with stars. That moment before the truck dropped seemed to suspend time, as if he could be up there forever, if only gravity didn't want him. But it did. Gravity pulled on the truck, and it lowered.

The buses came back into view. Two still needed to be cleared. If the truck came down too soon, he'd crash into the buses. Wrecking was an understatement. He could flip the truck. There could be an explosion. The engine could eject into his seat. There were too many possibilities for injury and death.

The truck sailed over one of the buses, but as it did so, it fell even more. He tried to gauge if he'd make contact with the last school bus. The back tires could touch the roof. Gripping the steering wheel, he eyed the final school bus. The truck inched over it. The tires cleared, but the rest of the truck wouldn't. He braced for the rear bumper to clip the bus's roof.

But he didn't feel a thing. Not even a tap.

The tires slammed into the ground.

Relief filled him when he realized he must've passed the bus with inches to spare.

Cheers erupted from the stands.

He performed wheelies in front of the stands that sent mud flying toward the fans. The cheers grew louder. Once, Donovan had lived for the applause. Although it was still great, other things were better, like what waited for him at home.

Donovan finished the show by running over a couple of cars and doing a race against four other trucks, which he won. Crossing the finish line, he hoped Nathan had seen it. He imagined the boy on his father's shoulders, whooping with his fists in the air. Donovan lived for this, for giving people excitement. Being viewed as a hero by a child was a gift. One he'd never take for granted.

After the show, the truck was loaded up for the night, and Donovan laid out on the bed in the cab of the semi-truck. He called Beth for a video chat before he hit the sack. She answered quickly. Her hair was knotted into a messy bun, and she had an eye mask high up on her forehead. He chuckled. "What are you doing?"

"Leighton's here. We're having a girl's night. We have ice cream, *Breakfast at Tiffany's*, and a lot of nail polish, which was Leighton's idea."

"I guess I'm glad I'm not there."

"You're lucky." She leaned in to whisper, "I kinda wish I wasn't here. How was your day?"

"Good. I made the day for about a dozen kids."

Beth grinned. "I bet. You're so good with kids."

In the background Donovan heard Leighton shout, "Beth, the male strippers are here!"

Beth's smile didn't falter. "I gotta go, honey. We have guests."

"All right. There's a bunch of ones in the safe."

His answer made her laugh. "Call me in the morning."

"I always do. Have a fun night. Don't go crazy."

"With this belly, there's only so much crazy I can do. Goodnight."

"Night, baby."

She kissed her fingertips and pressed them to the screen of her cell phone. Then the screen went black as the video call ended.

Donovan set down his phone. These nightly video chats, like the morning ones, had sustained him throughout his trip, but they weren't enough anymore. He laid back and put his arms behind his head. He had seven more days to go.

Seven was such a big little number.

Chapter Three

Beth padded to the living room where Leighton sat cross-legged on the couch, wearing a pink silk nightgown with a bowl of popcorn on her lap. In one hand, she held the remote to the DVD player. Beth hadn't wanted to be home by herself tonight. She couldn't ask Amanda to spend the night because the poor woman was still dealing with her own demons and a real fear her ex-boyfriend would find her and harm her. Corissa, Beth's receptionist at The Fighting Chance, was working on her psychology thesis. By asking Leighton, Beth got roped into a list of girly activities that would normally make her cringe and scream, but being pregnant, cringing and screaming wasn't a very good thing to do around other people. Not to mention the fact that she had lost the will power to argue out of pure desperation to not be alone. Being pregnant was seriously messing with her hormones.

"Did you have to mention male strippers?"

Leighton grinned. "Yes, yes, I did." She patted the cushion beside her. "So, how is your fine specimen of a husband?"

Beth sat down and tossed a throw pillow at Leighton. "Stop calling him that."

"You have a sexy husband, girl. Own it. If he were my husband—"

"Okay. You're restricted from seeing him until

further notice."

Leighton laughed. "Party pooper."

Beth couldn't help but laugh, too. "Pass the popcorn, crazy."

Leighton handed her the bowl. "That's okay. Thorn is a sexy beast, too."

"Thorn is taken," Beth said.

"What?" Leighton's plump lips pouted. "When did that happen?"

"Well…it hasn't officially. Yet." Beth frowned as she thought of how to phrase this. "Thorn is head over heels for Amanda. He's been…I guess you could say…courting her."

Thorn was committed to taking it slow, for Amanda's sake. He didn't know how much she had been hurt, but there were a lot of wounds there—visible and hidden. Thorn was a fierce protector, and Amanda was the woman who had unknowingly captured his heart.

"That. Is. So. Adorable." Leighton shook her head. "Damn. I missed out. Twice."

Beth grabbed a handful of popcorn. "All right. Let's start the movie."

They watched *Breakfast at Tiffany's* and gorged on ice cream and popcorn, which Beth decided to put all into one bowl. Then Leighton painted Beth's fingernails the brightest shade of pink Beth had ever seen. Apparently, Leighton hoped the pink would influence the baby's gender.

"You do realize the baby already has all of its parts, right?" Beth asked.

Leighton recapped the nail polish. "Haven't you ever heard of the power of persuasion?"

"I don't think that's what that means."

"Whatever. This polish"—She waved the bottle in the air—"is my way of hoping the Big Man Upstairs will sway things in Auntie Leighton's favor."

"I don't think He cares so much about what Auntie Leighton wants."

"If He was a mortal man, He would." She winked.

Beth shook her head. "That's so wrong."

Leighton popped to her feet. "I'm going to get some more wine. Is there anything you'd like? Milk? Ginger Ale?"

"No, thanks. I'm good."

Leighton's fuzzy slippers made little scratchy sounds on the tile as she walked to the kitchen. Beth examined her fingernails. The pink was *very* pink. It made her wonder if their baby was indeed a girl. Or if it was a boy.

Since they were waiting to find out the sex of the baby, they were going to pick a boy and a girl name, but they hadn't been able to agree. Donovan liked Dante for a boy, and she liked Ethan. For a girl, Donovan liked Sabrina, after the hurricane that brought them together. Beth objected, considering how devastating that storm had been. Personally, she liked the name Emma. She suspected they'd end up playing rock, paper, scissors once the baby was born, and the winner would get to put the name he or she wanted as the first name on the birth certificate, while the other would get the middle name. That would be their style.

A clatter sounded from the kitchen, and Leighton hurried into the living room. "Beth, Beth, there's someone outside."

Beth's insides froze. "What?" Although she had

been afraid, she hadn't believed the person, if it was a person, would come back to taunt her. And not so soon. "Did you see him?"

"Him? No. There's a car in your driveway. The lights are flashing."

Frowning, Beth pushed to her feet. Surely Leighton was mistaken. Someone could be having car trouble and put on their flashers. Or maybe it was her neighbor and their car's blinker was on as they backed out of the driveway.

As she approached the kitchen, she saw the glares coming through the window, filling the room with yellowish flashes. She slowed her steps instinctively. Her hand flattened onto her belly, like a shield. She stopped behind the wall and inched closer so she wouldn't be seen.

"Beth, be careful," Leighton whispered.

Keeping her belly safe behind the wall, Beth peeked past the corner. All she could see was the flashing lights dominating the window space. Needing to be sure the lights were malicious, she made her way to the kitchen window.

"Beth, don't."

She shifted to the side and peered out the window. A dark-colored car was parked in her driveway. The inside of the car was pitch-black, and the front headlights came on and off. She studied the flashes, seeing if there was a pattern—like SOS—but there wasn't. As soon as the lights went off, they came back on again. It was a deliberate act. Someone was sitting in that car, flashing those lights into her home.

Mouth dry, heart pounding, she backed away. "Leighton, go upstairs and call Thorn from the landline."

"No way," Leighton said. "I'm not leaving you."

"I can't move as fast as you."

"Then I'll move slower than you." She took Beth's hand and pulled her to the staircase. "You first. I'll catch you if you fall."

"If I fall, I'll squash you."

Beth did her best to hustle up the stairs. In her bedroom, she pointed to the landline. "Call Thorn. Keep the light off." She went to the window. Using the tip of her finger, she lowered a blind at eyelevel. The car was still there. The lights switched on, off, on, off. Squinting, she tried to see inside the car, catch a glimpse of the driver, but she couldn't see the figure's outline, the color of clothing, or the sheen of light on skin. Nothing. It was as if the driver was a ghost.

If the driver got out of the car, what would he do?

"Thorn, thank God! It's Leighton. I'm at Beth's house. No, no, she's fine, but there's a car in the driveway. It keeps flashing its lights into the windows. Yeah, hold on." She scurried to the window. "He wants to talk to you." She held out the phone to Beth.

Beth took it. She kept the blind lowered with her other hand. "Thorn."

"Beth, what's going on?"

She spoke softly, as if the driver could hear her. "Yesterday, someone was outside my house, knocking on my window where I was sleeping in the guest bedroom. I called the cops, but they didn't find anyone. And none of the cameras caught a glimpse, but I know someone was there."

"I believe you. What is the car doing now?"

"It's just sitting there, flashing its lights."

"Whatever you do, stay in the house."

"You don't have to worry about me." Now that she was pregnant, she was a lot more cautious. Even being versed in self-defense, she would never risk her child's life by venturing outside to lay into a creepy intruder. "But Leighton may go out to throw her fuzzy slippers at the windshield."

On the other line, Thorn breathed hard. A bang reverberated through the ear piece.

"What are you doing?" she asked.

"I'm coming. What the hell do you think I'm doing?"

Another bang sounded. "Well, don't knock down your house."

"Why are you making jokes? I think I'd rather talk to Leighton. She's at least having an appropriate reaction to this."

"I'm pregnant, Thorn. My hormones are wonky. Be glad I'm not hysterical."

Thorn grumbled something under his breath that she couldn't make out.

During their exchange, she hadn't looked away from the car. Leighton huddled beside her, almost sheltering behind Beth, the one large with child.

Light gleamed off the car when the driver's door opened.

Leighton gasped and clutched Beth's shoulder.

"Thorn, the driver's door opened," Beth whispered.

"Fuck." Another bang sounded. Thorn's breathing quickened. The next bang Beth made out to be his car door slamming shut. "I'm coming. Did anyone get out of the car?"

"Not yet, but the door is wide open." She wondered

what was taking the driver so long to get out of the car. Then again, it was a good thing he wasn't getting out so fast. The longer it took, the more time Thorn had to get there. If the culprit did get out of the car, she didn't know what he'd do to her house...to her...to Leighton.

"Do you have somewhere to hide? When Donovan was having the house built, did he have a panic room installed?"

"No."

"You guys had Jackson's men after you, and he didn't think a panic room would be useful? What the hell was he thinking?"

"I don't know, but he probably didn't think we'd have bad guys to hide from our entire lives."

"And how's that working out for you?" A horn blared in her ear. "Get the hell out of the way!" His yell made Beth flinch; he hadn't lowered the phone when he shouted.

She kept her eye on the car and the space below the door for any sign of a shoe stepping out onto the driveway. Suddenly, the car's headlights flashed off and stayed off. Darkness enveloped the car. Beth straightened, not liking this change. "Thorn, the lights turned off. The door is still open, but I can't see anything around the car."

"Five minutes."

Her mouth went dry. "Five minutes might be too late."

"Beth..." Leighton tugged on her arm. Fear radiated off her friend.

"Here." She passed the phone to Leighton. "Talk to Thorn."

Leighton took the phone from her, and Beth

stepped away from the window, heading toward the bedroom door.

"Where are you going?" Leighton called after her. "No, not you, Thorn. I meant Beth. I mean she's leaving the room. I don't know. What do you want me to do? Tackle a pregnant woman?"

Beth paused at the door. "I'm not going to engage the man, but I have to do something. I'll be right back."

She padded down the stairs, gripping the railing with her hands. On the ground level, she made her way to the front door. Her heart tripped in her chest with a fresh dose of fear. The man in the car could be anywhere outside her house. With soft footsteps, she tiptoed up to the door. For all she knew, the intruder could be on the other side of it. She angled her belly to the side, so it was positioned behind the wall instead of the door. People tended to shoot through doors, and she'd rather take a bullet than her baby.

Carefully, she laid her ear against the door, searching for the sound of someone on the welcome mat. Her hand elevated toward the panel on the wall. The alarm was already set, but that panel operated many things. She pushed a button. From inside her house, there was no indication that anything had happened. She backed away from the door and hurried to the staircase. In her bedroom, she joined Leighton at the window.

"Girl, you're funny," Leighton said.

Sneaking a look through the blinds, Beth watched the sprinklers as they shot water in all directions. Even at the black car. The driver's side door was shut now.

"Did anyone come out?" she asked.

"I don't know, but the door shut as soon as the

sprinklers came on."

Beth took the phone from her. "I'm back," she told Thorn.

"Next time, stay upstairs." Thorn ground the words out between clenched teeth. "I'm coming up on your neighborhood."

As if the driver knew he was about to get caught, the car's lights activated, and it started to reverse down the driveway.

"The car is leaving."

"Damn it."

With a squeal of tires, the car was gone.

A moment later, Thorn's car came from the opposite end of the street and blazed into the driveway. "I'm going to make sure he didn't leave anything. Can you turn off the sprinklers?"

"Sure."

With Leighton by her side, Beth descended the stairs and went to the front door where she deactivated the sprinklers. A few minutes went by as she suspected Thorn checked the guest bedroom window and the porch.

"Beth." Thorn's voice came from the phone still pressed to her ear. "You can open the front door now."

She opened it to a soaking wet Thorn. Water coursed down his face, dripped from his hair, and plastered his shirt to his body. Apparently, Beth hadn't been fast enough.

"Hello, ladies."

Leighton nudged Beth with her elbow. "Good girl."

Beth found one of Donovan's T-shirts and a pair of jeans for Thorn to put on. Luckily, the two men had similar builds. "Here. You can change in our

25

bathroom." She gave him the clothes along with a towel. "I'll keep Leighton away."

Thorn's shoulders lowered. "Thank you," he whispered, and she knew he wasn't thanking her for the clothes or the towel.

After Thorn changed, he put his wet clothes in the dryer. Then he met Beth and Leighton in the living room. "Thanks for coming," Beth said.

"I'm doing my job."

She tilted her head, wondering if he referred to his law enforcement job or the job Donovan had left him with before he went on the road. She rubbed her stomach.

"Are you okay? You're not going into early labor, are you?"

She chuckled at his panicked concern. "No. Rubbing the belly is a pregnant woman's habit. I'm fine."

"Good." Thorn let out a breath. "Do you have a sleeping bag?"

She frowned. "Sure. Why?"

"You didn't think I'd be leaving the two of you after all that, did you?"

"Yeah," Leighton said. "You didn't think he'd leave us after all that?" She leaned in to whisper in Beth's ear, "Do you have a sleeping bag for two?"

Beth glared at her before addressing Thorn. "You'll have to get it for me. It's on a top shelf in the garage." She showed him where it was. With the sleeping bag tucked under his arm, he followed her back inside. "You know, you don't really need a sleeping bag. You could sleep on the couch or in the guest bedroom."

"No, I'm good with this. Why don't the two of you go upstairs, try to get some sleep? I'll be down here. If anyone tries to get in, he'll come face to face with me."

"Okay. Night, Thorn." Beth shooed Leighton upstairs and into her bedroom.

Leighton dropped heavily onto the bed. "I don't think I'll be able to sleep tonight."

"I know what you mean. I'll be thinking about that person all night."

"No, I mean because a fine man will be sleeping downstairs. So close, and yet so far."

Beth rolled her eyes.

****

In the morning, they left her bedroom and stopped at the sight they saw. Thorn was sound asleep in the sleeping bag at the foot of the stairs. On the floor next to him, Beth spotted his holstered weapon. He had stayed there all night.

"He's like a faithful, protective dog," Leighton whispered.

Beth made her way down the stairs. When Leighton tiptoed by to start the coffee, Beth lowered onto one of the steps. "Thorn," she whispered. "Thorn, wake up."

Thorn sat bolt upright. "What? What's happening?" He glanced left and right before peering at Beth with groggy eyes.

"Nothing. It's morning." She felt bad for Thorn. Sleeping on the floor, on high-alert all night, couldn't be comfortable or restful. "Would you like coffee? I've also got bacon."

Thorn perked up at that. "Bacon and coffee are the perfect cures for a long night's stakeout." He peered at

27

his surroundings. "Or, more precisely, a stake-in."

In the kitchen, Leighton helped Beth fry bacon, scramble eggs, and butter toast. She also kept topping off Thorn's coffee. When Donovan's video call alert popped up on her cell phone, she held the phone close to her chest, but she didn't answer it. "No mention of what happened last night from either of you."

"You're not going to tell him?" Thorn said. "Haven't you learned anything?"

"It'll worry him, and he'll be home in seven days anyway." She pointed at them. "Not a word." With a final glare of warning, she switched her facial expression for a smile and answered the video call. "Hey, handsome." Seeing his face always brightened her day.

"Hey, did you sleep better last night?"

Beth didn't so much as glance at Thorn or Leighton or else Donovan would notice and guess something was up. "Yup. Like a baby."

Leighton snorted.

Beth kicked her in the shin.

"Ow!"

On her phone's screen, Donovan's brows furrowed. "What was that?"

"Oh, Leighton singed her tongue on her coffee. She's fine." At her words, she sensed Leighton's glare. Wanting privacy, Beth got up from her chair and walked into the living room. "How are you doing?"

"Good. Anxious to be home. I can't shake the feeling that I'm needed."

She smiled at that. "You are needed. You'll always be needed."

"When's your next check-up?"

"Three days."

Donovan winced, and she knew it was because he wouldn't make it in time.

"I'll show you the ultrasound images as soon as I get them," Beth said to placate his disappointment and watched him nod.

"Thanks," he said. "I should go. I have a lot of miles to clock."

"Drive carefully."

His smile brought out the dimples on either side of his mouth. "Don't I always?"

"No."

He chuckled. "Well, I'm coming back home to you, so I'll be careful."

"I love you."

"I love you, too. Tell our little urchin I love him or her, too."

"I do every day."

His eyes dimmed; he wanted to be the one to do that himself. "Bye."

She blew him a kiss before ending the video call. Back in the kitchen, Thorn and Leighton eyed her over their cups of coffee. "What?" she asked them.

"Do us a favor and leave us out of your deception," Thorn said. "I promised Donovan I'd tell him everything that had to do with your safety. If...*when* he finds out about this, he'll want to beat the shit out of me. And if he tries, that's assaulting an officer. Just remember that. In the meantime, what do you plan to do? Staying here at night might not be safe."

Beth shrugged. "I could sleep over at Leighton's every night until Donovan gets back."

Leighton's face paled. "What if this sicko follows

her to my house?"

"He won't," Thorn promised, "because I'll be in my car, keeping an eye on your place. Every night."

Beth swallowed. She felt awful for putting them in this mess.

Chapter Four

Three days later, Donovan pulled his truck into the driveway, behind Beth's car, and stared up at their two-story home. As soon as the fan day ended, he and his team had taken turns behind the wheel so he could get home faster. After being gone for a little over a month, their home was a sight for sore eyes. He turned off the engine, grabbed his duffel bag, and climbed out of his truck. His heart pounded with excitement as he slipped the keys into the locks and opened the door. Once inside, he peered toward the kitchen. It was empty.

No longer able to contain his happiness, he called out her name. He made his way to the staircase, eyeing the second floor. When Beth stepped out of their bedroom, his breath left him. Damn, she was gorgeous. And, damn, was her belly big.

She put her hand to her chest. "Oh my God. Donovan. What are you doing here?"

He dropped the duffle bag to the floor and took the stairs two steps at a time. In a flash, he was in front of her. He put his arms around her, tucking her close to his body. Having her in his arms again felt amazing. He regretted the next time he'd have to hit the road, after the New Year, and then Monster Jam World Finals in Orlando would be in May. He'd be busy for a long time, and they'd have a four-month-old baby by then. What would he be missing during that time? How much bigger would his son or daughter get? Would he or she even remember him when he came back from his trips? His throat tightened. But he didn't want to think about any of that right now, not when Beth was finally in his arms. He leaned back, framed her face with his hands, and kissed her in the way he had imagined kissing her all those days and nights he'd been away.

Beth clutched his shoulders. Her belly dug into him, but he didn't mind. Not one damned bit. A soft moan slipped from her mouth. She shifted forward, knocking him back a step and disconnecting their kiss.

"I'm sorry," she said, reaching for him again and taking his arms. "I was trying to get closer, but this belly is too big." She looked down at it, drawing Donovan's attention to her stomach, too.

He lowered to his knees and placed his hands on either side of her pregnant belly. "Hey there, little one. Do you remember me?" He hoped so. Whenever he had the time, he would ask Beth to hold her phone's speaker close to her belly, so he could talk to their baby, but over the phone and in person were two different things. "I missed you. And I missed your mommy." He gazed up at her, and she smiled.

A thump on either side of Beth's belly connected with his hands and had him peering back at her belly. "Whoa. Do you think this kid can perform splits like you can, but in utero? Because I felt a kick over here"—He massaged his fingers in the spot on the left of her belly—"and over here." He did the same on the right.

Beth laughed. "One of them was probably an elbow. I'm telling you, this kid likes to dance, and I'm beginning to think The Funky Chicken is his or her favorite dance number."

While watching her belly in awe, he hummed the tune for The Funky Chicken, causing Beth to laugh louder. He laughed along with her when the baby really did seem to dance beneath his hands. And this was the stuff he had been missing.

Beth put her hand on his shoulder. "Enough play time with the baby." She glanced at her belly. "Sorry, kiddo, but now it's Mommy's time to play with Daddy."

Her gaze on him steamed with lust, and she curled her fingers around the collar of his jacket to draw him to his feet. He rose and captured her lips with his. The heat intensified tenfold. If she weren't pregnant, he'd lower her to the ground right there and take her, but considering she was with child, he wouldn't be that aggressive. So, he bent his legs and lifted her into his arms.

"You're going to break your back doing that."

"That's nonsense." He chuckled while carrying her to their bedroom. "You're not that heavy."

"Uh-huh. I've seen the scale at the doctor's office."

In the bedroom, he set her on her feet. With his gaze on hers, his hands slipped beneath her shirt, seeking the band to her maternity skinny jeans. He worked the band down over her belly. Then he knelt at her feet and pulled the jeans down her hips. She put a hand on his shoulder as she stepped out of the legs one at a time. Underneath, she wore bump bikini underwear, but he didn't remove those yet. Instead, he backed her up to the bed, where she lowered onto the edge.

On his knees, he lifted her shirt above her head,

revealing her belly. His hands moved to her smooth skin, caressing her and following the curve of her belly. While staring into her eyes, he removed her lace maternity bra. He cupped her full breasts with his hands and rubbed his thumbs gently over her nipples. Then he bent his head to take one of them into his mouth.

Beth arched her back and let out a moan. He moved his tongue over the taut point. Beth's hands touched his face. Her fingers trailed down his stubble-covered cheeks. At his neck, her fingers interlocked. His name came out on a sigh.

He lavished kisses over one breast before moving on to the next, giving it the same attention. He finished with a trail of kisses down her middle, over her bump, and to the band of her panties. On his feet, he stared down at Beth. He was sure he exuded hunger as he removed his boots, without so much as looking away from her. As he did that, Beth scooted back across the bed, all the way to the pillows. She didn't tear her gaze from him, either.

He stripped down and made his way to her. On the bed, they lay on their sides, facing each other. After Donovan peeled away her underwear, he put one of his legs between hers and the other on top of hers. He entered her without breaking eye contact. They made love in the way Donovan had been dreaming about since he had left. Having her pregnant belly between them made it that much more intimate. He watched her closely as he varied the speed and depth, being sure not to cause her any discomfort. She gripped his shoulders and gyrated her hips. Sounds of pleasure escaped her. Her fingernails bit into his skin when she came. To the tune of her ecstasy, he released himself.

Lying in bed beside her, with his arms around her, was heavenly. He drifted off to sleep, more content than he had been while on the road. Sometime later, he woke up to Beth combing his hair with her fingers.

"I'm sorry," he said and rubbed his eyes. "I didn't mean to fall asleep."

"It's okay. I've been enjoying this." She brushed his hair from his forehead. "It's really nice to have you back. Speaking of, how are you here right now?"

"I didn't want to be away from you any longer, so my team and I drove straight here. Only stopping to change drivers, use the restroom, and get food. And I postponed the meeting to talk to management and my team for Friday."

"I'm glad you did, but you're exhausted. You don't have to come to my appointment."

"No, I want to." He lifted onto one elbow. "I missed too much already. When is it?"

"Two hours."

"I'll be there."

Two hours later, Beth lay on the examination table, with a sheet over her legs and her shirt lifted over her belly. Donovan stood next to her, holding her hand and leaning close to her with his arm above her head.

Doctor Kerry moved the ultrasound wand across her belly, slipping it through the warm gel on her skin. "Everything looks good, perfect, in fact."

He showed them images of their baby's face. Seeing the tiny nose and mouth amazed Donovan. Would the baby look like him or Beth? Or would the baby have a perfect blend of both of them? It was hard to tell whose features the baby had inherited, and Donovan couldn't wait to see their baby in the real world.

The doctor showed them the baby's hands, which were raised, and the baby's right foot, which appeared as though the baby was tapping it up and down to a beat.

"I told you." Beth smiled. "The Funky Chicken."

Chapter Five

That night, Donovan picked up Beth's duffle bag from where she had left it on the floor of their bedroom that morning. "What's this?"

She had meant to put that away before Donovan saw it. "Oh, I spent the night at Leighton's house last night." In fact, she had spent the last couple of nights there, returning home each morning. "I didn't like staying here at night by myself."

Donovan's brows drew together. He sat on the bed next to her and took her hand. "I'm sorry."

She shook her head. "It wasn't your fault...something happened while you were gone."

Concern stole Donovan's face. "Something with the baby?"

"No, no. Nothing like that." She squeezed his hand, took a deep breath, and told him everything. She ended with, "I know we promised not to keep anything from each other anymore, especially something that could be dangerous, but your job and the happiness it brings you is important to me. I didn't want to do anything to jeopardize it. I knew you'd be coming home soon, so I thought waiting to tell you until you were home would be better than causing you to panic when you were miles away."

Donovan nodded. "I understand why you didn't tell me."

Beth blinked. That wasn't the reaction she had expected. She thought he would've been enraged to find out she had kept something this important from him.

"You're right that I would've panicked, but you bring me more happiness than my job. You and our baby. I wouldn't ever want anything to happen to you." He paused. "But someone was trying to scare you while I was away, and that does not sit well with me."

"Me, neither, but you're back now, and whoever it is may not have the guts to come back and try that again."

"They better not."

Donovan's oath rang in her thoughts again and again during the night. She could count on Donovan to keep her and their baby safe, but she didn't want him to have to do that anymore. Day-to-day protect, sure. But not the sort of stuff they'd contended with since they met. She had hoped they were beyond that. She needed for them to beyond that, and she prayed that whoever had been outside their house two nights in a row had gotten their kicks out of terrifying a pregnant woman and wouldn't do it again.

Having Donovan across from her at the kitchen table the next morning made her smile. "It is so good to have you here in person and not on a small cell phone screen."

"Tell me about it." He reached out and took her hand. His thumb rubbed over her knuckles. "I lived for our video calls, but every time they were over, it became that much more evident you weren't close."

"I felt that, too."

They fell silent as they ate breakfast and drank

coffee. Except, this morning, Beth had opted for herbal tea. The smell of Donovan's coffee tempted her cravings, though.

"What do you plan to do today?" Beth asked.

"Sleep."

Beth pouted in sympathy. "You need it."

"Do you have plans for the day?"

"Yeah, I was going to go to The Fighting Chance. I may not be able to kick ass in my present condition, but I like to check in. Mostly I do office work, but I can stay here with you."

"No, you go. I'll try to catch up on some sleep, and if you're still at The Fighting Chance later, I'll pop in for a visit. It'll be nice to see everyone again."

"They'd like that. See you later." She kissed him before leaving.

At The Fighting Chance, Beth found Corissa and Amanda prepping for the day. "Hey, Mama Bear," Corissa said.

Beth smiled. "Hey."

"You know you don't have to come here every day. Amanda and I have this under control."

"I know, but I like to get out of the house." Her studio was her second home. When she felt lonely at the house without Donovan, The Fighting Chance gave her solace, a place to be with people she considered family.

She did what she could to help them prepare for the first class. During the lesson, she stood back, offering words of encouragement. Every once in a while, she stepped onto the mat to assist them with their poses and correct their maneuvers. Even though she couldn't bust out the boxing gloves and kick ass, that didn't mean she was useless. Far from it. She hated how people coddled pregnant women. She may be pregnant, but she wasn't breakable. Except, she did tire out faster than normal.

Behind the receptionist's desk, she took a load off her hurting feet. She double-checked the books and made a few calls to check in on students who hadn't been to a lesson in several days. Luckily, they were all okay. In the past, that wasn't always the case. Since then, she made it a point to make calls if a student went missing. As their instructor, it was her duty.

Shortly after lunch, Thorn arrived.

"Hey, didn't Donovan tell you? He came home yesterday. You don't have to check up on me anymore."

"What are you talking about?" Thorn feigned innocence. "I like to come here." He shifted toward the class taking place, the one Amanda was teaching.

Beth looked, too. "Uh-huh. I know why you like to come here." She smirked. "You're not just checking up on me, but on Amanda, too."

Thorn slipped his hands into his pockets and lifted a shoulder. "What can I say? I take my job seriously."

She tilted her head at him. He was in love. This was what a man did when he was utterly, hopelessly in love, regardless of his profession. Maybe he didn't realize that yet. Or he did, and he wasn't ready to admit his feelings. She wondered if he had ever been in love before. By the petrified look on his face, she doubted it. This was new to him, and a guy treating her good was new to Amanda. They were venturing into uncharted territory.

"Well, she appreciates you coming here every day, too. Even if she is too shy to say it."

Thorn stared at his feet. "I'm taking it slow. I'm trying to be her friend right now."

"I know you are. And she needs that."

The bell behind Thorn jingled. He turned, and Beth peered around him to see a delivery man holding a crystal vase. It held two dozen red roses. "Hi there, I have a delivery for Beth Goldwyn."

"That's me." Beth scribbled a messy signature with the tip of her finger on his tablet.

"Have a good day," the delivery man said.

"You, too." Beth positioned the vase to the far side of the counter beside the wall.

"Donovan makes every man in the world look bad," Thorn said.

She checked the card and smiled. It read, "To the love of my life."

"Yes, he does," she mused and leaned in to give the roses a nice, long sniff. They smelled divine. "I think I'm going to go home and thank him."

"Ew." Thorn scrunched up his face.

She retrieved her purse. "This class is almost over if you want to stick around for a bit." Her wink told him he'd have a few moments with Amanda. Grinning, she went to her car parked behind The Fighting Chance. Donovan had come home mere hours ago and had already done something sweet. Now, she wanted to spend time with her husband, who she shouldn't have left after not being near him for weeks.

In the front seat of her car, she slipped the key in the ignition and twisted it. Nothing happened. She tried again, but the radio didn't even turn on. Groaning, she leaned her head back against the head rest. Her cars never gave her a break.

She dug the phone out of her purse to call Donovan.

He answered on the fourth ring with a groggy, "Hello?"

"Did I wake you? I'm sorry."

Donovan mumbled. A rummaging sound met her ears. "I overslept."

"You're exhausted. It's understandable. Look, my car isn't starting, but don't worry. Thorn is here. I'll have him look at it, and I'll text you what he finds."

"Okay. Love you."

"Love you, too."

She hung up and went back inside. Thorn stood on one side of the counter, and Amanda stood on the other. The counter acted like a barrier, keeping them safely apart, where they were comfortable—close but not too close. Beth hated to disrupt their conversation. Seeing the two of them exchanging words without her or Donovan nearby meant they were making tremendous progress.

"Hey."

They turned.

"I thought you were leaving," Thorn said.

"So did I, but my car says otherwise. It won't start. Can you take a look at it?"

"Sure." He followed her to the back parking lot.

"Sorry for interrupting," she whispered.

"That's okay. I can't leave a pregnant woman stranded, now can I?"

"I'm not exactly stranded. It's not as though I'm on the side of the road somewhere."

He popped the hood of her car and fiddled around with things she couldn't identify. "Give it a try."

She wrenched the key, but the engine didn't crank.

"I'll bring my car around and give yours a jump. Stay put."

Where else would she go? She waited by her car for him to return. The cold snap from last week was gone without a trace. The November sun warmed her skin, and a breeze blew down the alley, tossing the scent of hot asphalt at her.

Footsteps drew her around. "Thorn, I thought you were…" She went silent when she saw the alley empty. "…bringing the car." Frowning, she peered back and forth. No one was there.

Must've been the wind, she thought as another gust came and sent crumpled newspaper rolling on the ground.

Thorn's car came around the corner. He parked it beside hers and hooked up jumper cables to their batteries. "Okay, try it now."

She twisted the key. The engine made a cranking sound and turned over. "Yes!"

Thorn disconnected everything and lowered the hood. He came over to open her car door. "I'll drive you home, or else you really will be a pregnant woman stranded on the side of the road. I can call a service to bring me back here to get my car."

"If you're sure. Do you want to say goodbye to Amanda?"

Thorn checked his watch. "The class has already begun. I'll tell her goodbye later."

Driving her home was all a ruse so he'd have to get his car later, giving him a reason to see Amanda one more time today. Beth smiled.

He let out a sigh. "What?"

"Nothing."

"Good. Keep it that way."

Thorn drove her home. After saying a quick "hi" to Donovan, he left to get his own car.

Beth sat next to Donovan on the couch and put her arms around him. Coming home to him felt wonderful. Every day he had been gone, she missed him more and more. Having him home now showed her precisely how much she had yearned for him to come back. Next time he had to leave, she'd have a hard time letting him go. Was that what the roses were for? A gift for his return? An apology for being gone?

"Thanks for the roses. They are beautiful."

"What roses?"

She shifted back to see his frown. "The roses you had delivered to my job today."

He shook his head. "I didn't send you roses."

Chapter Six

Donovan had no clue who sent the roses to Beth. Or why. Either way, he didn't like it. The only one who should be sending roses to his wife and calling her the love of his life was him. End of story. Whoever did it had done something he hadn't thought of doing himself.

"Your mystery sender is making me look bad," he said while driving Beth's car to his mechanic's shop.

"What are you talking about?" Beth sat in the passenger's seat, with the shoulder strap to her seatbelt behind her because her belly was so big.

"I should've sent you the roses."

"No. You came home. That's better than roses."

At a red light, he reached over to touch her belly. "Pretty soon, you're not going to be able to drive."

Beth groan. "Don't say that." She peered down at her belly. "I don't want to get any bigger. I'm huge as it is. But, on the plus side, you'd have to drive me everywhere. It'll be like old times." She grinned.

When they first got together, Donovan had to drive Beth to and from work because her car had been out of commission, and he had enjoyed it. Seeing Beth after hours of working out in sports bras and workout pants had been the highlight of his day. Now, he simply craved more time with her before their baby came, and, of course, he wanted all the time he could get with their baby once he or she was born.

While Scotty, Donovan's mechanic—the one man he trusted to work on his vehicles other than himself—checked out Beth's car for issues, they stayed in the waiting room. Beth picked up a magazine from a table. She lowered onto the chair beside him. "Wow. He's hot," she said as she examined the cover.

Donovan groaned. "I don't want to know."

"Are you sure?" She batted her lashes and grinned. "You could fulfill some of my wildest fantasies."

He cut a glare toward her. "You have wild fantasies?"

Beth inhaled between her teeth. "With this man, I do." She turned the magazine around to show him the man on the cover. He didn't want to look, but he had to see who his competition was for his wife's deepest desires. What he did not expect was to see her holding a truck magazine. He was the one on the cover, in his fire suit, with his helmet under his arm, standing next to Venom.

"I forgot they had interviewed me."

Beth lowered the magazine after taking another look at the cover. She cast a look at him. "You are one sexy man, Donovan Goldwyn."

He winked. That's all he had to do to have her blushing.

They waited together for an hour. While he watched the news on the flat screen TV hanging on the wall, Beth read his interview and flipped through the magazine. Then Scotty came into the waiting room with a rag stained with motor oil draped over his shoulder. Donovan stood and helped Beth to her feet.

Beth held up the magazine. "Do you mind if I take this?" she asked Scotty.

"Nope. Feel free. Well, I've got good news. It was a spark plug. I replaced it, and now your car is good to go."

"You didn't find anything…strange?" Beth's voice was low, so no one else could hear.

Scotty glanced at Donovan, who peered at Beth. She stroked her belly with her hand, but it was her face that gave him pause. Her features were pulled into tight lines. Her lips were flat. That question sparked his memory from months before, when Scotty had found a snake head painted on the underside of Venom's hood. It had been Viper's calling card, his way of letting them know he was out, he was close, and he was coming. For Beth. But Viper was gone…dead. He couldn't come after Beth again.

"No, I didn't find anything weird," Scotty said.

Beth's shoulders lowered. Would she forever suspect car complications to be the fault of criminals out to get them? If so, they may need to consider replacing her older car for a new one, although there was no guarantee that a new car wouldn't have issues. Car problems were inevitable.

"Oh, but I did find this stuffed between the driver's side door and the car seat."

A single sentence had Donovan's spine snapping straight. What could it be? A package with a dead snake coiled inside it? A message scrawled in blood? Both of those scare tactics had been employed before to frighten Beth.

Scotty pulled out a strip of fabric from the right pocket of his stained coveralls. "I didn't know you wore ties, Goldwyn." Scotty grinned in a way that only a long-time friend could do to make fun of you.

Except, there was a problem…

"I don't wear ties." Donovan took the fabric from Scotty. It was a burnt orange with horizontal lines of autumn colors. If he did wear ties, it wouldn't be this one. In fact, he owned two ties—the one he wore to Ryan's funeral and the one he wore on their wedding day.

"Oh," Scotty said. "Well…"

Donovan noticed him glance at Beth.

"I better get back to work." Scotty wheeled around and whistled discreetly as he went.

Donovan swore inside when he realized Scotty assumed Beth was having an affair and that's how the tie had wound up in her car.

"Maybe it's Thorn's," he said to Beth. "He drove you home yesterday. He could've dropped it."

She shook her head. "He doesn't wear ties."

"We'll ask him anyway." Maybe he had to wear a tie for work that day and had stuffed it into his pocket the first chance he could remove it. Donovan wanted to believe that, because any other explanation for how a man's tie got into Beth's car wouldn't be an answer he'd like. He didn't believe, not for a second, that Beth was unfaithful. She didn't have that quality in her. Although he had been gone for a month, and several times since they've gotten together, he knew without a shadow of a doubt Beth loved him and would never have an affair. But how exactly did that tie get in her car?

At home, Beth video-called Thorn. She sat in a chair at their kitchen table, and Donovan leaned over her shoulder.

Thorn's face popped up on the screen when he

answered the call. "Hey, Goldwyns," he said. "What can I do for the two of you?"

Beth held up the tie. "Is this yours?"

Thorn scrunched up his face. "That thing is ugly."

Donovan snorted.

"No, it's not mine. If you haven't noticed, I'm not the tie-wearing type. I have the tie for my formal officer's uniform and the one I was forced to wear to your wedding."

"Aw. You kept it?" Beth asked.

Thorn rolled his eyes. "Yes, I kept it. I figured it might make a good tie to wear on a date."

"And have you...worn it on a date?" Beth's question hinted at Thorn's obvious infatuation with Amanda, her sweet, vulnerable assistant.

"Not yet," Thorn said. "One day, though. Hopefully." He shrugged. "Anyway, why did you want to know if that butt-ugly tie is mine?"

Beth considered it. "It's not that ugly. I like fall colors."

Donovan shifted into view. "Scotty found it in Beth's car between the driver's side door and the seat. I thought you might've had it in your pocket and it could've fallen out when you drove the car home yesterday."

Thorn shook his head. "It's not mine." His eyelids fell to slits. "What are you thinking?"

And that was why Thorn was a detective. He could sense what wasn't being said.

"Just wondering where it could've come from."

"Uh-huh."

They fell silent.

Beth studied Donovan from over her shoulder.

Then she peered back at Thorn. "Okay. You two are going to make me paranoid. It's a used car. Whoever had owned it before me could've lost their favorite tie."

The problem with that theory was Donovan had detailed the car from top to bottom after Beth had bought it. He had polished the interior, waxed the exterior, vacuumed and shampooed the rugs and upholstery, and he had even moved the seats as far back as he could to get every last crumb. During the cleaning, he had found a couple of old crumpled up receipts and several pennies, but that was it. He most certainly would've found a tie, especially since Scotty was so easily able to find it. However that tie had gotten there, it had happened recently. But he didn't want to voice that.

"That's a possibility," he said.

"Good. Now that that's settled, I'm going to take a nap," Beth said.

"Sweet dreams." Smiling, Thorn ended the call.

Beth got up. She still had the magazine from the mechanic's shop.

"What do you plan to do with that?" The last thing he needed was for her to show it to Leighton and the women at The Fighting Chance.

"You mentioned our baby during the interview, so it's going in the baby book." She paused to look at the tie, lying limply in his hand. "And what are you going to do with *that*? Maybe we can dry clean it and give it to Thorn for Christmas. He obviously loves it."

Donovan smirked. "I'll throw it away."

"Okay." She kissed him on the cheek. "Wake me up in a couple of hours."

"I will. Have a good nap." He faced the trashcan,

pushed the level down with his foot to open the lid, and held the tie over the opening, but he didn't let it go. After a moment, he glanced over his shoulder to make sure Beth wasn't around. When he didn't see her, he lifted his foot, closing the trash bin's lid. He carried the tie over to the pantry where he pulled a large zippered plastic bag from a box. He opened it, slipped the tie inside, and zipped it closed. Holding it behind his back, he crept up the stairs and went to their office. He hid the plastic bag beneath a Manila folder in the filing cabinet.

No, he did not know where the tie came from. He didn't even know if there was a reasonable explanation for it or not, but he did know there may come a time when they could need it as proof.

Chapter Seven

Beth lowered onto the bed for her nap. Before she could stretch out and get comfortable, her phone dinged with a text message.

See you tonight.

Beth frowned. She didn't recognize the number. It wasn't programmed into her phone, and she didn't have any plans tonight other than to relax on the couch with Donovan and binge watch episodes of their favorite TV show. She had sworn to him she wouldn't watch a single episode while he was away, and she had kept that promise.

She fired off a quick text in reply. *Sorry. Wrong number.* Then she put her phone on silent so it wouldn't disturb her again.

The next morning, a new text came in. *Last night was amazing.*

Her finger sped across the screen of her phone as she tapped out a response in all caps. *WRONG NUMBER!!!*

Seconds later, a reply popped up. *Right number.*

Beth frowned. *Who is this?!*

The little balloon with the three dots in it appeared, indicating the person was typing in the messenger. After a moment, the balloon disappeared, and a new text took its place. *I'm the man of your dreams.*

Beth shivered in disgust. *Ew. What a creep.*

She sent a final text, hoping to shut him down. *I know who the man of my dreams is. I'm MARRIED to him!* Once she sent that text, she blocked the number from further contact.

Jeez, some men are real pigs, she thought. Social media made it that much easier for men to target women. They send inappropriate messages that usually started with "Hey gorgeous," "Hey beautiful," or even "Hey honey" to strange women, and all in the hopes of getting laid. The messages could get quite lewd, too. What made these men think they could do that? Would they want strange men to send the women in their lives messages like that?

Later that evening, she got another text. This time, from another number.

Send me a pic I can look at in bed.

Why did men think it was a good idea to request sexy pictures from women? She was tempted to send him a picture of her middle finger. Instead, she blocked that number, too. That didn't stop other creepy texts from coming in, though.

A third number sent, *I love you.*

Those three words, from an unknown man, gave her the chills.

This time, she replied. *Who the hell is this?*

Without pause, the texter replied back with, *I know you love me, too.*

If you don't leave me alone, I'm going to report all of these numbers. She didn't know if it was the same person or not, but she was fed up.

The bubble indicating the person on the other end was typing something appeared. Heart pounding, she closed the text, went to the number's info, and blocked it.

She carried her phone to the living room where Donovan sat on the couch, with his feet on the coffee table, working on his laptop. "I think I might need to change my phone number. I keep getting creepy text messages."

Donovan looked up from the computer screen. "What do you mean?"

She set her phone down on the coffee table and joined him on the couch. "Like the kind of messages men send to women on social media when they want to hook up. I've blocked three numbers since yesterday. I think my number got out somehow."

Donovan's brows drew together. "Let me see."

"No." She pushed her phone farther from him. If he were to read those texts, he'd fume. Understandably, considering she was his pregnant wife, but still...she didn't want him to blow this out of proportion. "The last person who texted, I shut down. I told him I'd report all the numbers, so I shouldn't hear back again, but if my number got on some list for sicko men to contact, we should change my number."

"Okay. We can do that later today."

Her phone dinged.

They eyed it.

Donovan dropped his feet to the floor and snatched up her phone. He entered her passcode and opened up her text message. She leaned close to see.

"That's a different number." She pointed. "Those are the other three numbers that have texted me since yesterday."

He activated the recent text, pulling it up so it filled the screen. "I want you," he read.

She swallowed uneasily. "That's sick."

Donovan tapped on the keys, writing out a response.

"What are you going to say?"

He didn't respond. His jaw was set with aggravation. He jabbed the send button, and then he held it up for her to read. *This is her husband. Why don't you tell me what you want to do with my wife?*

"And that's how you shut down a sick perv," Donovan said.

She had to give it to him. That worked; she didn't get another text that night.

****

In the morning, Beth found Donovan in the bathroom with his shaving kit. She leaned against the doorjamb. "Hey, you going to shave?"

Donovan examined his face in the mirror and ran a hand down his cheeks and neck. "Yeah. I think it's time. Plus, with the baby shower tomorrow, I should look presentable."

"Mm." She scanned him from head to toe. He wore faded jeans and a white tank top with a few tiny holes in it. The term "ruggedly handsome" came to mind. "You look quite presentable to me right now."

The corner of his lips lifted.

She went to him. Reaching up, she ran her hands through his long, brown locks. "But keep this," she said. "I'm liking this longer hair on you."

"Oh, yeah?" He put his arms around her and slid her over so she stood in front of him.

She gazed up into his eyes. "Oh, yeah."

Grinning, he leaned down to kiss her. When he took her mouth, she looped her arms around his neck.

55

He kissed her as if he hadn't lost an ounce of passion for her, as if he didn't care she was huge with pregnancy. For that, she was grateful. She'd heard stories of how husbands and boyfriends often didn't want to be intimate with their pregnant partners, no longer seeing their wife or girlfriend as a sexual being, or…worse yet…desirable. The fact Donovan didn't shy away from her but seemed as turned on as ever relieved her.

She was dizzy with his love and attention when he pulled back. "Oh, yeah," she repeated. Only, this time, her voice was deeper.

Donovan chuckled. "Okay, I guess I'll leave the hair."

"You better."

She left the bathroom to let Donovan do his thing. In the kitchen, she steeped a cup of tea and dug out chocolate chip cookies from a plastic package. A knock at the door interrupted her mid-morning snack. Nibbling a cookie, she walked to the door. Thorn stood on the other side. She opened the door for him. "Welcome, would you like a cookie?"

Thorn squinted his eyes. "This baby is making you loopy."

She laughed out loud. "It's called being happy, Thorn. I know…strange concept with the state of this world, but it still exists."

"Uh-huh." Thorn followed her into the kitchen. "But…um…I would like a cookie."

Smiling, she held out the cookies. He took one.

They were eating cookies when Donovan entered the kitchen, clean-shaven, with his hair brushing his neck and framing his face. He still wore the faded jeans and beaten-up tank. She lifted a brow as her core liquified with lust. "Mommy like."

Donovan's eyes sparkled with equal passion.

"Oh, come on," Thorn grumbled and covered his ears with his hands. "I don't need to hear this."

"What's wrong, Thorn? You used to flirt with my wife all the time."

"Yeah, but that was before she became a mom."

Beth glared. "That's offensive."

"That's not what I meant." Thorn lifted his hands in defense. "It's just…okay, I'm going to insert my foot into my mouth now before I get into further trouble."

"That would be wise," Donovan said.

"Uh-huh," Beth agreed, still scowling at Thorn. Thankfully, Donovan didn't share his sentiments. Then again, she didn't have the same relationship with Donovan as she did with Thorn. With Thorn, she was a best friend, sometimes sisterly. With Donovan, she was his lover, his equal partner, his everything. And he was that for her.

"I'm assuming I'm here for a reason other than to eat cookies and get into trouble."

Beth dusted off the cookie crumbles from her hands. "You are, my friend." She picked up her phone and went to the text messages. "I've gotten a bunch of weird text messages, all from different numbers."

Thorn studied each text a few times over. "Could be the same person using a burner phone. The tone reads the same. Grammar, too. He could be swapping out sim cards to change the number."

"Would you be able to trace the numbers?"

Thorn made a wincing face. "Maybe. Maybe not. Burner phones are known as 'throwaway' phones.

People buy them when they don't want to be tracked or to have the ability to change numbers quickly. Burner phones protect their identity. The NSA wouldn't even be able to track them. In most cases, carriers don't even have the callers' identities, because they don't require a real name, or any name, even. But…"

Beth and Donovan glanced at each other. "But?" they said together.

"I might be able to triangulate a location using signal strength from whatever three cell towers this guy was closest to when he was using those numbers. The next time you get a text, Beth, let me know, and don't block the number. The longer he has a number and has his phone on to receive texts from you, the better of a shot I'll get."

"How close of a location could you get?" Donovan asked.

"Within twenty-five to one-hundred meters."

Donovan frowned at that, probably hoping to get an exact pinpoint.

"But we'd at least know where he is or has been," Thorn said. "The important thing is to make sure this guy isn't close."

Just like that, realization jabbed Beth in the gut. The tapping at her window. The man in the car outside her house. The text messages. Could it be the same person? Looking at Donovan and Thorn, she realized they were on the same page as her.

"Couldn't I just change my number?" she wanted to know.

Donovan took her hand.

"I know getting texts like this is disturbing," Thorn said, "but if you cut off his one line of communication, that could escalate things in a way we don't want it to."

Beth swallowed. She knew what stalkers were capable of from her studies and from the stories of her students, knew how their obsessions could rise to dangerous, deadly levels. Was that what this guy was doing? Was he stalking her? That single word sent ice through her veins.

Stalked.

****

Luckily, Beth had her co-ed baby shower the next day as a distraction. Donovan, Thorn, and Donovan's monster truck buddies were invited along with Beth's friends as well as her students. They had planned her baby shower closer to her due date since they'd be leaving for Michigan before Christmas and would be having a holiday party prior to their trip. There'd be a no-gift rule for the holiday party because of the baby shower. That way, guests wouldn't have to shop twice so soon. Besides, Beth and Donovan didn't want anything for themselves anyway.

The baby shower would be held at The Fighting Chance. Amanda, Corissa, and Leighton had been decorating all morning. Beth wondered what they had planned. She had requested the baby shower be less shower and more party, with finger foods Donovan's buddies would like and decorations that wouldn't make them cringe to be close to them. She also asked for there to be no games, rather for this to feel like a casual get-together, involving baby gifts.

When she stepped onto the sidewalk outside The Fighting Chance, she glimpsed gold and white star-shaped balloons through the glass windows. Donovan opened the door for her, and she stepped through. She stopped in the entrance as her eyes went wide. The blue mat where her students kicked ass had been moved from the large room, and round tables with light gray tablecloths had been brought into its place. Yellow and white napkins, paper plates, and cups were set out. In the center of each table, yellow roses filled small, white ceramic containers. The gold and white balloons she had seen outside lined the walls.

On the front desk, where orchids usually bloomed, was a display of food. She was happy to see platters of chicken wings—barbecue, mild, and butter garlic parmesan. Bowls of potato salad, coleslaw, and baked beans lined the countertop with trays of veggies, deviled eggs, and fruit kabobs. On the other side of the counter, where Corissa usually worked, stood a three-tier gray, white, and yellow cake, decorated with stripes and polka dots.

Beth loved everything about it.

"How's this for a guy-friendly baby shower?" she asked Donovan.

He nodded approval. "It's not half bad."

"Hey, Beth." Amanda hurried over, wearing jeans and a cute blue and pink blouse. "How do you like it?" Corissa and Leighton were right behind her.

"It's awesome. You three did an amazing job. I don't even recognize The Fighting Chance. If it weren't for the Wall of Signatures, I wouldn't believe this was the same place."

After all the guests had arrived and pigged out, Beth sat at a table to open the baby gifts. Donovan occupied a chair beside her, but he had insisted she have the job of opening the presents. Amanda held a notebook and a pen, ready to write down names and gifts for thank you notes, which were apparently a thing.

The first gift Beth opened had come a long way. It was from Meredith, Donovan's mom, who had sent a baby book after Beth had told her she wanted to keep one. Donovan's magazine cover and the article were the first things she planned to put in it. From Lily, Donovan's grandmother, they received a yellow and lavender hand-knitted baby blanket. Beth put her cheek against it and wondered what her parents, if they were alive, would've given their first grandchild.

She imagined her dad would've gifted a tiny tool kit, which she doubted would be plastic, but the real thing that the baby could use once he or she was older. And she had a feeling her mom would've created a special painting for the nursery, something the baby could keep up on his or her walls forever. Beth wished they could be there to witness this, to see their only daughter become a mother.

Trying to not let her thoughts dampen her mood, she refolded the blanket, laid it in the box, and set it aside. Luckily, the next gift she opened was the ticket she needed to distract her. From a bed of tissue paper, she lifted out red lace underwear, with cutouts where the breasts should be. Beth's eyes widened. She dropped it back into the box and covered it up with the tissue paper when she realized Donovan's friends, and Thorn, were all staring at it.

"Leighton!" Mortified, Beth gaped at her friend, the gift-giver. "That's not an appropriate baby shower gift. That's more of a private bachelorette shower gift."

"Are you kidding?" Leighton said. "The baby and Donovan can both benefit from that. Am I, right?" She winked at Donovan.

Beth covered her face with her hands.

Sensing she needed to be saved, Amanda stepped forward with another present in her hands. "Here. Open this one next. It says it's from Daddy." She beamed at Donovan as she passed the box to Beth.

Donovan was the most considerate gift-giver she knew. Every gift he'd ever given her had a meaning behind it that related to their love story, and she couldn't wait to see his gift to their first baby. She ripped off the paper. Underneath sat a thin garment box. The lid slipped up the sides as she raised it, and the white tissue paper crinkled when she folded it away. What she found beneath that paper made her smile. With her fingers, she lifted up a white onesie that said, "Daddy's Little Girl" in pink, cursive font. She turned it around for everyone else to see. All the women in the room broke out into a chorus of, "Awwww…"

Beth laid the onesie against her belly, imagining their little girl wearing it while sleeping in her bassinet. But there was something else in the box. Her smile grew as she revealed a second onesie. This one was blue with white, block letters that said, "Daddy's Mini Me."

The women erupted into another wave of, "Awwww…"

Beth shifted to Donovan. "A perfect gift. Either way, we'll end up using both onesies." She gave him a wink, hinting she hoped this little bundle would not be their last.

With pink cheeks, Amanda handed Beth a small white bag with curls of colored ribbon. "This one is from me."

Beth pulled out a wad of tissue paper and peeked inside the bag before reaching in to get the gift. "Oh my gosh." Laughing, she pulled out a tiny pair of black boxing gloves, attached by white laces. "Amanda, this is the cutest thing I've ever seen."

Amanda shrugged. "It's symbolic. You can hang them on a rearview mirror or in the baby's room."

Donovan took the baby boxing gloves from Beth. "I like these. They'll be perfect in my truck. Or maybe Venom." He grinned at Beth.

"Hey, who said you get to have them?"

"The fact that all the other gifts were exclusively for the baby or for you, especially Leighton's gift."

"Au contraire," Leighton said. "Beth would wear it, but it'd be your gift."

Beth shook her head at Leighton. Her mind always had to go *there*.

A throat clearing had everyone turning back to Amanda. "I had a feeling this might happen, so…" She presented a second, identical bag and gave it to Donovan. Inside it was another pair of black boxing gloves to represent their baby, their little fighter.

After opening several more gifts, Amanda came forward with a tiny box that rested in the middle of her palm. "This one is also from Donovan."

Beth smiled at Donovan. "Another one?"

He nodded. "Open it."

And she did. What she found made her heart flutter—a sterling silver baby rattle charm.

"For your bracelet," Donovan whispered.

She closed the jewelry box and held it clasped in her hands, close to her chest. "It's beautiful." She leaned toward him. "Don't take offense to this, but this is better than the onesies, and those were really cute."

Donovan touched her chin, drawing her closer, and they shared a sweet kiss, forgetting they had an audience.

A clap had them jumping apart to see all the women in the room watching them with dewy eyes, and the men in the room looking away awkwardly. Leighton dabbed at her eyes with a piece of tissue paper. "Okay, everyone," she said. "Time for cake."

Donovan stood. "Can you take care of that for a moment? I want to talk to Beth in private."

Leighton nodded. "Sure." Then she inched closer. "Would you like the lingerie?" She nudged Donovan with her elbow.

"Not right now," Donovan said, before leading Beth to her office. He shut the door behind them, giving them privacy. "I have to tell you something."

Beth leaned against her desk, still clutching the jewelry box, as she waited for Donovan to turn around. When he did, he swallowed. A look in his eyes told her the joy of the previous moment was long gone. But why? What happened? What changed?

He paused before her. "That charm is from me."

"I know." Her grip on it tightened. "And I love it."

Donovan stepped closer, putting his hands on her shoulders. "I'm not finished." He pointed at the jewelry box. "That's from me, but those onesies aren't."

Beth's brows furrowed, not understanding. "What do you mean? The onesies say 'Daddy' on them."

He lowered his voice. "I didn't buy those."

"Amanda said the card was written out as 'Daddy.' And no one corrected her."

Shaking his head, Donovan continued to stare

straight into her eyes.

A queasy feeling washed over Beth. Her palms dampened, and her heart rate rose. "If those onesies aren't from you, then who brought them?"

Chapter Eight

That was the question.

Once again, someone was messing with them, but unlike the other times, this sicko was targeting their unborn child. What kind of man would do something like that? Not one right in the head, that was for sure. But why their baby? Why Beth? None of their threats remained. They were either dead or locked up, never to get free. The past several months since Viper's end, everything had been quiet. Their lives had been filled with happiness as they planned for the arrival of their firstborn. Were they cursed to always have someone after them?

Donovan shook his head and raked his hands through his hair. *Don't think that. Your relationship with Beth is not cursed.*

And yet, a part of him still thought about the things that never would've happened to her if they hadn't met, if he hadn't turned his car down her street and crashed into that tree. He had brought a lot of shit into her life—pain, scars, fear, death. But he had brought a lot of good, too—love, passion, joy, and now...their baby. Knowing that, though, couldn't stop him from thinking what her life would be like without him. Surely, it would be peaceful. No doubt, she'd have a few less scars, no nightmares, no anxiety, no bad memories.

He should be home more often; he shouldn't have

left Beth while she was pregnant, and he shouldn't leave once their baby was born. Except, it was his job. A part of his job meant he had to leave, had to be gone, had to miss out on things that all fathers should witness. And he'd be doing it again, so he could participate in the Monster Jam World Finals in Orlando.

That didn't make it right, though. Or even necessary.

Sighing, he sat back on the couch. His life was different than when he had first started his monster truck driving career. Now, he had a lot to live for, to be present for. A change might be the answer. At some point in everyone's lives, they realize they need to go a different course, and maybe Donovan was reaching that fork in the road. He could give up traveling the world to compete and perform in monster truck shows. But what the hell would he do to support his family and to feed his hunger for adrenaline? Something that wouldn't take him away from his loved ones or put his life in danger. Except, the thought of leaving monster truck driving forever caused his chest to tighten. He loved it. Plain and simple. He enjoyed the risky stunts, loved his fans, and, as sad as it sounded, Venom was his first child. Could he really abandon all that?

He thought of little Nathan he had met while on the road. The awe he had seen in that child's eyes had energized him. He didn't want to stop inspiring kids. Quitting what he loved, that had been a part of his life for so long, and that which defined him was not something he wanted to do. But he didn't want to quit being a good husband or father, either.

No, *good* wasn't even the half of it. He wanted to be a *great* husband and father. To be those things, he'd have to give up being a great monster truck driver.

****

Come Thanksgiving, Donovan had made up his mind. He would quit monster truck driving in order to fully embrace and accept his new duties. Although, he still didn't know what he'd do with his time and to earn a paycheck, but he had time to figure that out. For now, he wanted to enjoy this day with his wife.

He put the lid back on the deep fryer. The smell of hot peanut oil and frying turkey swirled around him. He inhaled the scent deep into his lungs, relishing it. Years ago, he'd either be ordering pizza or Chinese takeout as his Thanksgiving feast, not cooking a turkey. Boy, how the times had changed.

"You're growing up, Donovan," he said to himself, imagining Ryan to be saying those words to him with a teasing smile and a playful jab to his side.

Donovan didn't envy those lonely Thanksgiving Days. He wouldn't trade his life with Beth and every holiday they would share for anything.

Standing before the fryer, he gazed around the backyard. Green, fresh palmetto branches had grown in the woods since the fire had ripped through there, charring everything it touched. Even the trees had green needles at their tops, but he could still see their blackened trunks and a layer of ashes and burned nature on the ground. Seeing the signs of that fire reminded him of how much they had to be thankful for on this day.

A gentle breeze stirred the trees' branches and swept past Donovan, lifting his jacket. The day was actually chilly for Florida, and Donovan was happy about that. He hated going through the holidays and it being blistering hot outside; it just wasn't the same. Growing up in Michigan had spoiled him. He missed the seasons. Florida was summertime nearly three hundred and sixty-five days a year, with a few sporadic winter days, springtime for about a week, and virtually no fall. Fortunately, they would be traveling to Michigan for Christmas, before Beth was too pregnant to fly. He couldn't wait to see his mom and grandma again, and he wanted to give Beth a better white Christmas than the first time they went to Michigan in December. That time, he had been riddled with anxiety over Buck being in the wind and suffering from PTSD. This year, however, would be different.

With that plan on his mind, he went back inside to check on Beth. She was in the kitchen, peeling and chopping up potatoes and sticking them in a crockpot of water to cook.

"How's everything going in here?"

"Good," Beth said. "I'm almost done with the potatoes. I have the green bean casserole and marshmallow yams put together and ready to go in the oven when it's time."

"Do you remember our first Thanksgiving together?"

Beth sliced the knife's blade through a chunk of crunchy potato, and then she dropped the potato pieces into the crockpot with a small splash of water.

"I do. We had Cornish hens and instant potatoes." With a laugh, she picked up a whole potato and waved it in the air. "Luckily, I've become more domestic since then." And she started to peel away the earthy, tough skin of the potato.

"So have I. I had to Google how to cook a Cornish

hen in the oven."

"You had to Google how to deep fry a turkey."

Donovan joined in on her laughter. "That was years ago. I'm a pro at it now."

"Just like I am a pro at digging out eyes from potatoes." She set down the potato she had been working on. "Although, I admit, cooking isn't my favorite thing to do."

"You pull it off well, though, baby." Donovan kissed her temple.

She chuckled. "Thanks. I think."

"Do you need any help in here?"

"Sure, don your apron and chop onions for the turkey dressing."

"You were waiting for me to come in and ask so you could pawn that job off on me, weren't you?"

She gave him a big, toothy grin. "I don't know what you're talking about."

"Uh huh." He slipped the apron on and tied it behind his back.

"Okay, so, I was really hoping to see you in that apron."

Donovan turned to see Beth with her head tilted to the side, smirking.

"You look incredibly sexy in that apron."

He peered down. "In this apron?"

"Uh huh."

He moved toward her. "Can you tell me what it says?"

Beth's eyes twinkled as he inched closer. "It says 'Kiss the Chef'."

"Then maybe you better do that."

"Maybe I will." She looped her arms around his

neck, lifted on tiptoe slightly, causing her belly to bump into him, and brought her lips to his.

He cradled her face in the palm of his hands and savored her lips and the warmth and flavor of her mouth. *It couldn't get any better than this*, he thought.

But it could, he realized. Their baby will make next Thanksgiving even better than this one. And he couldn't wait.

Beth pulled away enough so their lips weren't touching, but not enough his hands were no longer holding her face. She gave him a little shove. "Okay, to the onions, Chef."

He kissed her lips once more. "Yes, ma'am." When she swatted his arm at his use of the word "ma'am," he chuckled.

Together they finished the rest of the Thanksgiving feast preparations. He lit three candles before he started to chop onions; better to be safe than teary-eyed from the onion's fumes. Once Beth finished with the potatoes, she chopped up celery for the dressing, too. Then they tore up dried bread into one-inch pieces, filling their largest pot.

Donovan took care of putting the dishes into and taking them out of the oven so Beth wouldn't have to bend over the hot door with her pregnant belly. Finally, it was dinnertime, and the entire house smelled amazing. He carved the turkey at the dining room table, a bird that was probably too big for the two of them, but Beth insisted that, with her cravings and his bottomless-pit of a stomach, it wouldn't last long. Still, while they ate, he couldn't help but notice the empty seats around the table, where Ryan and Beth's parents would likely be sitting. It seemed too quiet, even with the sounds of their forks and knives tapping their plates as they ate.

"Should we have invited Thorn and a few others for dinner?" he wondered aloud.

Beth peered from across the table.

"I mean…it's just the two of us."

"You forget, next year, it won't be just the two of us." She laid a hand on her belly.

A smile stretched his lips. "I could never forget that."

"Besides," Beth added, "we saw everyone for the baby shower, and they'll be here on December 15th for an early Christmas party. If we had invited them today, they'd be sick of us. And I like these quiet moments with you. Soon, we'll have a house full of kids making us pull our hair out on Thanksgiving. Every. Single. Year."

Donovan chuckled. "That doesn't sound so bad."

"I'll remind you that you said that." She lifted her wine glass of sparkling cider. "To our future noisy and chaotic Thanksgivings."

Donovan got up with his glass, tapped it to hers, and then planted a kiss on her lips. "To all of our Thanksgivings together."

****

Later that night, Donovan was making a leftover Thanksgiving feast sandwich with all of the fixings when their house phone rang. He paused to answer it.

"Hello."

On the other end, a man's voice said, "So, you're the husband."

Donovan's back snapped straight. "Yeah," he growled. "I am the husband. Now, who the hell is this?"

The man sniggered in a mocking tone that had

Donovan clenching his hand into a fist. "I'm the other man."

Rage rolled through Donovan.

"Happy Thanksgiving, Beth's husband."

The call ended, but his anger did not vanish. He lowered the phone and smashed it against the kitchen counter. It shattered. The batteries fell onto the tile. Pieces of plastic scattered around the room.

"Donovan?" Beth hurried into the kitchen.

He put up his hand. "I'm fine. I'll clean this up."

She didn't move from where she stood. "Donovan, you murdered our home phone. You're not fine. What's going on? Who called?" Her eyes widened. "Is it your mom? Your grandma? Are they okay?" She took a few steps toward him.

"They're okay. It's not them." He veered from her to brace his hands on the counter. Fury burned beneath his surface. How he wanted to pound this asshole's face. How he wanted to make this man suffer for the sick game he was playing.

"Then what is it? Who was that?"

With his neck bent, he shook his head. "I don't know who it was." He turned to look into Beth's eyes. "But he said he's the other man."

She blinked. "The other…" Her eyes widened. "Oh my God, Donovan. No. There is no other man. You know I'd never cheat on you."

It wasn't a question, but a statement.

"You know I love you," she continued. "You know this baby is yours. And you know you're all I need."

Donovan went to her, walking around the shards of the broken phone, and wrapped his arms around her. "I do know that. This person is just pissing me off."

"That's why he's doing what he's doing," Beth said with her cheek against his shoulder. "He's doing it because he knows it'll rile you. Whoever it is, he wants you to think I'm having an affair with him. He wants to drive a wedge between us."

Donovan shifted back and cupped her face. "That'll never happen. If he thinks it will, he doesn't know us, and he greatly underestimates us."

She nodded. "But he's ballsy, though. Considering all the people who have come after us, none of them attempted to tear our relationship apart."

"They were smarter than this fool. Let's forget about him."

"Okay." She peered down at the demolished phone. "You know, we probably don't need a home phone anyway. This idiot cut our bill down by thirty dollars or so."

"I'll be sure to send him a text to thank him."

The problem was they couldn't forget about this nameless, faceless man, because he wasn't giving up on his perverted ways. On the first day of December, a knock sounded on their front door. Donovan opened it to see the delivery guy hopping back onto his truck. He waved before hefting the box left on their doorstep. While he stepped back inside, he read the scribblings. Black permanent marker spelled out Beth's name on the brown cardboard. But there was no return address.

"Hey, Beth, there's a package for you." He brought it into the living room, where she was sprawled out on the couch, and set it on the coffee table.

Beth sat up. "It's probably another baby gift." They had already received a few in the mail from long-distance family and friends. "Can you open it for me?"

"Sure." He removed his keys from his pocket and sliced open the packaging tape with one. Then he pulled apart the sides so Beth could take a look.

She scooted to the edge of the couch and tipped the box toward her.

"Oh my gosh." She pulled out a transparent white bra. That wasn't all, either. A sheer bodysuit, a cup-less bra, a beaded thong, and three sets of skimpy lingerie complete with garter belts and sheer stockings in red, black, and white lace. "This has to be more from Leighton. We should be thankful she didn't wrap all this up for the baby shower."

She took a picture of the box and its contents with her cell phone and sent it to Leighton with a text that said, *Ha-ha. Very funny. It may be a long time before I wear any of these, though.*

A moment later, Leighton's reply came through. Donovan expected her to make a joke. Instead, Beth met his gaze with unease. "Leighton said it's not from her." She showed him the text on her phone. "If it was from her, she wouldn't be shy about admitting it."

"No, she wouldn't be." He stared at the box. "It's from him," he said in a low voice. "It's from that bastard."

Unable to contain his anger any longer, Donovan snatched the box out of Beth's hands and stormed into the sitting room where the electric fireplace stood. He jabbed a button, and flames erupted inside the fireplace. In the next moment, he was ripping open the grate's door, about to toss every last bit of fabric into the fire to burn to nothing, but Beth grabbed the box, stopping him.

"You can't burn it."

"I sure as hell can, and I will."

"No." She kept the box from him when he reached for it.

"I don't want that in our house," he growled.

"It doesn't have to be in the house, but you can't burn it. I'll take care of it." She carried it off. A few minutes later, her voice met his ears as she talked softly.

Still seething, he stayed in the sitting room, pacing back and forth.

Beth rejoined him, but she stayed by the entrance. "I called Thorn to come and get it."

"I don't want to give that lingerie to Thorn," Donovan hissed.

"It's not like I wore any of it, and we're not giving him lingerie. We're giving him a package that some sicko sent me. We've done this before."

Donovan couldn't dispute the logic. They had done this before. Except, the package had never contained anything intimate intended for his wife.

While they waited for Thorn to arrive, Beth kept the box out of Donovan's reach, as if protecting it. And she very well was. Every minute that passed, Donovan thought about lighting it up, destroying it for good. What else could be done with a bunch of lingerie, anyway? What could the police do with it but joke, laugh, and blush at the image in their minds of his pregnant wife wearing those bras and thongs?

Sitting in a chair, Beth shifted the box around on the floor and lowered the flap. She eyed it for several seconds. "Um, Donovan?"

"Hm?"

"I recognize this handwriting."

Donovan shifted away from the flames in the fireplace. "What do you mean?"

She pointed at the permanent marker. "This handwriting is Craig's."

"Craig your ex?"

She nodded.

Craig, Beth's ex, had cheated on her when they were engaged to get married. Beth broke up with him and never saw him again, but some years ago, Thorn had uncovered that Craig had become obsessed with getting Beth back, according to his co-workers. Donovan had paid Craig a visit, warning him to never come around Beth or think about her. Since then, he hadn't been a problem, but people with obsessions didn't stop wanting what they wanted with a snap of the finger.

"Are you sure?" Donovan's voice was gruff.

"I used to watch him fill out forms for work all the time. That's his handwriting."

Shortly after Beth's realization, Thorn arrived, and they got him up to speed with everything that had happened since they'd last spoken to him. To say he was livid would be an understatement.

"Why the hell didn't the two of you tell me about the package from the baby shower as soon as it happened?" he wanted to know. "I was there, damn it." He stalked the length of the room in big strides. "Let me ask you this…did either of you realize he would've had to come into The Fighting Chance and put that package on the gift table? Did either of you realize he was inside long enough to deliver that package, but not long enough for Beth to notice him?"

Donovan and Beth glanced at each other.

Thorn nodded. "I thought not." He put his hands on either side of his head as though he wanted to rip out his hair in chunks. "I thought the two of you were smarter than this."

They stared at him from their seats, taking their scolding, because they had been stupid. Why hadn't they said anything to Thorn? Because The Fighting Chance had been packed with people there to celebrate their baby, and they hadn't wanted to cause a scene. Then, Donovan supposed, they had forgotten...forgotten to tell their best friend, the detective.

But why hadn't Donovan called Thorn after that phone call? The best answer Donovan had was he had been too enraged to think clearly. Obviously, his rage would've had him burning the lingerie and ripping the box to shreds to feed to the fire. Beth had been in her right mind, whereas he had been relying on his emotions, not his logic. And that wasn't like him.

"I'm not just angry you were putting yourselves at risk by not telling me," Thorn continued, "but you were putting Amanda at risk."

Donovan winced at that. If the tables had been turned and Thorn had done something to put Beth at risk, he would've punched out his lights. Thorn loved Amanda, even if she didn't know it yet. Hell, he might not even know it. But Thorn was all about Amanda and her safety, and he was more than justified in his anger toward them.

"You were putting Corissa at risk. You were putting all your students at The Fighting Chance at risk. He could've been there more times than we even know about."

Beth averted her gaze. Never would it be her intention to hurt her students and employees, all of which were her family.

"Let's back up here and see if I have everything straight. First, someone hung out outside the guest bedroom window where Beth slept while she was home alone. The next night someone came to the house and flashed headlights on and off while parked on the driveway. This person then had roses delivered to The Fighting Chance for Beth."

Beth looked back at that. "The roses?" Her eyes widened. "Oh my God. I forgot all about them. You think he sent the roses?"

"The card said, 'To the love of my life,' right? And Donovan didn't send them?"

Donovan shook his head.

"Whoever this is, he is doing things to make himself seem like your lover, Beth, hence the roses."

That simple, reasonable explanation had Donovan clenching his teeth. If this really was Craig, the bastard was deluded to think Beth would be his lover again. And no one would believe it, either.

"Then this person sends Beth texts from a bunch of burner phones, making it sound as though he were keeping up a conversation with her and meeting her for an affair."

Donovan's hands balled into white-knuckled fists.

"He comes into The Fighting Chance to drop off a baby present that says 'Daddy' all over it, as if he's the baby's father. Days later, he taunts Donovan on the phone, saying he's the other man. Now he's sending Beth a box full of intimates." Thorn peered at them. "Have I got everything?"

They nodded silently.

"Right." Thorn picked up his keys from a side table where he'd flung them earlier. "Come on. We're going to The Fighting Chance."

Chapter Nine

Beth sat next to Donovan in his truck and stared out the passenger side window. She was mad at herself for not keeping Thorn updated, but, damn it, pregnancy brain was a real thing. She had forgotten, but forgetting to tell authorities about contact from a stalker was not smart. Thorn was right; she sure as hell knew better. She hadn't even told Leighton about what had happened since the night someone had showed up to taunt them with his car's headlights.

"Are you okay?" Donovan's voice reached Beth.

She nodded, but she didn't look away from her view out the window.

"Thorn shouldn't have yelled at you like that."

"I wasn't the only one he yelled at."

"You're right. He yelled at the both of us. We're both at fault. Myself more so than you."

Beth turned. "That's not true. I knew about the phone call and the baby gifts, and I didn't tell him, either. I didn't even warn the girls about the chance of someone coming into the studio looking or asking for me."

"You didn't know how far this guy would take this."

"I should've guessed it was a possibility, though. Learning about what stalkers do, how they think, and how they victimize their obsessions was a big part of my studies in college. They will do anything to see their victims, to give their victims so-called gifts, and to communicate with them. No place is off limits. Not their homes. Not their jobs."

Donovan reached over and rubbed Beth's leg. "We should be thankful that nothing happened. He didn't do anything to anyone at The Fighting Chance."

That's because I'm his objective, she thought. *Me and our baby.* She knew better than to say any of that out loud to Donovan, though. He could be thinking it himself and didn't need her to voice it, adding to his stress.

Donovan followed Thorn's car into the parking lot and parked next to him in front of the wide windows for the studio. When Beth opened her door, Thorn was there with a hand to help her down. She smiled gratefully; it was getting more and more difficult for her to maneuver her bulk of a belly.

"Hey, I had time to cool off in my car, and I'm sorry for yelling earlier," Thorn said. "I shouldn't have done that, but...the two of you are my best friends. I care about you, and I care about..." His voice trailed off.

Beth put her hand on his arm and said, "Amanda."

Brows bunched up and lowered, Thorn nodded.

"Also, you're carrying precious cargo. It's not just you anymore, Beth."

She put her arms around her belly, as if to embrace her baby. "I know."

Donovan joined them on the passenger's side of his truck. "From now on, Thorn, we're going to tell you about everything, every phone call, text, or package."

Thorn nodded. "Good." He glanced toward the

entrance of The Fighting Chance. Beth looked, too, but she didn't see anyone looking out at them. "Speaking of which, I made a call on the way here. Since the sender of that package had used the Postal Service to send it, I was able to track it to where he had dropped it off for delivery. It came from the Post Office down the road from you guys…which means he's close."

A chill roped up and down Beth's spine, knotting her insides with fear.

"So, what we're going to do now is go straight to your surveillance equipment and view the footage from the day of the baby shower. The camera could've caught him entering and leaving the studio, and we'll be able to identify the perp. We'll go straight to your office. Try not to do anything to tip anyone off that something is up."

Beth nodded.

"Lead the way, Beth."

Thorn fell in behind them as they walked one by one through the doorway. "Hey, Cor," Beth said. "We'll be in the office for a bit."

From behind the receptionist's desk, Corissa gave them a thumbs up. She didn't even look up from the book she read. So far, so good.

She led Donovan and Thorn toward the back hallway. As they passed the blue mat where Amanda taught a class, Beth waved. Amanda waved back. Her gaze shifted from Beth to the back of the line, where Thorn was, and a smile formed on Amanda's face. Beth couldn't help but smile, too. The two of them would make the cutest couple, if they'd do something about it.

In her office, Beth switched on the lights. Thorn went right to her desk and booted up her computer. She stood back so he could do his thing and locate the footage that showed their front door during the time of her baby shower. When he found it, he waved them over. Donovan moved an extra chair beside Thorn's, indicated for Beth to sit, and stood behind her chair, leaning forward to see the screen.

Thorn hit the play button. "If you see Craig or anyone who shouldn't be there, let me know."

Beth nodded and shifted as close as she could with her belly sticking out so far. On the screen, party guests arrived alone or in clusters. Each one carried a present of some sort—a wrapped giftbox or a colorful bag. Thorn showed up on the feed, carrying a bag in one hand, with his other hand stuffed into his pocket.

Beth reached forward and paused the footage.

"What are you doing?" Thorn rotated in his chair. "If you say I look like Craig, I'm going to beat you silly. Figurately speaking, of course."

Beth rolled her eyes. She pointed at the screen. "You gave us a gift card. What is that?" She tapped the tip of her finger on the image of the bag.

Thorn cleared his throat. "Well, that's um…the second pair of baby boxing gloves."

Her heart warmed at those words. "Really?" She tilted her head. "You and Amanda conspired together on a joint baby gift for us?"

"Conspired, really?" Thorn groaned. "We talked about it nonchalantly one day while standing at the front desk. Amanda brought it up. She was going to get both pairs, but when she found out I was going to give a card, she took pity on me and suggested I get the second pair. I agreed."

"The bags and ribbons and tissue paper are

identical," Beth pointed out.

He shrugged. "That was all her. She gave me the bag pre-made. All I had to do was stick the gloves inside it."

"She said they were both from her, though."

"Yeah, well, it was her idea. I didn't want to take any of the credit."

Beth reached over, slung an arm around him, and laid her head on his shoulder in a sideways hug. "You're sweet."

"Okay, okay, okay. Can we get back to this?" Thorn indicated the footage.

"Please," Donovan said. "Let's."

Beth peeked over her shoulder at Donovan. Humor lit his eyes. He enjoyed seeing Thorn uncomfortable with affection as much as she did.

Focusing back on the screen, she continued to watch guests arrive. A smile dawned on her face as she thought about the baby shower—the food, the laughter, and the gifts each of them held. They had spoiled the two of them with everything they needed. And in Leighton's case, more than what they needed. Her thoughts had drifted into a daydreaming state as the sound-less video played. Then she caught sight of the purple bow atop a box wrapped in shiny, silver paper.

"Pause it!"

Thorn jumped at her command and stopped the video.

"That's the package that had the onesies in it."

The three of them inched closer. They could only see half of the box, and the man holding it was blocked by Smith, Gordon, and a couple other of Donovan's monster truck buddies. All Beth could make out was a pair of dark jeans, a black shirt, and golden tan. She shook her head. "I can't tell if it's him or not."

Thorn started the feed back up, and they watched the package and the man carrying it disappear from the camera's view.

"He used my own friends as a shield to get in undetected," Donovan said through mashed teeth. "It's as if everything he does, it's a big ole middle finger up in the air at me."

Beth couldn't dispute that, although she was the one the stalker wanted, everything he did was a purposeful jab at Donovan—calling himself the baby's daddy, claiming he was the "other man" in her life, and doing whatever he could to make Donovan believe she was having an affair. Except, this stalker didn't know a thing about their relationship and how strong it was. The two of them were soulmates, and that was something this man would never be able to understand.

A couple of minutes later, a black shirt reappeared on the screen, heading out of the studio. His head was angled away from the camera, so they couldn't catch a glimpse of his face. Thorn paused the footage anyway.

"What do you think?"

Beth shook her head with uncertainty. The man on the video didn't resemble the man she had known years ago. Everything about him was different. "If it is Craig, he's changed a lot. His shoulders appear wider, and I wouldn't say that he was a wimp before—"

Donovan snorted.

She reached behind her to slap him.

"—but he didn't have muscles like that before, either. I know muscles can be built, but he even looks taller. He's tanner, and he never used to style his hair like that." In the video, his hair was longer and windblown. When they had been together, he had been an adamant user of hair mousse.

"Craig may not be the stalker then. Or, if he is, he could've gotten someone else to bring the package inside," Thorn suggested. "It certainly would've been smarter and safer for him if he had a friend deliver it for him."

"Good point." Beth studied the frozen image again. "Yeah, because I can't say this man is Craig, but I swear it is his handwriting on that box."

"Okay, so here's what we're going to do now." Thorn shut down the program they were using to view the security footage. "Do you have a picture of Craig we can give to Amanda and Corissa, so they can be on the lookout for him if he does show up here?"

"You think I kept a picture of the piece of shit who cheated on me?" She gave Thorn a look that said, "Are you crazy?"

"I burned every single picture of him right after I threw his crap out of my house," she added. "I don't have a thing of his anymore. We could see if he still has his social media profiles, though, and print out a copy of his profile photo." She took the mouse in her hand and directed it to the browser. "I blocked him from my profile, so I'll stay logged out. I should be able to find him that way."

A few Craig Mitchell's popped up, and one of them was his account. She clicked on it.

"There he is." His profile picture was the same from all those years ago, a business photo. In it, he wore a navy-blue suit, and his dark blond hair was slicked back to perfection.

Thorn leaned forward, squinting his eyes. "You dated a man who used mousse in his hair?"

Beth slapped her palm to her forehead and bent her neck toward the desk. "You met him earlier this year before the fire, remember?" He had gone to question Craig when a bloody note wishing Beth a happy birthday had been found on their porch.

"Excuse me for not noticing a dude's hair when I'm questioning him."

Teasing him, she shook her head. "And you call yourself a detective."

They printed out three copies of the photo. One they'd give to Leighton, and the other two were for Amanda and Corissa.

"Wait," Beth said as they started to leave her office. "What are we going to say to them? You know very well how Amanda might react to this…an ex stalking me…"

Amanda's ex had nearly taken her life once.

Thorn let out a breath. He didn't want to cause Amanda to regress. She was a strong woman, but she was fragile, and with every right to be after the nightmare her ex had put her through. Unfortunately, she was still in the middle of that nightmare; Damon was out there, tormenting Amanda every chance he got.

"Maybe we don't have to tell them who he is or what he's doing," Donovan suggested. "They don't need to know the details."

"They'll be curious, though."

"Curious is better than afraid," Thorn said.

She couldn't deny that. Except, curiosity could lead to questioning, and the two of them knew Beth and Donovan's track record with bad people coming after them. They could put two and two together.

"You know what? I have an idea," Thorn said. "Follow my lead."

The class Amanda had been teaching had ended, and all the students were filtering out the doors as they chatted with each other and said goodbye to Corissa and Amanda. A couple of them turned to see the trio coming out of the office.

"Bye, Beth."

"Bye, Donovan."

"Bye, Thorn."

Beth called out a goodbye in return.

A few steps ahead of her, Thorn made it to the front desk where Amanda and Corissa stood talking. Amanda was using a dry towel to pat down her sweaty arms, neck, and chest. Thorn glanced away, and Beth pressed her lips together. *Poor guy.*

He cleared his throat, which had Amanda and Corissa rotating around. Amanda's cheeks, which were already pink from her workout, brightened a shade. She draped the towel quickly over her shoulder and wrung her hands.

"Hey, ladies," Thorn said. "I need to ask the two of you to do something for me." He handed each of them a printout of Craig's photo. "This man robbed the cigarette shop a few doors down early this morning."

Beth's eyebrows went up a fraction before she schooled them back into place.

"We haven't caught him yet," Thorn continued. "So, we're letting everyone know in this strip mall to keep an eye out for him."

Amanda and Corissa examined the paper in their hands.

"A man in a suit robbed a cigarette shop?" Corissa said.

Without missing a beat, Thorn replied, "He fell off the wagon."

Beth let out a snort that would've turned into a chuckle if she hadn't caught it in time and masked it with a short coughing fit. She patted her chest with her hand.

The four of them regarded her. Thorn's glare bore into her, warning her not to tip them off that his story was a coverup. "Sorry," she said. "I swallowed wrong."

"How'd you get this picture," Amanda wanted to know. "It's not from a security camera."

Uh-oh. Beth waited for Thorn's quick answer to that one.

"The security camera feed was too grainy. We couldn't make out his face, but the owner recognized him from when this guy was a regular. We were able to track down one of his social media accounts."

"If you got this off a profile, then you know his name." Amanda eyed Thorn.

Damn, she's smart.

The corner of Thorn's mouth twitched, no doubt thinking the same thing. "His name is Craig Mitchell."

Hearing Thorn use his actual name surprised Beth. She had expected him to give a false name to go along with his fabricated story.

"Look, I need the two of you to be on the lookout for him in case he comes around this strip mall again or comes into the studio. We're not sure what this guy might do next. We suspect he robbed a convenience store in a strip mall up the street." He paused. "Even a man in a suit can have a screw or two loose."

If Craig were stalking her, he definitely had a screw or two loose.

"Since you don't have a cash register or supplies, The Fighting Chance should be safe, but it's better to be prepared."

Amanda and Corissa nodded.

"If I see him around, do you want me to lay his ass down?" Amanda asked.

Beth flattened her lips together to halt the smile that wanted to take them over.

"'Cuz I am trained to do that," Amanda added.

Unlike Beth, Thorn let his grin dominate his face. "No. Don't engage him. If Beth is here, one of you should go quietly and calmly to tell her. And she'll call me. If she's not here, call me first, so I can get here right away, and then call Beth. This guy likes to ask for management and do his thing while the employee is gone, so whatever you do, if he asks for Beth, say she's not here and stay behind this desk." He tapped on the countertop with his finger. "You still keep your cell phones on the shelf under the counter, right?"

They nodded.

"Good. If he comes around and doesn't leave right away, try to discreetly get to your phone and call me. Make sure I'm on speed dial. You don't have to say anything specific. If I answer and you don't respond to me, I'll know you're in trouble." He met Amanda's gaze then. "I'll come right away."

His words told Beth he was telling Amanda what to do not only if something happened at The Fighting Chance, but if Damon ever came around. All she'd have to do was call him, and he'd come.

Amanda swallowed. "Okay," she whispered.

"All right." Thorn knocked on the countertop. "Keep those photos face-up on the shelf beside your phones at all times, so you can take a peek at it if necessary."

Right away, Amanda bent over to set her copy of the photo on the shelf.

"Take care, both of you." Thorn shifted to Beth and Donovan. "I'm gonna get going. I still have a couple more shop owners to talk to."

"I'll see you out," Beth said.

Once outside, Beth asked Thorn, "Why did you tell them Craig's real name?"

"Because they need to know his real name. If he introduces himself to them, they'll know who he is right away. A fake name wouldn't help them. Or you."

"Makes sense."

Thorn touched her arm. "Don't worry. You have me on the streets, Donovan at home, and a fierce woman in there who'll do what you can't right now and 'lay his ass down' if he tries anything at The Fighting Chance."

Beth smiled at that. "She is a warrior, that's for sure."

Thorn peered at the studio's door over Beth's shoulder. "She is." He cleared his throat. "I'm outta here. Remember, call me if anything happens."

"I will." She gave him a fast hug. "Thanks."

"It's my job," he said while climbing into his car. He waved at her before pulling out of the parking space.

"It's more than that," she whispered as he drove away. Thorn was her best friend, her brother from another mother, and her second shield, right behind

Donovan. One day, she hoped he wouldn't have to worry about them so much or always have to come to their rescue. One day, she hoped he got his own happy ending.

****

During the next few days, Beth spent more time at The Fighting Chance. She didn't want Amanda or Corissa to be alone if her stalker paid a visit. Except, she didn't exactly want to be there, either. If this was Craig, she had closed that part of her life long ago when she threw her engagement ring at his back. Seeing an ex-boyfriend after breaking up was one thing. Seeing your cheating ex was another. And seeing your cheating ex turned stalker was lightyears away from both of those scenarios.

She didn't know what she'd do or say if she came face to face with her stalker, and she didn't want to find out. So, she stayed in her office most of the time, hiding away. How she hated that he was stooping her to this level. If she weren't pregnant and at her usual caliber, she wouldn't be hiding. Instead, she'd face him head on, shoulders squared, chin up, fists on hips.

Behind her desk, she stroked her belly. She had other concerns now, though. Once, she may have put herself in the line of fire and braced for a punch, but things changed when she became a mother. Her priorities were different. From the moment her pregnancy tests showed positive results, her life altered. Forever her children would come before herself.

She focused back on her computer where she was drafting her newest business idea—to offer classes exclusively for young kids and teens. According to her notes, she could do two classes every Saturday. The first would be for kids ages twelve to fourteen. And the second would be for kids ages fifteen to seventeen.

Being a mother now, she realized the importance of not only adults being able to defend themselves, but for children to be able to do the same. The lessons would be vastly different, suited to their ages. Each lesson would be divided into verbal and hands-on. She'd discuss tips with them on what to do if someone was bullying them, or if they saw someone getting bullied, as well as how to handle violence at home.

Then she'd teach them easy techniques, being sure to lecture them not to use anything they learn in class on friends or to start fights. She'd stress that these lessons would be to boost their confidence and teach them what to do if their safety was ever at risk. Every child would also get a safety kit, complete with a whistle, a mini flashlight, fun bandages, and candy to make it kid-friendly. One of her other plans would be to create another Wall of Signatures for her young students to sign after their first lesson.

On cue, the baby moved, pressing onto her bladder. She scrunched forward with the pressure and squeezed her legs together. "Okay." She let out a breath between her teeth. "Bathroom break. I got the message, kiddo. Thanks."

While in the bathroom, she thought about her business plan and wondered if she could convince Donovan or Thorn to pitch in during the Saturday lessons. Young boys might feel more inclined to participate if a man was there to offer them guidance and teach them the moves. The problem was, Donovan and Thorn had jobs that took them away for stretches of time, but maybe it'd work out that at least one of them would have the time. She had a feeling Thorn wouldn't want to pass up a chance to be near Amanda for a few hours.

A noise from the office had her looking toward the closed bathroom door. "Amanda? Corissa?" No one responded, but she could've sworn she heard footsteps and a shuffling sound. Her gaze lowered to the doorknob. She hadn't locked it.

"Hello? Is someone there?" Not wanting anyone to bust open the door while she sat on the toilet, she grabbed a wad of toilet paper. Then she pushed to her feet and righted her clothes.

"Hello?" She inched toward the door. Pausing, with her hand on the knob, she pressed her ear to the wood. Whoever had been there, she couldn't hear them now. Nevertheless, she cracked open the door and peeked through the widening gap at an empty room. She stepped out of the bathroom and eyed her open office door. It had been open to begin with, so that wasn't any different. A scan of her office revealed it to be in order. Nothing was missing, and nothing had been added. There wasn't even a note on her desk. Except, someone had been in there.

She walked to her office door, poked her head out, and glanced up and down the hallway. Empty. At the far end, the back door was secure. At the other end, she could make out Corissa sitting behind the front desk. The sounds of Amanda teaching a class reached her. Curious, she made her way to Corissa. "Hey, did someone come into my office a moment ago?"

Corissa looked up from the spiral notebook she was writing in. "Nope. Oh, but a guy did come in to use the restroom. Chang's Restaurant wouldn't let him use theirs since he wasn't a paying costumer."

Beth knew all about Chang's strict bathroom policy; they often got people coming in to ask to use their bathrooms because of it. Beth was about to turn to go back to her office when Thorn's words replayed in her mind.

He could've been there more times than we even know about.

She froze in her tracks. "Did he look anything like the man in the picture?"

Corissa glanced at the picture in question. "No, this guy was more rugged."

"Rugged? How do you mean?"

"You know, like ruggedly sexy. Tall. Muscular. Dark, messy hair."

That description had Beth's palms dampening. *Son of a bitch.*

"Thanks, Corissa." She went back to her office, resisting the urge to run. As soon as she was there, she shut and locked her office door. She accessed her surveillance feed and backtracked it until she spotted a man wearing a baseball cap enter The Fighting Chance. With the image paused on the screen, she snatched up her phone to call Thorn.

"Everything okay?" he answered.

"Um. I'm not sure. You remember the guy in the surveillance feed from my baby shower?"

"Yeah."

"Well, he was just here."

Chapter Ten

After Beth called him, Donovan met her and Thorn at their house. Together, they sat in the living room, discussing what the appearance of this man meant.

"He's connected somehow," Donovan said. Whether or not Craig was the stalker, this man was involved.

"I agree," Thorn said. "I still don't have proof Craig is behind it, but if he is, this man could be working *for* Craig. He sends this guy in when there's a chance he'll be made."

"Sounds like something Craig would do," Beth added. "He's a business man. When we were together, I saw how much he loved to boss his assistant around and make the poor kid do all his chores. Craig didn't like to get his hands dirty or be bothered with meager jobs. It'd be just like him to hire a man to do his grunt work."

More and more, Donovan disliked Craig. What a pathetic excuse for a man.

Thorn set down his glass of water. "Did this guy leave anything behind?"

"I looked everywhere and didn't see anything."

They were silent a moment, trying to figure out what that could mean. Why was he there if he didn't have something to deliver?

Donovan finally broke their silence. "What do we do now?"

Beth let out a breath. "Well, we can't tell Amanda and Corissa to watch out for another man. They'll be suspicious and know we've been keeping the truth from them." She stared down at her clasped hands. "I think I need to close down The Fighting Chance."

Donovan whirled around, surprised.

"At least until this is over," she added. "Who knows how many more times this guy will come into the studio? And he could become dangerous if someone gets in his way to stop him from getting to me." She met Thorn's eye. "Like Amanda."

Thorn's jaw flexed.

"That could hurt your business, though," Donovan pointed out.

She shrugged. "Hopefully, my students will understand and be there when I reopen. I'll tell them the truth, why I have to shut down. I'll tell Amanda and Corissa the truth, too."

"You don't know how long he'll be a threat," Thorn said. "Some stalkers roam free forever. Even the ones who get time for serious criminal activity get out eventually."

Beth nodded. "I know that. I'll close down for as long as it's necessary. I can't put my students or employees at risk. It's my job to keep them safe."

Thorn let out a sigh. "When you tell them, I'll be there."

Donovan took her hand. "So will I."

"Thanks. I'll do it tomorrow. I'll tell Amanda and Corissa before we open. Then I'll tell each class before they leave. I'll have to refund them for lessons they won't be able to attend." She chewed her bottom lip. "We have enough to cover the space and paid leave for all employees for a few months. After that, I'll be in trouble."

"It'll be okay," Donovan told her.

It better be okay, he vowed silently.

The next day, Donovan, Beth, and Thorn were there, waiting for Amanda and Corissa to arrive. Amanda came first. When she saw the three of them, she stopped short.

"Hey, what's going on?" She peered over her shoulder, as if expecting someone to be there.

"I have some…difficult news to share with you and Corissa. And everyone who comes for a lesson today."

Amanda gripped her purse and twisted the strap in her hands. "Okay."

After Corissa showed up, the two of them stared at Beth, waiting for the news. Donovan rubbed Beth's back. She took a deep breath, but before she could get a word out, Thorn spoke. "What I told the two of you the other day about the man in the photo wasn't one hundred percent accurate. I am looking for him, but not because he robbed the cigarette store or a convenience store."

Beth cut in then. "He's my ex, and he might be stalking me."

Amanda and Corissa gasped.

"Do you remember the onesies from my baby shower that said they were from 'Daddy'?"

"Yeah," they answered together.

"Not from me," Donovan said.

"We're not positive who it is, but *someone* is stalking me at my house and here at the studio. Because of that, I think it's best I shut down The Fighting Chance until further notice."

Their jaws dropped even more.

"It's for your safety," Thorn explained. "And I am going to do everything in my power to find this guy, so he won't bother Beth or any of you anymore."

Thorn's promise seemed to calm them. They peered at one another. Then, with her shoulders back, Amanda said, "What can we do to help?"

Donovan smiled at that. No one would let Beth go out of business. No one would let this bastard win. Even her students were on the same page. They wanted whatever was best for Beth, and none of them asked for refunds. What they did ask for, was for Beth to call them as soon as she reopened. Having them behind her made her decision to close easier, and Donovan fully supported her choice.

At the end of the day, the five of them parted ways, for who knows how long. Donovan hoped, for Beth's sake, it wouldn't be too long. Not only did Beth need The Fighting Chance, but many people relied on it...relied on her.

For the next few days, Donovan stayed home with Beth, keeping her company. She insisted he didn't have to babysit her, but he didn't want to go off to work when she couldn't do the same. Nor did he want to be away if the perp came around again.

On December 6th, the two of them were lounging on the couch, watching TV, when a car horn sounded from outside. It beeped in the "Shave and a Haircut" tune. Beth turned to Donovan. They stared at each other a moment. Then the horn beeped out "Two Bits."

"That's him," Beth said with a breathy voice.

That's all she had to say to have Donovan leaping to his feet. He ran to the front door and threw it open.

Sitting there on the street in front of their house was a black car. It sped off with squealing tires, throwing smoke into the air that reeked of burnt rubber. Donovan raced down the length of the driveway to the road, but by the time he got there, the car fishtailed around the curve and disappeared from sight.

"Damn it!"

The bastard had been right outside their house. Again. Who knew how long he had been out there, spying on them, listening to them? And he had wanted them to know he'd been there, too. He could've left unseen, but he announced his presence to them. Letting them know he was close by was part of his game. Where could he be and when? That's what he wanted them to worry about, day in and day out, as any true stalker would.

"Donovan."

Beth's voice calling out to him had him turning back to the house. In her bathrobe, on the doorstep, she pointed down at the welcome mat. "He left something."

Donovan jogged back up the driveway. Lying on the doorstep was a Manila envelope. Written in bold letters across the front was "Donovan."

"Apparently, it's for me.

Beth bent closer. "I swear it's Craig's handwriting. If Thorn could get his hands on a document from Craig's job, he'd be able to prove it's a match. I know it."

Donovan nodded. Believing her. If she said it was Craig's handwriting, he took her word for it. "I'll be right back. Don't touch it."

He retrieved a box of latex gloves, brought it back to the front door, and put on a pair. Then he picked up the envelope carefully, holding it by the edges.

"What does it feel like?"

Donovan felt the contents through the envelope. "It's thick. Maybe a document or booklet of some kind." He ran his hands over both sides of the envelope. "No wires. No lumps. It's smooth."

"We should call Thorn anyway."

Donovan eyed the envelope. The last package had contained lingerie for Beth. He didn't know what this envelope held, but he wanted to take a peek at it before showing it to Thorn.

"I'm going to open it."

Beth shook her head. "We need to let Thorn do his job."

"I will, but I want to see what it is first, especially since it's about you."

"You're too stubborn for your own good." She sighed. "Fine. We'll sneak a look, and then, we'll call Thorn regardless of what we find, but we should do it inside over the kitchen table. If there's something small in it, the table will catch it, and it won't blow away."

In the kitchen, Beth sat in a chair, but Donovan was too wound up to sit. Standing across from her, he slit open the envelope with a knife. Before he slipped his gloved fingers in to pull out whatever the bastard wanted him to see, he ballooned the envelope by pressing on the folded corners and peered inside it. No powder, from what he could see. No odors, either. Nothing sharp that would cut him.

"Looks like large photographs." He pinched the stack of photos with his thumb and index finger, being careful not to disturb prints that might already be there. As he slipped them out, the first image revealed itself to him slowly. The photo was black and white. It wasn't until it was halfway out that he could make out the subject. A woman. A naked woman in the arms of a man. He grasped the stack of photos then, forgetting all about preserving fingerprints. His heart rate escalated. It pounded frantically at each of his pulse points. In his neck, it throbbed, making him nauseous. He breathed deeply to shove down the urge to vomit.

The photo exposed the woman's upper body. At the top of the photo, the image cut off at her chin, and the bottom stopped at her hips. The focus of the photo was of the side of her breast, half shielded by the man's arm so the most intimate parts weren't visible. Her ribs and navel were also uncovered. Donovan stared at it, with his mouth dry. He'd seen Beth's body enough to believe it was her in the photo.

"What is it?" she asked. "Show me."

Wordlessly, Donovan lifted the image and rotated it for her to see. When he did, the photo beneath it became visible.

"Oh my God." Wearing gloves, Beth took the photo from him.

Donovan didn't see her reaction, though, because he couldn't tear his stare from the second photo. This one was focused lower down, zeroing in on the couple's pelvises, which were pressed together passionately. He dropped the photo to the table.

"Holy shit. This is almost pornographic."

Still, Donovan didn't look at her to see her facial expression. Horror ricocheted inside him like a rogue bullet and settled right in the middle of his chest, where his heart beat frantically. "It's you."

"Excuse me?" Beth's tone had an acidic bite to it,

as if she were cursing him for voicing such an accusation, but he had the proof right in his hands.

He tossed down the stack.

Beth flinched as the photos scattered on the table in front of her. She bent her neck. For the first time, Donovan watched her reaction play out on her face. Her eyes widened. Her mouth popped open. She plucked up the photo on the top, the one that had caused Donovan such a reaction. The image showed a sideview of woman's neck and her face from the tip of her nose down. Her head was thrown back in ecstasy, and her mouth was open to release an erotic cry as an orgasm rippled through her. There was no mistaking the woman was Beth. That was her neck, her chin, her mouth.

That was his wife!

Donovan's hands formed fists.

Beth gawked. "Donovan, I…I don't know how this was taken."

Even though he was looking right at her, all he could see was red. He uncurled his hands and grabbed the chair in front of him. His fingers locked around it in a vise that he imagined around Craig's throat.

"He must've taken these photos when we were still together. Years ago. Way before you. And if he did, it was without my consent."

He didn't look at her, though. His attention was fixated on the photos spread out on the table. Slowly, his vision cleared, and a photo conjured a spear of agony in his heart that stole his breath.

"I'm so sorry, Donovan. I swear I don't know anything about these photos."

Donovan opened his mouth. "They weren't taken before me." His voice was flat. Dead. The proof stared up at him, torturing him.

"What? How do you know?"

The anger swirling like a tornado inside him unleashed its energy, snapping his composure. He reached over, flung a photo aside, and jabbed a finger at the image it had been partially covering. "That's how I know!"

The photo was of Beth's chest, showcasing the scar that stretched across it, the one she got when Hurricane Sabrina hit, when they had met and their relationship had begun.

Beth picked it up. "It could be Photoshopped."

Her response broke whatever little control Donovan had inside. He marched around the table and yanked open her robe, baring her chest and the scar he loved to lavish attention on.

"Donovan!" Beth caught the sides of her robe.

He pointed at her scar. "It's identical." Then he backed away, all the way to the wall where he collapsed into it.

Beth got up and carried the photo over to the mirror hanging beside the front door. While holding it up beside her chest, she compared the two. After a moment, she said, "My scar has faded since then, but...you're right it is identical." She turned the photo to see it up close. Her back stayed to him as she inspected every inch of the photo. Suddenly, she whirled around. "You missed a few things. What's not in this photo?"

Your clothes, he thought bitterly but didn't say.

She tugged her robe off her left shoulder. "This. My bullet wound. The picture was taken before we were married."

"You think that makes it better?"

Beth surged forward. "Did you notice the bedspread beneath me? It's the one from your bed, before we moved in here."

Donovan examined the photos on the table. True to her word, the black and white pattern on the bed in the corners of the images were of the set he had used years ago in his apartment.

"And don't you dare think I had sex with another man in your bed!" She slapped the photo on the table, grasped his hand, and smacked it down beside the image. Then she tugged the glove from the back of his hand. "Because you're the one with me!" Her finger tapped the side of the image where a man's hand cupped her shoulder.

He compared the photographed hand to the back of his own hand. They both had the scar from the burn he received in San Francisco. She was right; the man captured in the photos with her was himself.

"Ponder that," she spat and ripped off her gloves. "I'm going upstairs. I want to be left alone."

Donovan didn't move, couldn't tear his gaze off the damning evidence of his stupidity.

Their bedroom door upstairs slammed shut, causing Donovan to wince. Beth had every right in the world to be pissed off. How could he let Craig get in his head like that and fuck things up?

Donovan pulled out the chair and dropped into it. Of course, Craig would use photos of the two of them to make Donovan think the worst. He'd been trying to do that this entire time.

But how the hell did he get those pictures in the first place?

He removed his phone from his pocket and called Thorn. "An envelope of photos was dropped off," he said as soon as Thorn answered. "We opened it."

Thorn let out a curse. "What kind of photos?"

"Photos of Beth. And me. Being intimate." He inhaled. "Beth stands behind the handwriting being Craig's. And I believe her."

"I'm on my way."

"No." Donovan covered his eyes. "No offense, but I don't exactly want you to see these pictures."

"No offense right back, but I don't exactly *want* to see those pictures."

"He cropped them so I'd think it was him. And I did."

There was a pause on the other end before Thorn shouted, "Are you a fucking moron?"

"Yes." Donovan let out a sigh. "I have a mess to clean up here."

"I bet."

"Come on, Thorn, what do I do?" He was desperate. "I don't want to hand these photos over. I want to destroy them."

"Don't. Keep them. I know you don't want to, but those photos could be the evidence we need to show Craig's unraveling mental stability. Can you date the photos?"

"Yeah. Somehow, they were taken from the bedroom of my old apartment."

"Angle?"

"Up, pointing down."

"Okay, so here's what I'm going to do. I'm going to go to your old apartment, talk to the manager, and see if I can figure out where that camera might've been.

As for you, you're going to get down on your knees and let Beth kick you in the nuts. Then you're going to plead for her forgiveness."

"Sounds like a plan, but she wants to be alone right now. I'll give her some space. Call me back with whatever you find."

"Will do."

Donovan disconnected. For several minutes, he glared at the photos in disarray on the table. Then he gathered them up and shoved them back into the envelope. While he waited for Thorn to call him back, he roamed the first floor restlessly. He even ascended the stairs and stood outside the bedroom door, listening for signs of Beth crying and working up the courage to knock, but not finding it in him to confront her yet. For two hours, he suffered this excruciating tug of war and sense of powerlessness.

Back downstairs, cradling his head in his hands on the couch, his cell phone sounded. The screen indicated a text from Thorn. *I'm on my way. I'm going to need those photos.*

"Shit," he hissed. The fact Thorn needed those photos meant he found something.

Donovan got to his feet and took the stairs one at a time. At the bedroom door, he braced himself. Then he knocked.

Chapter Eleven

Sitting on the edge of the bed, Beth held a pillow to her stomach. She had wailed on that pillow, pummeling it with her fists. Then she sobbed into it. Now, she was embracing it to comfort herself. She didn't look toward the bedroom door when she said, "Come in."

The door creaked open. Donovan's footsteps made soft noises as he moved cautiously toward her. He came into her line of vision, but she kept her head down, so she could only see his feet. When he knelt in front of her, she could see his shoulders and neck, but still, she didn't raise her head to see his face, to look into his eyes.

"Beth."

He said her name in a whisper that tugged at her heartstrings.

"I'm so sorry."

For a moment, he said nothing else, letting his apology hang in the air.

"I can't explain what's going on inside my head," he finally said. "He's messing with me. Everything he's done has been aimed to chip away at my rationale, to make me believe you're..." His voice trailed off.

"Say it," she prompted.

"Having an affair," he said in a voice that was barely audible. He laid his hands on her knees. "I'm so sorry, Beth. I wasn't thinking clearly. It wasn't until I saw those photos that I started to doubt what I know to be a fact, that you'd never do that."

"But photos can be damning," she concluded.

"Yeah." He slid closer, trying to see her face. "Those images made me sick inside. I couldn't even see the things you saw, because all I saw was my wife, the love of my life, being physically intimate with a man that, for all I knew, wasn't me, but was *him*."

Beth lifted her head then and eyed him. "For you to believe for one second that I'd do such a thing…" She paused. "Even with what Craig is doing, I'd think you'd believe in me more. You're the man I want. Period. To think I could cheat on you with another man, and Craig of all of them, hurts me, because you should know better."

"I do." He framed her face with his hands. "I swear I do. I know that deep down."

Beth shifted her gaze, but she didn't pull away from his touch.

Silence lingered between them.

Donovan leaned back on his heels. He lowered his hands to his side and dropped his chin to his chest, defeated.

That same silence between them continued on until Beth found the strength to speak. "Stalkers are good at getting into their victim's heads. They cause fear, confusion, rage. It's what they do." She stared at his face. "You're right that he's targeting you." Donovan's gaze met hers. "He wants to break us apart. He wants you to leave so he can get me alone. And, if I have anything to say about it, that's not going to happen." She reached for him and pulled him into a kiss.

Donovan flinched in surprise. Then he rose onto

his knees, slipped the pillow out from between them, and took her into his arms. Something wet and warm touched Beth's thumb on his cheek—a tear. She couldn't even imagine the emotions he felt at that moment, after fearing he'd lost her, and being terrified that what he'd accused her of was irreparable. All she knew was how she'd felt—betrayed, heartbroken, enraged, torn. No doubt that was what he'd experienced when confronted by those photos, which were meant to make it look as though she'd been playing with Donovan from the start.

Beth deepened the kiss. Could their lips erase what had happened between them? She hoped so. The doorbell interrupted them from taking it further.

"That'll be Thorn," Donovan said.

She stopped him from getting to his feet to answer the door. With her forehead against his, she said, "I love you."

Donovan pressed his lips to hers once more. "I love you, too."

They went to the front door together. Thorn peered from Donovan, to Beth, and back to Donovan.

"So," he said. "Are you black and blue?"

"No."

"You got off easy."

Donovan moved his head slightly in a half shake and half shrug. "I wouldn't say that." Then he led them into the kitchen where the envelope sat on the table. "There they are."

Thorn picked them up. "I won't personally look at them, but they will be examined." Beth grimaced at that. The only person she wanted to see her like that was her husband. It was bad enough knowing Craig had seen them, taken them, watched them making love. She didn't want anyone else to see those moments when she was in the throes of intimacy with Donovan.

"Sorry it took me so long to get here," Thorn said. "After I went to your old apartment, I looked into Craig and went to the last known place he was staying." One at a time, he peered at them. "Are you ready for this?"

They nodded.

Thorn took something out of his jacket pocket and set it on the table. "I found this in the air vent in your old apartment bedroom. It's a wireless, pinhole covert camera that works with most smartphones. With this, he could see and hear everything that went on in your bedroom on his phone or PC."

Beth stared at the tiny, black camera no bigger than two inches. Revulsion rolled through her. Knowing Craig had spied on them every time they were in Donovan's apartment bedroom sickened her. Every time they had private conversations. Every time they made love. Every time they slept side by side.

"This device is as high-tech as you can get and nearly impossible to find if you're not looking for it. There's remote playback capabilities, infrared night vision, and motion detectors that alert you with email or text."

"Holy shit," Beth said. Equipment like that was dangerous. Sure, it could help someone to keep an eye on a nanny, assist with elder care, watch an ex during custody battles, or even to catch burglars in the act. For stalkers, however, it was the perfect tool to spy on their prey, to memorize their routine, to feed their mania.

Donovan took Beth's hand in his. "How long could it have been there?"

Thorn shrugged. "Maybe not long because it ran on batteries. It also has a power adapter plug in, but he would've had to keep coming in to connect it to the power adapter to charge."

Beth swallowed. He could've watched them for weeks. "So you believe me when I say it's Craig?"

Thorn's jaw ticked. "Yeah, but more on that in a minute. Do either of you have any idea how he could've gotten into your apartment to plant this?"

"No," Beth said. "I mean, we had someone break in during that lightning storm, remember? But he wouldn't have had time to put that in the vent. Donovan was patching up the shattered bedroom window, and I was lowering the blinds in the guest bedroom. Whoever got in stayed in the front of the apartment."

"She's right," Donovan said.

The three of them contemplated the possible ways Craig could've managed this extreme breach in privacy. Every scenario Beth had disturbed her and gave her the chills. It didn't really matter how Craig achieved it, because, in the end, he did it. The mere thought Craig had invaded their home, or had someone else do it for him, and saw things he had no business seeing was something she couldn't shake.

"I remember something."

Donovan's voice drew her back to the present.

"Months after we got back from San Francisco, a man came to the apartment to check and clean the air vents."

Beth sat up straighter.

"He wore coveralls and a hat and said he was checking every apartment in the building that day. They often had people come to check on things or do random inspections, so I didn't think anything of it. He worked on all the vents, even the one in our bedroom." Donovan met Beth's eye. "You weren't home."

"Did the man look like Craig?" Thorn wanted to know.

He lifted his hands. "I saw Craig that one time, and the man who came to check the vents had a beard."

"A man can grow a beard quickly to disguise himself," Beth muttered.

Thorn inclined his chin. "Once again, she's right."

Except, Beth didn't want to be right. Her knowledge aided them, no doubt about it, but she hated that what she'd learned as a self-defense instructor came into play so often in her life. Had she jinxed herself by teaching self-defense? Had she welcomed men like Buck, Jackson Storm, Viper, and Craig into her life by opening The Fighting Chance? Was this the balance the universe required when she taught students how to be strong and stay alive?

"That's not all," Thorn said.

Of course, it's not.

"After I left your old apartment, I looked into Craig. Months ago, Craig sold his house and quit his job. He doesn't have a current job, either. And the apartment he did have, he apparently vacated a couple of weeks ago, with months of back-rent owed. The manager let me in to look around. They're waiting a couple more weeks before they clear out his stuff. It was mostly empty, but he left behind his suits and ties."

Donovan's eyebrows lowered. "Ties?"

"Yup. About a dozen or more."

"Hold on." Donovan got up and hurried upstairs.

Beth shrugged at Thorn.

When Donovan came back downstairs, he had a plastic bag in his hand. "Ties like this?"

Inside the bag was the stripped tie Donovan's mechanic had found stuffed beside the driver's seat of Beth's car.

"A lot like that tie, actually," Thorn said.

Beth's mouth fell open with what that meant. "How could he get that in my car?"

"He apparently has the means." Thorn took the plastic bag to add it to his stash of evidence. "And he's been learning."

"Which is clearly dangerous."

Thorn nodded. "Among newspapers and mail, I found the instruction manual for the same covert camera I found in the vent. A sticker on it matched the product number on the bottom of the device. Not only that, but I spoke to a couple of Craig's co-workers again. They said that over the past couple of years, he'd changed his looks drastically and bulked up. He doesn't look anything as he did when he first started working there."

Beth swallowed. The words "bulked up" sent fresh alarm through her. "So, it could've been him on the security feed. He could've been the one who came into The Fighting Chance?"

"It's a strong possibility."

That was a possibility Beth didn't want to be true.

****

The days, even though they were shorter, dragged on and on for Beth. Without The Fighting Chance, she didn't have anything to take up her time. She spent a lot of time in the baby's room, rearranging the decorations and folding freshly-washed clothes that she laid in the drawers of the white dresser. They hadn't decided on a theme for the baby's room, since themes change constantly as a child gets older. Instead, they put whatever they liked into the room—a stuffed giraffe, a stuffed panda bear, an animated map of Florida in a white frame, a painting of the full moon, and a dragonfly mobile. A shelf on the wall had framed photos of Beth and Donovan, Beth's parents, Meredith and Lily, and Ryan. And in one collage on the wall was every single ultrasound photo of the baby so far.

Beth enjoyed spending time in the baby's room, doing what people referred to as "nesting." But there wasn't much one could do in a baby's room that didn't have a baby in it, so she was relieved when Amanda texted asking if she'd like to meet for lunch.

Beth texted back, *YES!!!!*

Then, she followed up with, *Sorry for the yelling all caps, but I need this.*

Amanda replied, *I thought so. Without needing to go to work, I'm going bonkers.*

They decided on a Japanese restaurant for hibachi. Beth went downstairs and found Donovan watching the news and drinking a soda. "Hey, Amanda invited me out to lunch." She paused when she noted the boredom on his face. "But maybe we should go out for lunch together, instead."

"No. Go meet Amanda and have fun. I'll be fine here."

She smiled. "Maybe you should call Thorn and have a boy's lunch out."

Donovan scowled. "Not happening."

She chuckled. "It was worth a shot." Unable to hide her smirk, she picked up her purse from the hook by the front door. When she went to get her keys from the dish on the stand, she stilled mid-reach. Her keys weren't there. "Have you seen my keys?"

"Nope. Are they in the kitchen?"

After scanning the countertop, she said, "No. I might've left them in the car. Again." She had left her keys in the car a couple of months ago, and she hadn't found them until after she searched the entire house top to bottom. They had been in the cupholder of her unlocked car all night. "I'll text you from the car if I find them in there."

"Okay. I love you. Drive safely."

"Love you, too." She went out to her car, which she found locked. "Damn." With her hands to the driver's side window and her face close to the glass, she stared inside it. Her keys dangled from the ignition. She hadn't even removed them when she'd parked the car! "Pregnancy brain is a real thing," she grumbled under her breath.

She pulled her purse straps down to her elbow and dug through it for her spare key. Usually, it could always be found at the bottom of her bag, in a corner that she'd already checked twice. "Ugh. Come on. Where is it?" She tucked her wallet under her arm and continued to rummage through the contents of her purse—lip balm, business cards, spare change, gum, a mini bottle of hand sanitizer, and a key card. A frown formed on her face. A key card? She pulled it out and examined it. When was the last time she and Donovan had had a hotel room? She recalled their stay in the motel following the fire. Thorn had paid for that room, and it had an old brass key, not a plastic key card.

"Radisson" was printed on one side of the card. On

the other side was information for a concierge app with a QR Code, their phone number, and website URL. Beth and Donovan had never stayed at the Radisson before, and she was pretty sure they would've wanted their key card back when they checked out.

She had no idea where the key card came from or how it got into her purse, but she didn't have time to solve the mystery now. Amanda was probably on her way to the restaurant, and Beth didn't want to stand her up. She dropped the key card back into her purse, and then she located her spare key beneath an emergency sanitary napkin.

"There you are!" A quick text to Donovan later and she started on her way.

When Beth arrived at the restaurant, Amanda was already there, sitting on one side of a large, u-shaped table alone. A loud family of six occupied the other side. Beth hurried over and took the chair next to her. "I am so sorry I'm late. I couldn't find my keys." She gave Amanda a sheepish smile. "They were locked in my car."

"That's okay. I haven't been waiting long."

The waitress came over right away. Beth ordered a chicken hibachi meal with extra broccoli, and Amanda ordered the shrimp and mushroom. Before they had a chance to catch up, the chef came over. He sprayed the hot iron plate with oil, which had flames shooting up toward the ceiling. Heat scorched Beth's face. She leaned away from the flames. The chef dumped a bucket of veggies onto the tabletop stove. With the veggies on, he then upturned a small dish of shrimp. He chopped off the tails of the shrimp with his spatula, flung the severed tails up one at a time into the air above his head, and caught each of them in his tall chef's hat.

While the shrimp and chicken breast cooked, he sliced a large onion into rings and stacked the rings from biggest to smallest. Then he squirted oil on the inside of the onion ring mountain. Fire shot out of the rings, creating a volcano that erupted for a minute before extinguishing and emitting steam like a train. Finally, he plopped a tub of rice onto the surface, added sauce, and mixed it up with the diced veggies. He scooped up the hot food with his spatula and piled it onto their plates. They thanked him when he finished, and then they dug in.

"How have you been?" Beth asked Amanda. "It's been weird not seeing you and Corissa every day."

"I feel the same way. I've been working out at home to make sure I don't get soft."

Beth chuckled. "Gosh, I am going to be so out of shape by the time I have this baby and can get back to work."

"Yeah, but you'll get back there. I'll help you."

"You'll kick my butt, you mean."

Amanda faked a hurt expression and laid a hand to her chest. "I would never."

Beth pierced a chunk of chicken with her fork. "I am sorry for the inconvenience this has caused you and Corissa. Not me being pregnant, but closing down The Fighting Chance, I mean. I swear you and Cor will receive paid leave until this matter is resolved."

"That's okay. We understand. You're doing what you have to do." Amanda picked up a mushroom slice with her chopsticks. "Speaking of which, how have *you* been? Have you heard from Craig? Has he done anything since you've left work?"

Beth swallowed a piece of carrot. "Actually, he came to the house."

Amanda's face paled.

"He left an envelope on the front step."

"What was in it?" Amanda's voice sounded as though she was being strangled, and she was…by fear.

"Photos of me." Beth glanced at the family across the way and lowered her voice. "Naked. I wasn't alone in the photos, though."

Amanda's eyes widened.

"He tried to make it seem as though the man was him, and I was having an affair, but the man in the photos with me was Donovan."

"H-how would he get photos of the two of you?"

Beth took a gulp of water. Her face felt flushed. "He had installed a wireless spy cam in a vent in Donovan's old apartment bedroom."

"Holy shit!" Amanda slapped her hand over her mouth and peered around to see if anyone had heard her. She leaned toward Beth to ask, "But how could he do that?"

"He pretended to be with the apartment, checking air vents. He came to the apartment when I wasn't there. Neither of us knew about it until now, and that camera was still in the vent, too. Dead, but there."

Amanda stared at her plate of food. "That's scary."

Beth nodded. "It is." She hated to tell Amanda these things, because she had her own stalker to deal with. Hearing about ways that he could harass her, spy on her, violate her could damage her fragile sense of security and induce paranoia. Beth didn't want to keep these things from Amanda, her friend, though. Amanda wanted to know, and she needed to know to understand the extent of how far a deranged stalker would go to achieve his or her goal. A little paranoia was better than being naive and unprepared.

"I…um…have something to show you." Amanda set down her chopsticks and pulled a piece of paper from her purse. Without a word, she handed it to Beth.

Beth unfolded it and read, "found you." The statement was written in all lowercase and lacked punctuation, but that didn't make those words any less threatening.

"I found that sticking out of the crack between my front door yesterday," she explained. "It's from him."

Damon.

"Did you tell the police?"

"No."

"You should tell them. Or at least tell Thorn."

Amanda's gaze lowered to her food again. "I don't know."

"Why not?"

"Because…" She sighed. "Because I don't want to drag Thorn into my mess."

"He wouldn't consider it that way. This is what he does, and whether or not you want to hear it or are ready to hear it, I am going to say it…he cares about you. A lot. He wants to be there for you. Believe me."

Amanda's cheeks flamed. "I'm ashamed."

"What could you possibly have to be ashamed of?"

Her friend gripped the napkin in her lap and spoke quietly, quickly, as if pushing the words out. "Ashamed I let it go on this long. Ashamed I can't handle it myself. Ashamed I'm weak, that he still has the power to frighten me, that he found me. Again."

"First of all, you are not weak." Beth took Amanda's hand. "You are brave and fierce and strong. Everything he has ever done to hurt you has made you into a warrior. Second, you shouldn't have to handle this yourself. You're stronger when you have others at your back. I never would've been able to survive what I have without Donovan and Thorn at my back.

"Third, nearly every woman dealing with domestic violence stays because they hope it'll change and get better. That's not a bad thing to hope for. It becomes bad if you never get out. You got out. As for him having power to frighten you, yes, he does. They all do. But you have the power and the will to keep on fighting, to keep on living. You have friendship and love, skill and knowledge making you powerful."

Amanda wiped away stray tears as they slid down her cheeks. "Thanks, Beth."

"I mean it. Every word of it."

"I know." Amanda lifted her napkin and used it to dab her wet eyes. "It's just…I don't know what to do so he won't be able to track me down again. I've thought of changing my name, but I'd still have my social security number. He would be able to use that to find me, wouldn't he?"

"He could, but you can change your social security number if you can prove that using your existing number will cause you harm, which you can easily prove with your hospital records, police report, and this note." Beth tapped on the piece of paper. "But you'd have to change your name, your phone number, move, and get another job."

Amanda's shoulders lowered. "And…I don't want to do that. When I moved here from North Carolina, I didn't think he'd be able to find me, but the Internet makes it easy to find out where someone lives. All you have to do is type in someone's name and a state, and websites pop up listing every record that closely matches the search. They list phone numbers, partial email addresses, and full mailing addresses. I looked up my name with 'Florida,' and there I was, with my current address on full display." She shook her head. "Those websites are dangerous and should not be readily available for anyone and everyone to use."

Beth knew all about websites like that. They were often the reason why her students would have encounters with the people they were trying to escape or forget. She wished websites that freely provided those details, without even needing to download a report, would be banned for safety reasons.

"The thing is, I don't want to move again, and I don't want to quit. I like it here, and I love my job. And, yes, one day, I'd like to have the courage to pursue something with Thorn." Amanda met Beth's gaze briefly. "But Damon knows where I live now. It's a matter of time before he knows where I work." Her shoulders drooped. "I'm so tired, Beth. I'm tired of running and starting over and hoping he won't find me or finally leave me alone."

"I know." Beth put her arm around Amanda's shoulders and pulled her into a hug. "I know." She rubbed Amanda's back. "One day, he will leave you alone, because he'll be in jail."

Amanda let out a bitter laugh. "That'll be the day." She eased back. "I can't even imagine what that day would feel like, or how long it'd take me to accept it." She took a sip of sweet tea before saying, "I have a pepper spray keychain with my car keys."

Beth took out her keys and set them on the table. "So do I."

"I have a stun gun in my purse." Amanda met her eyes.

"I don't have a stun gun, but I do own a gun," she said. "It's at home in the safe, but I have shot and killed two men."

"What was it like?"

Beth studied Amanda's face. Was she planning to shoot and kill Damon if he ever confronted her? She couldn't say he didn't have it coming, but that wasn't always the answer.

"It was unnerving that I could kill someone so easily, with as little as one bullet, with a mere squeezing of a trigger. I still have moments where I think back on what happened and have to remind myself it was in self-defense. If I hadn't shot Chewy, I would've been killed. Donovan, too. And if I hadn't shot Viper, the two of us *and* Thorn would've died."

Amanda was silent for a long time before she said, "I have a second stun gun that I put beside me while I sleep at night. I've memorized Thorn's phone number, but in a moment where I am terrified, I may not be able to recall it or be able to find his name in my contacts fast enough. I have Thorn's business card behind my phone, inside the case." She popped her phone out of the case to show Beth the card hidden there. "I have another one with me at all times, in case I drop my phone or run away without it."

Her voice lowered. "I made a slit in all of my bra's cups, and I slipped one of his cards into each pair. Every morning when I dress, I make sure it's still there, and, at night, I sleep with my bra on. Not exactly comfortable, but safety is more important. I also put his cards throughout my house, so whatever room I am in when Damon breaks in, I have several close by that I can grab. You know, in case the one in my bra gets damaged somehow." She shrugged. "I come up with a lot of 'just in case' scenarios."

"That's good. That means you'll be prepared for whatever happens."

Amanda shrugged. "Sometimes it makes me feel crazy. I have two bolts and three chains on my front door and the door to the garage. Hurricane shutters are screwed over my sliding glass door, black-out curtains cover every window, and I set up booby-traps at my windows that'll alert me of an intruder. If Thorn or anyone were to see that, they'd think I'm crazy."

Beth shook her head. "Thorn wouldn't. He'd probably applaud it, and even suggest a tin can of marbles in front of every door."

That had Amanda smiling.

"Believe me, if there's anyone who'll understand, it's Thorn."

And he'd sure love to know that his business cards were inside every single one of her bras, too. Beth had never seen him faint before, but he might while imagining that.

The two of them fell quiet while they picked at their food. It wasn't as hot as it had been before, but it was still edible, especially for a hungry, pregnant lady. With their check, which Amanda insisted on picking up since she'd asked Beth to lunch, came two fortune cookies.

Beth opened hers. *Happiness comes in twos.*

She frowned at that. *What the heck is that supposed to mean?* She left the slip of paper on her plate and crunched on the cookie fragments. "My fortune cookie is being all Sherlock Holmes with me. What does yours say?"

Embarrassment colored Amanda's cheeks. "Give love a chance."

Beth grinned, not even caring if she had cookie crumbs in her teeth. "You should listen to him. Mr. Fortune Cookie knows his stuff."

Her cell phone dinged as the two of them giggled. She flipped her phone over to see the notification on the screen, and her laughter dissolved.

Amanda also stopped laughing. "What is it?"

Beth swallowed. "A text. It says, 'Meet me at the Radisson in our favorite room tonight. I have plans for you. Eight p.m.'" She peered at Amanda from over her phone. "It's not from Donovan. Before I got here, I found a hotel key card in my purse. Craig must've put it in there."

"But how? When would he have had access to your purse?"

The answer came to Beth right away. Feeling stupid, she put her hand to her forehead. "When he came into The Fighting Chance to use the restroom. I had sworn I'd heard someone in my office. My purse had been on top of my desk. He must've stepped in, slipped the key card inside, and fled before I could come out of my bathroom."

"If he's going to be at the Radisson tonight, you need to tell Thorn. He could catch him."

Beth couldn't agree more. "Funny how telling Thorn about what's going on in our lives has been the theme of our lunch."

Amanda offered a weak smile.

"The police department isn't far from here. I think I'll stop by and tell him in person."

"I'll follow you there," Amanda said.

"That's not necessary."

"No, it is. If Craig is following you, I'll be a car between you and him. And…" She chewed on her bottom lip a moment. Then she held up the note Damon had left her. "I think I'll tell Thorn about this, too."

Beth squeezed her hand. "That's a good idea."

****

They arrived at the police department ten minutes later. Amanda followed Beth in, and Beth couldn't help but wonder if she did that so she could duck out and make a fast getaway if she changed her mind about talking to Thorn. Luckily, she stuck with Beth as she made her way through the bullpen to Thorn's desk.

Thorn glanced up to see Beth walking toward him. His head went back slightly in surprise.

"Hey, Beth."

In front of his desk, she stepped to the side, revealing Amanda.

He popped to his feet. "Amanda." He turned to Beth. "What are you two doing here?"

"We have to tell you a couple of things." Beth passed him her cell phone so he could read the text Craig had sent her. "And I found this in my purse." She handed him the key card.

"Do me a favor." Thorn held out the phone. "Text him back. Tell him you'll be there."

"What?" Beth and Amanda said together.

"If he's at the Radisson, I need him to stay there,

and he'll do that if he's expecting you to show up. Tell him you'll be there."

Not liking the idea of falsely leading Craig on and reinforcing his fantasies further, she did as Thorn asked.

"There." She showed him the screen with the text exactly as he had asked.

"Good."

At the same time as Thorn spoke, another text came through.

Beth read it. "He said he can't wait to see me."

"Reply back."

Beth glared at Thorn. "You've got to be kidding me. I don't want him to think we're secret lovers."

"He already thinks that." Thorn pointed at the phone she grasped in her hand. "Tell him something so he doesn't suspect you're tricking him."

Beth thought about it and tapped out, *Me neither.* And although it made her cringe, she added the winking emoji blowing a kiss.

"Happy?" She shoved the phone at Thorn.

"I am. The emoji was a nice touch." He let out a sigh. "Look, I know you don't want to egg him on, but it's crucial he be there when I arrive to arrest him. If you hadn't responded at all, he could've lost his temper and come to your house, instead. And we don't want that."

"No, we don't," Beth whispered.

"Why don't the two of you sit down? I need to make a couple of phone calls to figure out which Radisson he's staying at."

Beth and Amanda sat in the chairs on the other side of Thorn's desk. They stayed quiet as he made his phone calls and spoke to the managers, who all wanted confirmation from the police chief that Thorn was indeed a detective doing legitimate law enforcement work before they even considered giving him a smidge of information. At the end of the second call, Thorn rubbed his hands over his face.

"Hotel managers," he groaned.

"Did you find him?"

Thorn lowered his hands. "I did. He's staying at the Radisson Resort at the Port in Cape Canaveral, Room 202. But…" He stopped short.

Beth and Amanda glanced at one another.

"But what?" Beth wanted to know.

A wince took over his face, and he scratched the back of his neck. "Well, he put the room under Craig Goldwyn."

Hearing her married name paired with "Craig" made Beth's stomach whirl.

"Okay…yeah…" She swallowed. "That is creepy."

Thorn leaned forward. "I'll get him, Beth. If he texts you again, send back short replies so he'll be encouraged enough to remain in that room. With the evidence we have of him illegally recording you and Donovan, terrorizing you, and stalking you, he will be charged."

Although her mouth was dry, she said, "Thanks."

Beside her, Amanda cleared her throat. "I guess it's my turn now." She wrung her hands in her lap and kept her gaze low. "Beth encouraged me to tell you."

Thorn met Beth's eye, and she nodded.

Amanda slipped the paper onto Thorn's desk. "My ex left this for me outside my house."

Thorn picked it up and unfolded it. His jaw clenched as he read the few words. "When did he leave this?"

"Yesterday." Amanda's voice was small.

For a moment, Thorn glared at the note. Beth almost kicked him under the table to get him to rouse, but he pulled himself out of his rage-induced trance. "I can get an unmarked car and two cops to stake out your house for the next few days and nights to make sure he doesn't come around, and, if he does, they'll arrest him." He opened his desk drawer, took out an evidence bag, and dropped the note inside it. On the plastic he wrote with a permanent marker yesterday's date and Amanda's full name. He paused with the marker hovering over the bag. "What's his name?"

Amanda didn't meet his eye when she said, "Damon Hunter."

Thorn blinked. "Demon Hunter?"

That had Amanda bursting with laughter. "No. Damon." She spelled it out for him. "But you could say he's a demon."

Thorn recapped the marker. "Do you have a security camera by your front door?"

"No, but I have an alarm system."

"You need a camera in case he comes by again. If he does, you'll have proof. I have an extra peephole security camera. You can't even tell it's a camera. I can come by after five and install it for you if you want."

"That'd be nice. Thank you."

Thorn nodded. "Is there anything else?" He studied them.

"No, that's it," Beth said. "Although, you have your work cut out for you."

"It's my job." He always said it with a shrug, as if he didn't do the things he did out of love.

They said goodbye to him. On their way out, Beth's phone dinged with another text message. Her body chilled all over, but the text wasn't from Craig. It was from Thorn.

Thanks for convincing her to tell me.

Smiling, she sent off a heart emoji.

Later that night, Beth and Donovan waited for eight o'clock to come. Twenty minutes past, Thorn texted Beth words she did not want to read. *He's not here.*

Chapter Twelve

With Craig at large, Donovan hated to leave Beth, but since she wasn't alone, he felt better about attending a meeting with Mitch and his team. Except, Leighton was the one keeping Beth company, and that didn't really mean much. The one consolation was Leighton knew how to use handcuffs and, according to Beth, could throw a shoe far. Not exactly protector material, but Donovan didn't plan to be gone long. He had one thing to say.

At the head of the table, Donovan studied his team. These were the men and women who had helped him to go from an amateur to a professional, who had been as determined as him to build the best monster truck in the business, who had always had his back. He hoped they'd have his back now.

"Thanks for meeting me today. I've come to a decision about my future as a driver, and about Venom's future." He paused. "I'm going to retire after next year's Monster Jam."

Everyone's mouths fell open.

Mitch jumped to his feet. "Are you crazy?"

Donovan expected this reaction from him. Mitch had fought hard for him to get into shows when he was starting out and no one cared about a rookie driver.

"I was crazy to begin monster truck driving," Donovan said. "This decision is the least crazy thing

I've done as a driver."

Mitch's mouth opened and closed, like a fish gasping for water. "But...but...but you are in your prime. You're at the top of your game. You're the best driver in the world!"

It was true. Donovan won every competition he was in, and he was performing better than ever. But some things were more important than applause, even a stadium full of cheers.

"I realize this comes as a shock to all of you, but I've had my time and my fun. Now, I need to do something different. I need to pass on the torch."

He had more than enough trophies. A case held dozens of them in their office and a couple of his most memorable wins were displayed beside their electric fireplace.

"I want to retire as driver. I will continue to own Venom, but I want to coach a new, younger driver to take my place behind the wheel."

That had the room going silent. Then they all grinned.

"So, you're not quitting the team?" Miranda asked.

"Not if you still want me."

"We want you," they shouted together.

Donovan smirked. "Beth is going to love how kinky you all are."

Guffaws filled the room.

"But seriously," Donovan said when the laughter died down, "I'd like to coach someone to be Venom's new driver. I'd like to help a young person get the chance, and I'd like to help that person rack up the wins, as all of you helped me."

"I'll do you one better," Mitch said. "You can

manage the team."

Donovan blinked. "I don't want to push you out, Mitch. I want to work with you."

"Ah. You're not pushing me out." Mitch waved his hand in the air. "I've been thinking of retiring, myself. It is past that time for me, but I've been holding off because I didn't want to let you down. With you not driving and wanting to coach, this is the perfect time for me to step down and for you to take my place. I just have one request…free access to competitions."

Donovan pounded Mitch's fist. "We can do that."

He discussed with his team how they'd go about looking for a new driver and agreed they'd hold auditions right after Monster Jam. A few of them even knew of up-and-coming drivers hungry for a chance, who'd be thankful for the opportunity. For some reason, the idea of coaching a driver through his or her career thrilled Donovan more than when he had decided to be the one behind the wheel performing death-defying stunts.

Everyone agreed with what they had to do first— kill it at Monster Jam.

Donovan left the meeting prouder than ever of his team and excited for the future of his career. He arrived home to Beth and Leighton blasting Christmas music and decorating the house. "Whoa. What happened in here?"

Holly garland wrapped around the columns to the small sitting area and draped over the electric fireplace. Large, red, velvet bows were tied to the staircase banisters. Shiny, silver tinsel covered the surfaces of every piece of furniture. Over-sized silver and gold ornaments hung from curtain rods.

"We're decorating for your Christmas party," Leighton called out over the carols. "You know that it's in eight days, right?"

He tossed his keys into the dish by the door and headed in the direction of Leighton's voice. "Of course, I do." In fact, he was counting down to their Christmas party, because two days later they'd be flying to Michigan for their Christmas vacation.

In the living room, Beth and Leighton were decorating their artificial tree. It looked as though they had been decorating themselves more than the tree, though. Beth had a gold, plastic garland tied around her belly, and Leighton had a bit of garland around her head like a crown.

"You're lucky I'm here," Leighton said. "I've saved your party from being a complete and utter failure."

"It wouldn't have been a failure. There would've been food."

"That sounds so sad." Leighton twirled back to the tree and eyed it critically before hooking an ornament to a branch.

"We saved you the star to put on top of the tree." Beth held it up.

With the star on the highest bow and the lights on, it really was beginning to look a lot like Christmas.

****

The day of their early Christmas party, Beth and Donovan were busy making sure everything was ready before their guests arrived. They put out extra toilet paper and hand soap in the guest bathroom, positioned covered trash bins in every room downstairs, and made sure there was more than enough food, drinks, plates, napkins, and utensils.

Beth wore a floor-length, maroon maternity dress with a lace bodice and three-quarter sleeves. Donovan wore dark gray dress pants and a black suit jacket with white stars on it over a white shirt and gray tie. It was as festive as he was willing to get. He had to repeatedly decline Leighton's fashion advice for him to wear a full Christmas suit that would've made him look as though he wore pajamas. A jacket with stars on it he could work with, however.

Beth came up to him with a bundle of green leaves and red berries in her hand. "Can you hang this on the arch to the dining room?"

"Sure. What is it?"

"Mistletoe."

He arched a brow. "It's a ball."

"They actually call it a Mistletoe Kissing Ball."

"Who's *they*?"

"Everyone."

"Ah."

She whacked him in the stomach with the back of her hand. "Don't make fun of it. I made it from scratch with a Styrofoam ball and holiday bouquets from the dollar store."

"In that case, I love it."

"Uh-huh."

Donovan slipped a clear tack through the red ribbon at the top of the ball and reached above his head to push the tack into the plaster. "There." He lowered his arm. "It doesn't look so bad."

"No, it doesn't. And neither do you."

Beth gazed up at him. Her hair, set in waves, draped over her shoulders. Dark eyeshadow gave her eyes a sultry look, and her deep red lipstick to match the color of her dress made her lips look more seductive than ever.

"Guests aren't here yet, and we're under a mistletoe." She put her arms around his neck.

Donovan put one hand on her hip, drawing her closer, and the other on the side of her face. "Was this your plan in having me hang that?"

"It had to go up, but this is a bonus." She closed the distance between them. Their lips connected, as if magnetized.

The smell of Beth's sandalwood perfume invigorated his senses and had sparks of lust bursting throughout his body. Their kiss deepened.

"Is it too late to cancel the party?" Donovan spoke between her lips.

Right then, the doorbell chimed.

"Yes," Beth whispered.

Donovan continued to hold her and kissed her again.

Knocking had him finally pulling away.

"Can you let them in?" she asked. "You can move faster than me."

"Yeah, but after the party, if you're not too tired, we're picking this up right where we left off."

"I'll meet you under the mistletoe." She winked.

Donovan answered the door and scowled at Thorn. "Of course, it's you."

Thorn lifted his hands. "What did I do?"

"Never mind. Come on in. You're the first to arrive."

"Lucky me. I'm not exactly a holiday party kind of guy."

"Then why'd you come so early?" Donovan eyed him suspiciously. For a man who claimed to not be a holiday party kind of guy, he had on a black jacket and a tie with white reindeer on it. He did look more laidback than Donovan did, though, in his dark jeans. "And why are you wearing a Christmas tie? I thought you only had a couple of professional ties."

"What is this? An interrogation? I bought it for this party." He smoothed down his tie. "At least I'm wearing manly deer and not girly stars."

Donovan yanked on his collar, proud of his jacket. "Stars are exploding balls of gas. They're not girly. They're neutral."

"Fine then, we're even. Besides, if I would've come in a plain T-shirt, Beth would've punched me. And for your information, I came early to get credit. If I had come late, I would've gotten punched twice."

"Smart man."

"Thanks. Now is there anything to drink around here? I'm going to need alcohol to get through this thing."

"In the kitchen."

The doorbell rang as Thorn headed off to wet his whistle. Beth joined him at the door to help greet the early arrivals. Old friends from work and school, members of Donovan's team, staff and special members from The Fighting Chance, monster truck buddies, and even Officer Burnett, who had been there for them during the investigation into Ryan's murder, all came to eat, drink, and be merry.

Leighton arrived, fashionably late, in a short silver dress as shiny as chrome hub caps. She flounced by, jingling with bells she wore around her ankles. Beth covered her mouth and whispered to him, "She's hoping to leave here tonight with one of your friends."

"Oh, no," Donovan groaned. He craned his neck to see Smith and Gordon gaping at her and all but drooling. Hopefully, they wouldn't come to blows. It'd been known to happen when they wanted the same girl at a party.

April, one of Beth's students, came moments later in a black dress with a slit up the side. The crescent moon-shaped scar on her cheek was barely visible. She looked beautiful. Donovan glanced over at his friends. Smith nudged Gordon and discreetly pointed at April. Then he pointed at Gordon and Leighton before heading in April's direction. Donovan shook his head. Was everyone going to hook-up by the end of this party?

"I think that Mistletoe Kissing Ball is going to be seeing a lot of action," he told Beth.

She peered around him to see the couples forming among their friends. "Oops."

Donovan wasn't at all surprised by it, though. Their friends had mingled at their gender-less baby shower and now was the time to get closer. Just in time for Christmas and New Year's Eve.

A soft knock sounded on the door. Donovan opened it to Amanda. She held a wrapped Christmas present in her hands.

"We told you you didn't have to bring a gift." Beth ushered her inside and gave her an air kiss beside her cheek.

"Oh, I didn't. This isn't from me. I found this outside. Someone must've set it down to knock and forgot to pick it up. I didn't want to leave it there for anyone to snag."

Beth took it from Amanda. "Thank you, and your dress is beautiful."

Amanda wore a bright red dress that came off her shoulders. The layers were cut uneven so that the front came to her knees and the back went down to her shoes. Thorn would have a heart attack when he saw her. Donovan scanned the crowd but couldn't see him. He was likely hiding out in the kitchen, close to the booze.

"Go on and mingle," Beth told Amanda. "Food and drinks are in the kitchen. We'll be joining everyone soon."

"I could probably use some liquid courage," she said.

When Amanda left, heading for the kitchen—she and Thorn were more alike than either of them thought—Beth tapped on Donovan's arm. "The tag on the box is written out to me. In Craig's handwriting."

Chapter Thirteen

Donovan took the package from Beth, and the two of them went into the kitchen to hunt down Thorn. They found him standing next to the counter with Amanda, each holding a glass. Beth hated to barge in on this moment. The two of them were alone and talking. This was what Thorn had been hoping for, for months. And here Mr. and Mrs. Disaster were coming to disrupt that and put a damper on the festivities.

"Hey," Beth said. "Sorry to interrupt."

Thorn glared.

Sorry, sorry, sorry, she thought.

"But we need to borrow Thorn for a moment." She angled her head to indicate he was needed elsewhere.

Unfortunately, Amanda was a smart woman. Her gaze connected to the wrapped package in Donovan's hands, and she figured out the truth. "It's from Craig, isn't it?"

Thorn straightened off the counter he had been leaning comfortably against.

"I brought in a package he had left for you." It wasn't a question, but rather a statement. Amanda knew she had helped Craig achieve his plan by picking up that package and bringing it into their house.

Beth nodded. "It is." She peered at Thorn. "We need Thorn for a minute."

"No."

They turned their attentions to Amanda.

Her cheeks flamed. "What I mean is that I brought that thing to you, so I want to know what's in it. I already know what's going on, so you're not leaving me out of this."

Thorn bobbed his head and smirked to himself, as if he were saying, "She's got us there."

"It's up to you," Donovan told Beth.

She studied Amanda a moment. This was not the same woman she had met a couple of years ago who had been afraid of her own shadow and was skittish around men. Any man. It didn't matter who it was. She hadn't even liked to be touched back then. A mere handshake had been too much contact for her.

But now she was confident. Her own shadow didn't make her jump anymore, and she was able to give hugs. She had blossomed into the warrior goddess she was always meant to be, who Damon had tried to smother. The bastard may still frighten her, but she wanted to be there for her friends. Beth didn't want to take that away from her.

"Okay," she said. "Let's go upstairs."

In the closed office, with gloves on his hands, Thorn removed the bow and wrapping paper gently. His careful movements had Beth's heart racing. What could be in there? Did Thorn suspect it could be dangerous and didn't want to disturb it with quick movements? Her mouth went dry. The possibilities of what could be in there ran through her mind—a dead animal, a doll that looks like her with a knife in its heart, more intimate items, creepy gifts to the baby. Or the box could be empty. Beth didn't believe Craig would pass up the chance to give her something, especially not on the night of their Christmas party. Something was definitely in there.

Thorn took out a pocket knife and sliced through the tape. Then he eased back the sides.

They leaned forward to see packing peanuts filled the box to the rim. Thorn scooped out the peanuts in handfuls and deposited them into an empty trash bag, which he had confiscated from the small pail by the desk. Halfway through the box, nestled on more packing peanuts, he uncovered the back of a picture frame.

Beth inhaled deeply as he reached for it. He flipped it over so he could see it first. Once he did, he rotated it around for the three of them to see.

A gasp escaped Beth's lips. "Oh my gosh. That's the picture that went missing after the lightning storm, when that person broke into our apartment. It had been on the refrigerator, and then it vanished." She had always suspected that the person who broke in had taken it, but why would someone want a photo of her and Donovan on the beach when they could've walked away with anything in that apartment?

Now the who and why were clear. Craig had swiped it and replaced his face over Donovan's. He was trying to eradicate Donovan entirely and put himself in his place, as Beth's husband and the father of her baby.

"That's freaky," Amanda said. "But I am glad it wasn't a bomb or something bloody."

"Me, too," Beth said.

"I think we can all be thankful for that," Donovan agreed.

Thorn finished removing the packing peanuts and knotted off the trash bag. The framed, altered photo went into a Manila envelope, and the envelope and the bag went into the box. They left everything on the floor behind the desk. As soon as the last guests left, Thorn would retrieve it and take it into the department to be catalogued. Until that time came, they had a party to attend.

Except, Beth couldn't get the photo out of her head. Seeing an image of herself, smiling and in love, and seeing Craig beside her, gave her the chills. Once, she had thought she had loved him. After all, she had accepted his proposal. But, looking back, she hadn't really been in love. She'd agreed to marry him because that's what she thought she had to do. They'd been dating for a couple of years, and he had moved into her house. It seemed like the next logic step.

That's exactly how countless people made the mistake of marrying before they were truly ready for that step. They felt obligated. It wasn't until Beth met and fell in love with Donovan when she learned the difference. Craig had never been right for her. She had settled for him. If she had never caught him with the fortune-telling tramp, she would've married him and made the worst mistake of her life. Unfortunately, dumping him had caused consequences she had never foreseen. And because she had fallen in love with and married Donovan, those consequences involved him.

Donovan pulled Beth into his arms in the middle of the living room, which they had cleared out for dancing. "Have Yourself a Merry Little Christmas" by The Carpenters came on, one of Beth's all-time favorite Christmas songs. She closed her eyes and rested her head against Donovan's shoulder. More than anything, she wanted to forget about Craig. She was in her husband's arms, in his warmth, surrounded by his love. Beautiful Christmas decorations had transformed their Florida home into a Christmas palace. The air was scented with pine and cinnamon, and she wore a gorgeous holiday dress. She wanted to enjoy this moment and their house full of friends and laughter and love and—

Her eyelids popped open. And Craig. What if he had snuck in and was lurking in a corner, watching them? She angled her neck this way and that to find him. There were so many people around, though, that it was difficult to see past everyone. She'd catch glimpses of sweater sleeves and the backs of heads between the movement of bodies but couldn't spot that sleeve or head a second later when the bodies moved out of her line of vision. Chills coursed down her back, as if someone stared at her from behind, sending daggers of pure hatred into her spine. She twisted around to look, but Donovan cupped her chin in his hand and angled her head back.

"What is it? What's wrong?"

Keeping her voice low, she said, "What if Craig came inside?"

Donovan's jaw ticked. "He wouldn't dare come into this house."

"I used to say the same thing with The Fighting Chance, but he boldly walked into my place of business twice. And while I was there. Once while *you* were there. He even broke into our apartment with us inside it at the time." She dropped her voice even more. "He's not in his right mind, and he's becoming increasingly brave."

Brave or dangerous? Often, there was no difference

when it came to stalkers. Their bravery was dangerous for their prey.

Donovan laid his other hand on the side of her face. "Look at me."

She stared into his calm eyes, inhaled deeply through her nose, and released a long exhale, as if purging herself of Craig's memory.

"He's not in this house. You're safe. I'm going to make sure of that. He's not going to come near you. I promise. In a couple of days, we'll be in Michigan, and we can leave this behind us."

Their trip couldn't come soon enough. Except, Craig would be here when they got back, and he could be far more furious after having no contact with his obsession for weeks. Those moments where rage and mania feed on each other are the most treacherous. That's when they go too far—kidnap, torture, kill.

She squeezed her eyelids shut to banish those thoughts. They wouldn't help her now.

Donovan wrapped his arms around her.

"All I Want for Christmas Is You" came on next. When the beat picked up, Donovan rocked back and forth to it. Beth laughed. This wasn't exactly a great song to dance to in someone's arms, with its fast tempo, but Donovan had some moves, and her belly didn't even deter him. She bopped to the music, moving her shoulders, lifting her hands into the air, and shook her hips back and forth. Laughter bubbled out of her mouth.

Mariah Carey, the diva herself, and Donovan's dance moves were the two things that could get Beth out of her funk. The lyrics were perfect, too. All she wanted for Christmas was Donovan. Him and only him. This Christmas and every Christmas after it. Forever.

And ever. Dancing with Donovan to those lyrics was like a big middle finger up in the air at Craig. For a split second, she almost wanted him to be watching, witnessing her happiness, but that thought died quickly as she boogied to the beat and laughed aloud with Donovan. Dancing, she realized, really was a cure for anything, and this was her way of dancing it out.

When the song ended, Beth was breathless. She leaned into Donovan, panting and smiling from ear to ear as "I'll Be Home for Christmas" by Michael Bublé played. Donovan put his hands on her hips and swayed gently, leisurely rotating her in a circle. She thought of how they were in their home now, but would be traveling soon to Michigan, Donovan's second home where he grew up.

The more she made trips with him there and saw his mom and grandma, the more Michigan felt like her other home, too. She looked forward to being there again and spending Christmas in their home. The last time they were in Michigan for Christmas, it was right after Hurricane Sabrina and Ryan's funeral. Donovan had been in a hard place, plagued by PTSD, and wanting to catch Buck so badly that he saw the man everywhere he wasn't. This year, their Christmas would not have that anxiety, uncertainty, or tension.

They completed a rotation, and what Beth saw when they came back around had her eyes growing wide. Thorn and Amanda were dancing together. Thorn's arms were locked around her waist, with his hands flat on her back, and their faces were side by side. They appeared to be embracing each other rather than dancing, but their feet did shift slightly, revolving them with the tiniest of steps. Beth's heart bloomed for them. What each of them needed, they could find in the other's arms, as Beth and Donovan did with each other. They deserved happiness, and she suspected they were starting to get it. The going may yet be slow, but the important thing was that they got over that first hurtle.

Later that evening, after snacking on delicious hors d'oeuvres and chatting with their guests, Beth went looking for a free seat to take a load off. Literally. She rubbed her belly. Her feet were killing her, even barefoot. Plus, another one of her all-time favorite songs was on—"Where Are You, Christmas?" by Faith Hill—and she wanted to be able to lip-sync and act it out like a fool where no one would be able to see her. She headed for the dining room, where not many people had been all evening, planning to plop down in one of the chairs around the table and fake belt out this epic song. Except, someone stood beneath the arch, in a bubble of quiet where the chatter and noise of the guests didn't overwhelm. Two someones actually.

Beth froze before Thorn and Amanda could see her and backed away. She hid behind the wall that divided the dining room and the living room and peeked around the corner.

"I wanted to give you something." From his back pocket, Thorn pulled out a small, square box. Beth shook her head when she noticed it wasn't wrapped. Men. It didn't even have a bow on it.

"But I didn't get you anything," Amanda said as she stared down at the box in her hands.

"It's okay," Thorn told her. "I don't need anything. And you don't have to worry. It's something small." He shuffled his feet and dipped his hands in his pockets. Nervousness shot off him in every direction. Poor guy.

Amanda lifted the lid. Her brows furrowed seconds before her eyes alit with humor and a smile spread across her face. She tipped the box over into her hand. Beth squinted her eyes to make out what it was that Amanda held. She, too, smiled when she noticed it was a stack of Thorn's business cards.

"You laminated them?" Amanda said.

Thorn shrugged. "Beth mentioned you always have one on you."

Oops. Beth slunk back out of sight in case either of them sensed her close by.

"Why are you spying on them?"

Beth jumped. She gave Donovan a small shove and moved her hand up and down to keep him quiet. "Shh. And because I want to," she hissed. Not caring what he thought, she peeped around the corner again.

Donovan copied her.

Mm-hm, she thought. *Look who's spying now.*

Amanda's smile was warm and genuine. "This is perfect. Really." Then she did something that Beth would bet had Thorn's heart skipping a beat. She reached her finger into her bodice, removed the business card that had been there and replaced it with one that was laminated. Thorn lifted his chin higher, as if fighting to not look at her breasts. When he did that, Amanda glanced up at the arch.

"I think I know what I can give you."

Thorn frowned. "What's that?"

"Look up."

Silently, Thorn tipped his head back, and there was the Mistletoe Kissing Ball, dangling in the space between them. "What is that thing?"

"Mistletoe." Amanda's voice was soft.

"Really. Looks weird."

Beth scowled.

"Told you," Donovan whispered into her ear.

She rolled her eyes but didn't say anything, because Thorn had realized what that mistletoe meant.

He peered back at Amanda. "I had no idea that was there. I swear."

"It's okay." Amanda inched closer.

"You don't have to do this."

Amanda shifted even closer. "I want to."

Encouraged by her words, Thorn put one hand on the side of her neck and ducked his head toward hers. He searched Amanda's face for approval to continue, and she nodded consent. Their faces were inches apart and continued to draw nearer. Their noses brushed, and their lips were about to touch when Thorn stopped.

"Are you sure?"

"Yes." Her reply was barely audible. Then she took the final step and closed the distance between their lips, no doubt surprising Thorn. He recovered soon enough, though, and lifted his other hand to caress the side of her neck.

Beth's heart exploded with joy. She pressed her hands to her chest. If her heart could, it'd be shooting out rainbow-colored confetti.

A hand settled over her eyes, blocking her view. "I think we should give them some privacy," Donovan whispered and tugged her gently from her spot.

Of course, Donovan was right, but she couldn't stop her giddiness. Through the rest of the night until guests started to leave, she kept stealing peeks at them. Beth definitely had to give Amanda props for giving Thorn the best Christmas present this year.

At the end of the party, Thorn and Amanda lingered behind until everyone else left. Then Donovan retrieved the box full of evidence from the office and relinquished it to Thorn.

"I'll take this to the department first thing in the morning," Thorn said.

Beth gave him a side hug. "Thanks." She went to Amanda and hugged her, too. "And thanks for coming, Amanda."

"Thanks for inviting me." Amanda glanced at Thorn. "I had a great time."

Beth squeezed her hand. She didn't think anything more would come of that kiss tonight, but it was an amazing first step. Amanda had taken a chance, listened to her heart and not her head or her fear, and that took courage.

Thorn held the door open for Amanda. "I'll walk you to your car."

Ever the protector, Beth mused.

As Amanda slipped past Thorn, he caught Beth's eye and mouthed, "Thank you."

"You're welcome," she mouthed back.

On the doorstep, they waved.

"Merry Christmas, you two," Beth said.

They wished Beth and Donovan a Merry Christmas in return, and Thorn added, "Safe travels." He pointed at them. "And I mean it this time."

For the two of them, traveling to other states had never turned out well. It was a running joke, albeit a serious one, in their circle of friends that no one should ever, under any circumstances, travel with Beth and Donovan, but Beth felt differently about their impending trip to Michigan.

****

At the airport, Beth tugged a rolling suitcase behind her, and Donovan hefted a duffel bag. During the flight to Michigan, Beth had dozed off with her head on Donovan's shoulder, and him being such a good sport, he hadn't moved his arm a centimeter, so he didn't risk waking her. She appreciated how much he cared about her and their baby. So much so that his arm had cramped, and yet he had suffered through it until she roused.

Beth spotted Meredith and Lily waiting for them near the doors and waved. They rushed forward and surrounded Beth.

"Wow! Look how big you've gotten." Meredith's hands cupped Beth's belly. "You're beautiful. And glowing." She embraced Beth in a way that only mothers could.

"Thank you. This little one seems to grow another pound every day."

"When are you due again?"

"January 30th."

"Good. You'll make it back home before your final four weeks begin."

"That's the plan." Beth went to Donovan's grandma. "Lily." She stooped down to give Lily a tender squeeze. "The two of you look great." Beth touched Lily's sleeve. "And Christmasy."

Lily enjoyed letting her Christmas-loving flag fly for everyone to see in the form of wacky sweaters and skirts. Today, Lily wore a red sweater with green garland on it to look like a Christmas tree. Tiny silver and gold ornaments hanging from the garland swished back and forth whenever she moved.

"Mom has an ugly sweater for every day of December," Meredith explained.

"You're in time to see my favorites. I save the best ones to wear closer to Christmas," Lily chimed in.

"I can't wait." Beth smiled at Donovan. He loved his grandma very much. After all, she had helped to raise him, but she had a real knack at embarrassing her dear grandson.

Donovan held them one at a time and gave them each a kiss on the cheek. "I've missed the two of you."

"And we've missed you." Meredith reached out a hand to Beth. "And you, Beth."

Beth smiled. Not having her own mom to turn to during these new and exciting moments in her life made her that much more thankful to have Meredith. And Lily, too. "I'm happy we were able to come. We needed a break from Florida for a while."

Meredith looped her arm through Beth's. "Whenever you two need a break, we're here. Now, let's get home. I have a nice dinner planned."

Dinner consisted of Rouladen, sans pickles, the recipe which had been passed down from mother to daughter in Donovan's family for generations, along with cut potatoes cooked in the Rouladen sauce, green beans and sliced almonds, and hand-made rolls. For dessert, they had apple pie topped with a scoop of natural vanilla bean ice cream.

They lingered at the dining room table long after the pie crust crumbs and melted ice cream had been cleaned off their plates and their cups of coffee had been drained. Beth and Donovan had discussed whether to tell Meredith and Lily about Craig, and although neither of them wanted to cause needless worry, they also believed in not keeping anything from these two women. Ryan had kept them in the dark, and when the unthinkable happened, it had been almost too much for either of them to bear. So, Beth and Donovan shared everything with them.

Meredith covered her mouth with her hand. "Oh my gosh! That is—" Words failed her. She reached for Beth and clasped her hand. "Are you okay?"

"I am." Beth covered Meredith's hand with hers. "Donovan keeps me safe. And we have Thorn backing us up, too."

"Thank God for that." Meredith's prayer hung in the air.

Beth didn't want Craig to ruin their vacation or the wonderful dinner they'd consumed moments ago, and she knew exactly what would change the mood; something she'd thought about for a long time.

"Meredith, Lily, I have a question for the two of you."

"What is it dear?" Lily said.

Meredith nodded for her to go on.

Beth took a deep, stabilizing breath to fill herself with confidence. What she wanted to say had been building inside her since Donovan first introduced her to them. She linked her fingers over her belly to calm her nerves. "The two of you accepted me into your lives when Donovan and I had just started dating, and that meant a lot to me. More than either of you could ever know. I was worried about meeting you guys the first time because it was all so new, but also felt…" She met Donovan's eyes. "…intense."

He winked.

"And you both knew I loved Donovan before I

even did. Ever since, you've made me feel like a part of the family, as though I had always been in the family and always will be."

"That's because you are a part of this family," Meredith said.

"Thank you." Beth paused as her chest constricted. "I lost my mom and dad years ago. Some days, it feels forever ago. Other days, it feels like yesterday. And I never knew any of my grandparents. So, you ladies filled a void in my life and in my heart. That's why I would like to ask if I can call you Mom." She said that directly to Meredith. Then to Lily, "And you Grandma."

Once more, Meredith put her hand to her mouth. This time, though, it was out of delight, not alarm. Tears filled her eyes. "Of course. I would love that."

Lily lifted her hands. "I'm Grandma to everyone."

Their acceptance of her from the beginning had meant a lot to her, but this moment meant the world to her. She couldn't imagine her life without them. They were a part of her as much as Donovan was a part of her. Always.

Chapter Fourteen

Donovan led Beth by the hand upstairs to his childhood bedroom. He shut and locked the door behind them, and then he enfolded her into his arms. "What you did down there meant a lot to them…and to me."

Beth cuddled into his chest. "They are amazing women. I love your mom and grandma as if they are my own."

"That's because they are, from the moment they met you."

"I wasn't sure if they wanted me to call them Mom or Grandma, and knowing now that they'd love it…" She paused. "It feels as though I am fully a part of the Goldwyn family."

He frowned, furrowing his brows. Had she doubted her place in his family? He hadn't known she'd felt insecure about that. When he had asked her to come to Michigan the first time, he had made a step he'd never done before. Not for any other woman he'd dated.

As for his mom and grandma, Beth had become a permanent part of the family when she'd rescued Donovan from his crashed vehicle during Hurricane Sabrina. She'd prevented them from having to say goodbye to him *and* Ryan.

"You always were a part of this family, baby." He put a curled finger under her chin and lifted it so she stared into his eyes. "Before we even got married, you were a part of this family."

"Thank you for saying that."

"I mean it." He crushed his mouth to hers. Finding out Beth hadn't felt like a real member of the Goldwyn family until now struck him in his gut like an iron boxing glove.

"You're my family, Beth," he said through their kiss. "You're their family. You're everything to me." His lips locked to hers, and he angled his head, intensifying the kiss. He wanted her to feel, from her lips down to her toes, how much she was wanted and loved. And not just by him, but by the Goldwyns currently knitting downstairs.

"And you're everything to me," she said between his lips. "Everything and more."

Donovan pressed his body into hers, showing her another level of exactly how much he wanted and loved her. She leaned back in his arms. Her eyes sparkled with passion.

"Your mom and grandma are downstairs," she reminded him.

"They're occupied. And soon, we will be, too." He peeled off her sweater that doubled as a shawl. Underneath she wore a white, long-sleeved shirt. His hands caressed her belly, and not in the way he usually did when he wanted to have a moment with the baby, but in an intimate way. He slipped his hands under her shirt to touch her bare, warm skin.

"How can you want to have sex with them so close?" Beth wanted to know.

He shrugged. "I'm a man. I can have sex anywhere."

"That explains a lot."

Donovan smirked. It probably did.

Beth peered over her shoulder at his childhood bed. "That is a twin-size bed. We're not going to fit on it."

"We'll fit." He knelt on his knees in front of her and worked her pants to her ankles. She stepped out of them, one foot at a time. Her legs broke out in gooseflesh instantly. He rubbed her shins and thighs with his palms. Then he got to his feet and ushered her over to the bed where he pulled back the covers. When she lay down, he climbed in after her and pulled the covers over them. "Turn onto your side. Away from me."

She turned, and he moved in behind her so his body fit into her curves.

"Don't make a sound," he whispered.

"Ha. You're funny."

With a smile, he unfastened his jeans, pulled them down past his hips, and slipped into her. He rocked against her, and she moved her hips in response. Spooning allowed Donovan to get closer to her than he had been able to in a long time. From the front, her belly kept him about a foot or more away from her, so that even hugging her and feeling her body flush against his was difficult to achieve.

In this position, with his chest to her back, he could nuzzle her neck, smell her hair, and hold her hips. Because Beth could be sensitive, he kept his pace slow and steady. Each thrust was gentle, but effective. The sensation built inside Donovan, tightening his muscles as his body prepared for release.

Beth balled up a corner of the comforter and stuffed it into her mouth to muffle her cries of pleasure.

She held it to her mouth, and he buried his head into the pillow to stifle his own sounds of ecstasy. When Beth came, she clamped her hands over her mouth. Donovan let himself go as her body quaked. He pushed his face deeper into the pillow to catch the groan that burst from his vocal cords. Sated, he brushed the hair from Beth's neck and kissed her damp skin.

She finally removed the fabric from her mouth to say, "Damn. Who knew sex while pregnant could be so good?"

Donovan chuckled. "The two of us are just that good, baby."

****

The next day, Donovan had a surprise for her. Beth couldn't do most of the outdoor, snowy activities because they weren't safe. She'd love to go sledding, but that was out of the question. So was snowboarding, something he'd love to see her attempt. No doubt, she'd rock at it, since she slayed surfing. Even making a snow angel would be too difficult, as she'd have a hard time hefting her weight up from the ground. But he had plans for something she'd enjoy.

"So, you're not going to tell me what we're doing?" she asked.

"You'll see." He glanced at her from the driver's seat of their truck rental. "Patience."

"What's this 'patience' that you speak of?"

Donovan pulled up to a park, got out of the truck, and assisted Beth down. Hand in hand, they walked through the park. They were fortunate there was a light dusting of snow on the ground, so Beth was able to walk with ease. She didn't have to fight with deep snow or risk slipping on ice. They strolled in the crisp air.

The day was beautiful, with a blue sky overhead and soft, white clouds the sun peeked out of to shine its rays down on them. Blue Jays and Red Cardinals flitted from tree to tree, shaking loose snow from branches. One Snow Bunting bird flew into a tree with a bit of earth in its beak. It landed onto a nest settled high up in the bare canopy and added the brown grass to its nest.

"I guess I'm not the only one nesting," Beth said.

"Nope." Donovan put his arm around her waist to hold her closer as they walked.

"It's beautiful here in the winter. The earth seems so clean and fresh with the snow covering it. Is that why you brought me here?"

"Actually, I brought you here for that." He pointed straight ahead.

She looked, and her eyes widened.

On the path in front of them waited a white, horse-drawn carriage. The Morgan horses were brown with white legs. Red, velvet bows decorated their manes and tails and were tied to the leather straps that attached the horses to the carriage. Gold bells around their bellies jingled when they sidestepped in place. The seats of the carriage were red, plush, and empty.

"You brought me here for a carriage ride?"

"Mm-hm." He paid the driver and assisted Beth up the step and into the carriage. Sitting in the seat, he pulled the thick, fur blanket over their laps. She took the edge of the blanket, pulled it up to her chest, and cuddled into his side.

The driver made a clicking sound with his mouth, and the horses trotted forward at a relaxed gait. They lifted their hooves high in a sophisticated trot.

Donovan relaxed into the cushions. This was how

he had always envisioned spending Christmas in Michigan with Beth—snow fun and romantic ventures out on the town. He took Beth's chilly hands in his, rubbed them between his palms, and blew his warm breath onto them.

"This is nice," Beth said. "I never imagined doing this."

"I like to do things with you that you never imagined doing." He kissed her cheek.

They were silent a moment, and then Beth let out a giggle.

"What's that for?"

"I remembered something. When we were in San Francisco, after the quake, an elderly woman at the shelter told me about her late husband and told me to make sure I find a man who will take me on many adventures, even when I'm an old bitty. She said, 'A man like that will make life interesting. He'll make life worth living, because you'll never be disappointed.' She gave me a bit of advice, too. She said, 'A man like that is worth finding. But if you have to wait, he's worth the patience.' And right at that moment was when I saw you come into the shelter."

"You never told me that."

She nodded. "I love the adventures we go on."

Even our honeymoon? he wanted to ask but didn't. Bringing up the tsunami now would kill the romance.

"You make my life interesting, and I have never regretted a moment of it."

Donovan pressed his lips to hers. "I've never regretted a moment with you, either."

Although, he wished some things hadn't happened—the disasters, the crimes, the things that left physical scars on her body and haunted her memories.

"Thank you for crashing your car into a tree in front of my house."

Donovan chuckled. "Thank you for braving a category five hurricane and rescuing me."

"I'd do it again."

"So would I."

They kissed as the carriage rocked.

Something cold and wet landed on Donovan's check. He leaned back. Snowflakes spiraled down from the clouds. They danced through the air around them, settling on their clothes and laps.

Beth tipped her head back to watch them descend. "I'll just pretend you made it snow for our sleigh ride."

"I'd like to take credit, but I'm not that good."

She tucked herself into his side again. "Yes, you are."

He didn't want to argue with her, so he laid his head against hers and enjoyed the ride.

Chapter Fifteen

Beth stood behind the counter in Meredith's apple-red kitchen. She wore an apron made out of fabric decorated with teacups. The bottom of it flowed around her belly like a skirt. On the counter in front of her was a colorful bowl, containers and bottles of ingredients, and a baking sheet.

Meredith unfolded a worn piece of paper. "This is my family's snowball cookie recipe." She smoothed it on the counter with her hands. "I want to show you how to make them."

During their first trip to Michigan, Beth had sampled Meredith's snowball cookies and loved the way the powdered sugar had melted in her mouth. Being with Meredith in her kitchen reminded Beth of cooking with her mom. They'd chop up whatever vegetables they had on hand and toss them into a pot of water with bouillon cubes to make soup.

As a girl, Beth had mastered her own soup, which had far too many spices and herbs in it, but her parents would gobble it up all the same. She had also loved to bake bread with her mom. Punching the ball of dough was the first time she had exercised her self-defense skills...on innocent, self-rising dough, but it had excited her to punch that soft ball and watch her fist sink into it. Kitchen fun had been something special. Occasionally, her dad had joined in. He liked to marinate meat and brush thick globs of barbecue sauce onto ribs. To this day, the smell of barbecue sauce and Worcestershire sauce reminded her of her dad and their fun at the grill.

Now Meredith was giving her another kitchen memory.

She added the ingredients according to Meredith's instructions. With clean hands, she spooned up small portions of the cookie dough, with chopped walnuts in it, and formed them into small balls between her palms. She laid them out in neat rows on the ready baking sheet. As soon as the sheet got full, Meredith slipped it into the pre-heated oven and then pitched in to create the last baking sheet of cookies. They chatted about life and pregnancy and work while they went about making the tiny spheres of sweet dough. With the first batch out and cooling, the second batch went in. They stayed in the kitchen, sitting at the table, sipping spiced apple cider, and waiting for the timer to go off. The kitchen smelled delicious with the scents of vanilla and sugar swirling through the air.

"Here. I also wanted to give this to you." Meredith reached into her apron pocket and pulled out an index card.

Beth took it. On the top it read, "Rouladen— Goldwyn Family Recipe." It was the recipe passed down to all Goldwyn women.

"I should've given it to you a long time ago," Meredith said.

"I wouldn't have known how to make it if you had."

Meredith patted her hand. "When you make it the first time, we can video chat, and I can walk you through it."

"We may have to do that the second time, too."

"As many times as you need."

Beth tucked the index card into her pocket with the snowball cookie recipe. "Thank you."

"You're welcome."

The timer for the last batch of cookies went off. Meredith pulled it out of the oven, not knowing how much those two recipes in Beth's pocket truly meant to her. They were a Christmas present on their own, more valuable than anything that could be bought in a store.

"Come on, Beth. Now it's time for the fun part."

She joined Meredith at the counter.

"When I make these by myself, I usually push the cookies into a bowl of powdered sugar, but when I was little, Mom would put powdered sugar into a brown paper bag, drop in a handful of cookies, and have me shake up the bag to cover them." She opened a drawer and revealed a paper bag. They dumped a cup of powdered sugar into the bag and plopped in several cookies. "Okay. Now, give it a good shake."

With the top of the bag bunched up, Beth grasped it and shook it with vigor.

Grandma Lily shuffled into the kitchen. "I know that sound," she said.

Beth and Meredith laughed.

After the cookies were coated in powdered sugar, the three of them circled the table to enjoy the yummy spoils of their labor. Donovan came in moments later.

"Hey, you're not eating all the cookies, are you?"

"We saved you one." Beth picked up the single cookie left on her plate.

He bent over and caught the cookie between his

teeth. His lips grazed her fingers. When he straightened his back, he winked and bit into the cookie. "Delicious."

And still, even eight months pregnant, the man could arouse her with nothing more than a damn wink.

During the next couple of days, they visited Frankenmuth, an old-time German town, and shopped at Bronner's Christmas Wonderland, the largest Christmas store in the world, open year-round. Beth walked in wide-eyed and in awe. From the floor to the ceiling…Christmas. Every sort of Christmas decoration you could imagine, and dozens of trees decorated for different themes. One tree had a mannequin as the upper-half, and the bottom half of the tree was designed to look like a full skirt. The sheer number of ornament display racks could make you dizzy.

Beth picked out a personalized "We're Expecting" ornament that featured a snowman couple arm in arm. The snowwoman had a nice round belly. An arrow pointed at it and the word "Baby" was spelled out. At the bottom of the ornament, it said the month and year the baby was expected. She couldn't wait to put it on their tree at home.

Donovan also showed Beth frozen lakes, but when he drove onto the ice a little ways, Beth nearly had a heart attack. He reassured her it was okay, that it wasn't deep there and the ice was thick. Regardless of what he said, she gripped the door's side handle. Eventually, she relaxed. They stayed in the truck and stared out at the expanse of ice. It was so calm. She got the chills from how serene the frozen lake appeared to be, but beneath it, water moved and fish thrived.

Life went on, even under a thick layer of ice.

****

On December 22nd, Beth came downstairs in the morning to find Donovan, Meredith, and Lily sitting in the living room watching the morning edition of the news. "What's going on?"

Donovan pointed at the screen.

She turned to the TV to see a map of Michigan in green and a storm shown in shades of blues and purples creeping toward it. As a Floridian, she was used to forecasts that shadowed rain as green, with worsening parts of the storm as yellow, orange, and the most dangerous sections as red.

"What's that?"

"A winter storm coming down from Canada. It looks as though it'll sweep right across Michigan. It's coming fast, too." He got up and pinned a spot on the forecast. "This is where we are. Right now, we're in the winter weather advisory area, which means we'll get hazardous snow, freezing rain, and sleet, but we're not in the warning criteria of receiving four inches or more of snow."

"Well, that's good," she said.

Donovan shrugged. "I wouldn't be so sure. Worse weather in other areas could create dangerous flying conditions and ground airplanes."

"But we're not leaving for another six days."

"Winter storms can take a while to go through, and if this thing becomes a blizzard, we could be trapped inside for weeks."

Beth swallowed. That was the difference between a hurricane and a blizzard. A hurricane can shred your house to bits, but a blizzard could bury it whole.

"When is the storm forecasted to hit us?"

Donovan gave her a tight smile. "Christmas Eve."

"Well, I did want to have a true, white Christmas in Michigan."

"Be careful what you wish for."

No kidding, she thought.

By the end of the day, the storm had gained speed and strength. Its wind speed had increased to thirty-five miles per hour, firmly putting them into the winter storm warning area. The next morning, the day before Christmas Eve, the news wasn't good. All forecasts agreed; the storm was now a full-blown blizzard, and when it arrived, it would smother the state of Michigan. The Weather Channel map showing the intensity levels of the storm had their location right smack dab in the middle of the brightest pink. Meteorologists predicted they could get over twenty-four inches of snowfall, but with the size of the storm and how quickly its force escalated, no one could predict what it would do. The Weather Channel dubbed the storm Nemesis, the last blizzard of the year.

Chapter Sixteen

"I need to get us out of here."

Donovan grabbed his laptop from his duffel bag and booted it up. His fingers tapped on the keys as he went to a flight booking website, but every way out of Michigan was booked solid, from planes to trains. Oh, the joys of holiday travel. Everyone was trying to get somewhere in time for Christmas. Now with the blizzard coming, visitors were hastily beating an exit out of the storm's path while they still could.

Forecasts predicted the storm would slow down over them and linger, contributing to snow and ice accumulation, and likely forcing airlines to cancel flights due to uncertainty. They wouldn't be able to take off if the landing strips were buried under several feet of snow. Although their flight back home was on the 27th, that would be too late.

They were stuck.

"We're not going anywhere." He slammed down the lid to his laptop. "Damn it!"

"It's okay, Donovan," Meredith said. "We've weathered blizzards before."

"Well, my pregnant wife hasn't."

"Hey, your pregnant wife is right here." Beth moved her arms in a motion to indicate herself. "And she's gone through several category four and five hurricanes."

"After a hurricane blows through, you can get out of the house. After a blizzard, you have to dig yourself out. And then you're not going anywhere until the streets are plowed. That could take days."

"Everything will be fine," she told him. "We came now because it was perfect timing. I'm not due for another month, so we'll just hunker down and keep warm."

"That's right," Lily agreed.

Donovan wasn't convinced all would be okay. Beth didn't understand his worry because she'd never been through a blizzard before. He once endured two weeks trapped in this home with his mom, grandparents, and Ryan. Two words—cabin fever. There's nothing you can do while confined inside a house with the doors and windows frozen shut and snow drifts keeping you from opening them. You could play card games and boardgames in the glow of lanterns, flashlights, and candles, but that grew old a few days into the frozen imprisonment. Those conditions could drive a person with the most stable mind bonkers.

Already, he could feel the claustrophobic conditions settling in on him, squeezing his shoulders together. He shoved to his feet. "I'm going to chop firewood."

In the backyard, he found a decent-sized pile of dry wood ready to be chopped into firewood. His mother's cousins delivered wood throughout the year for her woodpile, and in the winter, her cousins took turns chopping them, so she wouldn't have to worry about it. Donovan was thankful for them every year, and even more so at this moment. Some of the logs were large, though, so he got out the chainsaw from the shed to cut them to length, about twenty inches. He sawed until he had a mound of firewood. Then he took a chunk and stood it on the old tree stump where his grandpa had taught Ryan and him how to chop wood. When he was really little, he had a tiny axe and would hack away at a block, creating nothing more than mulch and having a blast.

He tapped a sharp wedge into the wood's grain with a short-handled sledgehammer. A crack formed, and with two clean whacks, the round piece of wood splintered in half. He tossed it to the side. Again and again, he repeated the process, getting out his frustrations for a ruined Christmas vacation and for putting Beth in danger, something for which he seemed to excel. Gritting his teeth, he swung the sledgehammer, splitting a log down the middle.

His grandpa would've lectured him about not chopping wood while angry, as that was when accidents could happen, but he couldn't deny how great it felt letting out his pent-up aggression through a physical act. Splitting hard wood sure did the trick. The sound of the wood cracking and breaking apart was the sound of victory to his ears. With each hit, his muscles felt good—fluid and warm.

Soon, he had a heap of split logs. He set down the sledgehammer and filled up a wheelbarrow with the cut firewood. In the kitchen, he stacked the wood into alternating rows. The first row he laid flat vertically, and the second row he set on top horizontally. This would keep the pile from coming undone and spilling out across the tile. He continued this task until the wood pile came up to his chest, and he set the final piece on top.

Outside, he went back to work. Eventually, his arms grew tired from swinging, so he picked up the chainsaw to quicken his pace. Snowflakes started to fall around him, and a wind picked up. The wind pushed the snow where it pleased. Around the base of the tree stump, snow crawled up the sides.

But Donovan didn't stop. They'd need a lot of firewood to keep warm, to heat water and food. He wasn't the sole person relying on this firewood. Beth, Meredith, and Lily needed it, too. The more people in the house, the more firewood you'd need, and there was no telling how long the four of them would be trapped inside that house without electricity, without heat. One pile wouldn't cut it. One pile wouldn't last through days and nights, when they wouldn't be able to afford to let the fire go out. They'd have to constantly feed it and keep that fire going. One stack could be gone in twenty-four to forty-eight hours.

Yes, they needed more.

To speed up the process, he pushed the full wheelbarrow through the kitchen to the door that led to the garage. Along the wall at the back of the garage, he began a second stack of firewood. He made sure it was as close to the door as possible, so in case they ran out of the firewood in the kitchen, it would be easy for them to retrieve wood from the garage, without letting a ton of frigid air into the house.

As he did this, the women were busy gathering candles, testing flashlights, and hauling up canned goods from the basement. Every spring, his grandma went into a canning frenzy, preparing for the winter months. She'd can peaches, pears, strawberry jam, applesauce, beets, rhubarb, corn salsa, and dill and sweet pickles. She'd also make batches of apple butter. Her preserves had sustained the Goldwyns through many winter storms in the past, and they'd do it again.

They also prepared the house for cold weather by hanging up afghans in front of the windows to help block the cold from leaking through the rooms, checking for drafts, sealing any cracks with all-weather caulk, changing the filter in the furnace, opening the chimney's flue, and salting the sidewalk to the front door and the driveway.

Donovan finished the stack in the garage. Before he left, he counted the bags of sand that he'd need for after the storm to cover ice. Luckily, they had five bags, which should be more than enough. He also noted sheets of plywood leaning up against the wall. He considered boarding up the upstairs windows, but the wind was gusting already. Climbing a ladder with tools and plywood would be too dangerous at this point.

When he cut and split the entire pile of logs from outside, he brought in the final wheelbarrow to the living room where he unloaded the wood beside the fireplace. He dusted off his work gloves. "There," he said, and exhaled an exhausted breath. "That should do it." Or, at least, he hoped so, because that was all the wood they had. If they needed more, they wouldn't be able to find good, dry logs now. Not with everyone in the state of Michigan frantically buying the supplies they needed to get through the storm.

Which reminded him. "I'm going to check the generator and make sure it's ready to go." He hefted a red, plastic gas can and carried it to the porch where the portable generator sat in a corner beneath a tarp. Dust flew into the air when he whipped off the covering. The generator looked good. No rust. No dents. He filled the generator up to the fuel line and recapped the gas can. One by one, he went through the steps to turn on the generator. Then he flipped the engine switch and pulled the recoil cord. Nothing. He tried again. Not even a rumble.

"Come on." He yanked on the cord once more. Still nothing. "Damn it!" Something had to be wrong with it. On his hands and knees, he searched for a leak but couldn't find one. He double checked the fuel level. It was right where it should be.

Praying silently, he went through the steps again to turn on the generator. Another hard yank yielded no results. The generator wasn't even putting as if it wanted to turn on. He tried several times until he became breathless. "Piece of shit!" He kicked it, but not even that could jumpstart the hunk of metal.

He raked his hands through his hair. Without a generator, if they lost power, it'd get cold in the house. The fireplace and the wood he'd chopped wouldn't be able to chase off the chill.

Even more worried now, he went back into the house. "The generator is dead."

The women looked at him in alarm.

"It worked in January," his mom said.

"Well, it's broken now."

Beth stroked her belly. Her eyes reflected fear.

"Don't worry," he told her. "We'll just have to cuddle real close."

She gave him a smile. "I'd like that."

He returned her smile, but anxiety still buzzed inside him. They had to do whatever they could to keep out the cold. "Has anyone checked the attic for holes or cracks?"

"We were going to send Beth up, but when she tried to climb up the attic ladder, her belly got in the way."

Donovan blinked at his mom.

"It's a joke." Beth rubbed his arm.

"I was going to go up in a minute," his mom said, "after putting extra blankets on the beds."

"You do that, and I'll go up into the attic."

At the end of the upstairs hall, he pulled on the rope that dangled from the ceiling, lowered the attic door, and unfolded the ladder. With a small toolbox, he made his way up. The air in the attic was chilly and smelled a bit musty. Who knew what his mom and grandma kept up there to get moldy, damp, and moth-eaten?

Cardboard boxes lined the walls. Some of the corners had been scratched and gnawed on with little teeth. He wondered if they had mice. A few pieces of furniture filled the space, such as a trunk, which he assumed was packed with old clothes or books. Moving around the boxes and furniture, he checked for holes and cracks.

A cold draft hit him, and he side-stepped, searching for the source of it. He came up to a wooden rocker and reached over it to feel along the ceiling. A chittering noise came from below. He looked down to see a plump raccoon lounging in the rocker.

"Holy shit." Donovan leapt back.

The raccoon tilted his head, not understanding the response to seeing him sitting there, relaxing and minding his own business.

"How did you get in here?"

The raccoon lifted up a half-eaten, rotten apple.

Donovan shook his head. "No, thanks."

The raccoon lowered its arm and took a nibble from the apple. His stomach bulged out on both sides. However the creature got inside, it could get out, because it was well-fed, and apparently, it liked to bring its meal here to eat it in peace and out of the elements. Donovan couldn't blame him, but he couldn't leave a hole open during a blizzard for snow and ice to come through. He continued to follow the cold draft, and the raccoon didn't mind him one bit.

In the far corner, the temperature dropped significantly. The draft was there, somewhere. He moved aside a couple of stacked cardboard boxes and uncovered a hole that led to the outdoors and the tree growing beside the house in the backyard.

Donovan eyed the raccoon and pointed at the hole. "Is this your handy work?"

In reply, the raccoon purred.

"I'll take that for a yes. You know I'm going to have to patch this up, don't you?"

The raccoon jabbered at Donovan in his own language, but he didn't seem concerned or upset over Donovan having discovered his way in and out.

"As long as it's okay with you." Chuckling to himself, Donovan nailed small pieces of scrap wood across the hole. To make sure no frigid air could slither through, he taped a sheet of clear plastic over the wood. "There." He dumped his tools into the box and stood. "Now, you leave that alone. Understand?"

The raccoon, again, held out the apple he'd been snacking on. Except, now it was nothing more than a core and stem. Donovan held up his hand. "No, that's all yours."

The critter lifted its chin and peeled its mouth apart.

Donovan's brows lifted. *It's smiling at me.*

"After the storm, I'm going to take this down and shoo you out of here before I completely patch it up. I can't exactly have a raccoon loose in the house where my mom and grandma live. No offense."

The raccoon almost appeared to shrug. Then it set the apple core aside, sighed, and folded its arms across its wide belly.

"Good. I'm glad you're comfy. Don't leave that apple core there. You take care of your trash."

He made a little chirping sound and shut his eyes.

"Fine. Goodnight."

Shaking his head, Donovan left the attic.

Downstairs, he found the three women filling empty jugs with tap water. "Did you know you have a raccoon living quite comfortably in your attic?"

"Oh, you met Rodney," Grandma said.

"You named the raccoon? A wild…stray…filthy animal that likely has rabies?"

"He's not a stray, he lives in our attic."

Donovan glanced at Beth, who pressed her lips together to stop her laughter.

"And he doesn't have rabies. He's friendly."

"Please tell me you haven't been feeding him."

"Of course not!"

"Good. Don't."

"Speaking of food," his mom said. "I think we should run to the store to pick up some more provisions. These canned fruits and pickles won't last long."

"I can do that." Donovan picked up the keys to their rental truck from the counter.

"I'll come," Beth said. "I want to get out a little before I'm stuck inside for days."

The store's parking lot was packed with the vehicles of the people hoping to get food and water. One man came out with a boxed generator on a cart. He pointed at it and said to Donovan, "I got the last one."

Donovan ground his teeth. Every store was probably out of generators now. "Thanks for letting me know."

Inside the store, people were everywhere with carts stacked with cases of water, packages of toilet paper, piles of bread, and bags of pet food. "We have to move fast," Donovan said to Beth.

"Don't worry about me. No one would dare take something from a pregnant woman."

To prove it, Beth elbowed her way through the crowd, filling the cart with candles, batteries, the last loaves of bread, carrots, celery, a bag of apples, and a box of vanilla cake glazed donuts. The shelves that held canned goods were nearly empty. They picked out canned soups from the remaining selection. The snack aisles were even worse, but Beth snatched up a few bags of her coveted pickle-flavored chips. After they got all the non-perishable foods, they went over to the outdoor equipment. Donovan found thermal blankets, snow boots for him and Beth, and a wind-up radio, something he used all the time in Florida during hurricanes and tropical storms.

In the check-out lane, which was five carts long, Beth gasped and snatched something off the rack beside them. "I can't believe we almost left without this." She showed him her amazing find—cherry-flavored licorice sticks.

"How dare we leave without your licorice," he teased. "But are you sure one bag will last you?"

She thought about it a second and picked up another.

Chapter Seventeen

A blizzard was a first for Beth. She didn't know what to expect from this beast of snow and ice, from this monster that the clever meteorologists at The Weather Channel named Nemesis. That was exactly the kind of name you wanted a storm to be called that's headed right for you. Not! Every time they referred to the storm as Nemesis, she couldn't help but picture a creature with teeth and claws whose ass she needed to kick. She didn't like that Mother Nature enjoyed being her opponent. Everywhere they went, Mother Nature asked herself, "Hmm. What can I do to them now?"

A blizzard was the next step in Mother Nature's plan to give them hell.

On Christmas Eve, a day that Beth would be enjoying festive activities like watching her favorite Christmas movies, listening to carols, and decorating Christmas cookies, her attention was glued to the news. Just as in Florida when a hurricane was on the way, reporters were out and about, catching stories about the blizzard, talking about the current snowfall in certain areas, and interviewing local business owners.

Each update on the blizzard showed it to be growing in size and strength. When you didn't think it could get any worse, the next forecast came through, showing you it could indeed. Halfway through the day, the meteorologists started to refer to Nemesis as the new storm of the century. Perfect. That's exactly what they needed.

"They shouldn't have named it Nemesis," Beth said during a commercial break. "They gave it power by giving it a name like that."

Donovan arched a brow.

"What? Names are important."

He caressed her belly with his palm. "We still haven't decided on a name for this one."

"And that'll be something good for us to talk about when the power goes out and we get bored." She smiled. "Do you want a boy or a girl?"

Donovan considered her question a moment. "I'd love a son, but...I don't know. I'm looking forward to having a girl. I'd teach her to not take any crap from anyone."

"We can both teach our little girl that," she said.

"You can teach her how to whoop someone's butt, and I can teach her how to leave them in the dust."

Beth laughed. Then an idea popped into her head. "We need to put up one of your posters in the baby's room. Who knows? If we have a boy, he could follow in his daddy's footsteps, and if we have a girl, she could be like Linsey Read, but with Venom, not the Scooby-Doo truck."

"You wouldn't mind them wanting to race or perform in monster trucks?"

"Not if it's what they really want to do. I'd support whatever they decide."

Donovan's brows lowered, and he peered down at her hands.

"Wouldn't you?" She wanted to know. "If they wanted to be a cop or a teacher or an exotic dancer?"

"Of course," Donovan said automatically. When he processed that last one, he looked up. "Now, wait a minute. An exotic dancer?"

"Just making sure you were listening."

Donovan leaned back on the couch and put a hand to his chest. "Don't give me a heart attack. I had a flash of me lecturing our daughter, and she was wearing something that Leighton would wear."

Beth threw her head back in laughter. She patted his leg. "I don't think you'll have anything to worry about there, Daddy. We'll raise our kids right. And if one of our daughters feels empowered to have a risqué career, we'll deal with it then."

His face was still pale, despite her reassurances. His worries about being a parent and raising children made her smile, though. It told her she wasn't alone with her own worries. She cuddled beside him to watch the news. While they kept an eye on the storm as it approached, Meredith and Lily were busy in the kitchen, cooking up their Christmas meal one day early. They'd be able to eat a feast and enjoy leftovers later. A ham sandwich would be just as good with the power off as it would be with the power on.

That evening, they had honey-glazed ham, rosemary roasted potatoes, sautéed Brussel sprouts in butter and brown sugar, sweet carrots, and cornbread. Beth went to bed that night full and content and anxious about the storm. Outside, the wind howled as it rushed past the house. Every once in a while, the house let out a groan or a creaking noise that had Beth glancing nervously up at the ceiling. Although the ceiling couldn't be ripped off, it could cave in.

Lying in bed beside Donovan, she couldn't fall

asleep. Not with ice chips hitting the window and the room growing marginally colder. Beneath layers of quilts, she rubbed her belly back and forth, back and forth, not so much to soothe the baby, but to calm herself and ease herself to sleep. Except, every noise had her eyelids springing open. She'd react the same during a tropical storm, but she'd never been pregnant when one hit.

Eventually, her exhaustion pulled her into a light sleep.

She woke on Christmas Day with sleepy eyes. Snow had come down heavily through the night. She stood in front of the living room window that faced the front yard, with a cup of coffee in hand, and stared at the snow that came half-way up the mailbox's post. Not being from the North, she had no idea that snow could accumulate so quickly, but she figured it was similar to how quickly rainwater could flood an area. The more that fell, the more that built up, and Nemesis was unloading a ton of snow on Michigan.

Gusts of wind carrying snow and ice slammed into the house. A wet blast hit the window, causing her to flinch.

"Come away from the window, Beth," Meredith called out. "Snow and ice can knock down trees and powerlines."

"Right." Beth moved from her spot. She knew better than to stand directly in front of a pane of glass during a storm. Just because blizzards didn't have lightning or downpouring rain didn't mean they weren't dangerous. Blizzards could kill as easily as any other storm. It merely did it in different ways.

"What do you guys say about opening our

presents?" Meredith got up from the couch. "It is Christmas Day, after all."

Beth smiled. "Sure."

They passed out gifts to each other. Donovan received his grandfather's pocket watch from Lily and a new leather wallet from Meredith. They gave Beth a clay handprint-making kit to do with the baby and an album full of photos of Donovan. On the first page, he was a newborn, and on the last page he was a groom on their wedding day.

Beth grinned. "This is the cutest thing. Thank you."

"They're my favorite pictures of Donovan," Meredith said.

Hearing her say that made Beth pause. "These aren't the originals, are they?" She didn't want Meredith giving up beloved photos of her youngest son.

"No, sweetie. I made copies for you. And I have several albums full of photos. I'll bring them out later, and we can go through them."

Donovan groaned, and Beth smirked.

"Now our gifts to you," she said.

To Meredith, they gave a coffee cup with the word "Grandma" printed in cursive on the ceramic. Meredith hooted with laughter. She turned the mug around to show Lily, who also got a kick out of it. "I'm not the only grandma in this house anymore."

Their gift to Lily was a painted tree in a frame with her name, Grandpa George's name, the names of their two kids, including Meredith, and their grandkids' names on branches going down the canopy. There were enough empty branches for her great grandkids' names to be added. "This is precious. I love it."

"And we love our gifts," Beth said.

"Oh, but there's another gift under the tree." Meredith picked up a small box resting on the red velvet tree skirt. "I don't recognize it. It says it's to Donovan."

"It's from me." Beth watched Donovan take the tiny package from Meredith. "I snuck it into my suitcase and hid it under the tree when no one was looking."

"Well...you're not the only sneaky one." He moved a pillow on the couch and pulled out a small box, too. His didn't have wrapping paper on it, but a small white bow kept the box's lid secured. "Trade ya."

Beth took the box but waited for Donovan to open his present first. To Donovan, she gave a leather cord bracelet. In the middle of it was a silver bar engraved with coordinates.

"What are these coordinates for?" he asked.

"Our home...where we met...where we fell in love...where we live now."

For a moment, Donovan was silent. "It's perfect. Thank you, baby." He kissed her on the lips. "Can you put it on for me?" He held out his wrist to her, and she fastened the clasp.

When he rotated his wrist, she studied him wearing it. "Sexy," she whispered and winked in much the same way he'd wink to arouse her.

His dimples appeared when he grinned. "Open yours."

She untied the bow and lifted the lid to find a snowflake charm. A laugh bubbled out of her throat. "How appropriate."

"I got it to symbolize our Christmases here in Michigan, but I guess it can also symbolize our first blizzard together." He gave her a bleak smile.

Hoping to elevate his mood, she held the snowflake charm in her right hand and brought her bracelet to her heart. "I love all my charms. They're the reason why I got you that bracelet. You gave me *my* charm bracelet, so I wanted to give you one, too."

Right then, the lights dimmed, but they came back to full power a second later. Everyone peered around at the lights.

"I wonder how long our power will last," Meredith said.

None of them responded to that.

Outside, the wind screamed.

And just like that, the moment passed. Their little Christmas celebration was over. Now they were back to blizzard survival. Or, at least, waiting to see what it would do.

Hours crawled by as the storm intensified. The lights flickered every few minutes. They wondered when the electricity would snap off for good, leaving them to the dark and the cold.

"We better get the candles lit." Meredith got up from her rocker.

"I'll help," Donovan said.

They scattered glass jar pillar candles in clusters around the living room and brought over the battery-operated lanterns. Donovan handed Beth a flashlight. She held onto it, knowing from past experience that it was the moment when you set down the flashlight when the power always went out.

The TV's image dimmed but cleared to show Nemesis had firmly planted its bulk over Michigan, and the brightest pinks of the storm were directly over their area. With the size of the storm, they had many hours yet to go of enduring the storm's worst. For them, it was only beginning.

Icy gales punched the house.

Beth observed the conditions from the window. The wind was pushing snow drifts up against the house. Already, she could see a mound of snow in front of the window. The peak reached a few inches above the ledge, and Nemesis tossed more snow at it, adding to the growth. Seeing that made her nervous. As Donovan said, she was used to being able to get out of her house after a tropical storm. If the snow was up to the window, then it was surely piling up in front of the door and the garage, which were on the same side of the house.

Wondering what the back looked like, she got up from the couch, still grasping the flashlight, and went through the kitchen to look out the sliding glass door. What she saw wasn't good. The porch door was being plastered by a heap of snow, and the wind was forcing the snow around the porch's structure, so it came up along each side. Who knew what it would be like by the time Nemesis left?

Donovan came up behind her and looped an arm around her shoulders to hold her against his chest. He kissed the back of her head and spoke next to her ear. "It's okay. I'll dig us out if I have to."

"That's a lot of snow, Donovan. Even for you."

"I'll do what's necessary to get us out."

And she didn't doubt his word. When Donovan Goldwyn made a promise, he kept it. For better or for worse. Usually, it meant he'd risk himself to keep his vow.

"Don't worry," he added.

But she did.

A blast of snow-choked wind swept through the backyard. Several pine tree branches broke off nearby trees and fell to the ground.

"A lot of branches are going to fall during this storm. If not from the wind, then from the weight of snow or ice. Let's just hope none of them bring down any powerlines."

Walking through the snow where a downed powerline could be hidden would be dangerous. In Florida, powerlines often succumbed to the forces of a storm, and this would be no different. That also meant power would take even longer to be restored. Something none of them wanted.

They ate ham sandwiches for lunch while watching the news. Every squall that came and went caused the TV to fade in and out. As time went by, the picture became worse. Static distorted the forecast, and the meteorologist's words were cut off frequently. Then a roaring sound outside had Beth's ears perking up. The TV went pitch-black. A thumping noise reverberated through the house from upstairs. Whatever made it was moving, bumping along the length of the rooftop. A second later, something flashed out of the corner of Beth's eye. She swiveled to the window.

"Whatever that was, it fell into the front yard."

Donovan got up to look. He pulled back the curtain. "Well, no more TV. The roof-mount antenna is now in the snow. And the mailman is going to have a hard time making his deliveries. Snow is now covering your mailbox."

"Shit," Beth mumbled.

"At least we still have power," Meredith said.

Right at that moment, the power flickered.

Donovan put his back to the window. "Mom, don't jinx us."

"Sorry."

Except, they were fated to lose power. Not losing electricity in a storm like this would be damn near impossible of a feat. The way to ensure that was with a generator, which they didn't have. The lights went on and off on a loop, but the power fought its way back on every time. Until it couldn't. A boom resonated from miles away, and the electricity winked out. The candles and fireplace cast a reassuring glow through the living room.

"It's okay," Meredith said. "We've prepared for this."

"We have weenies we can roast," Lily piped up.

Beth laughed.

In the flickers of firelight, she cuddled next to Donovan on the couch and stared into the crackling fireplace. The sound of the logs popping mixed with the clicking of Meredith's and Lily's knitting needles as they made scarves to occupy their time. Nemesis wailed its fury as it jabbed the house with fists of snow and ice. Despite the blizzard raging outside, there was something cozy about being inside the house with the fireplace roaring and Donovan's arms around her.

For dinner, they indeed did roast hot dogs in the fireplace. Even though Beth had lived her entire life in Florida, she'd never gone camping before, never cooked hot dogs in a campfire or made smores from marshmallows melted by fire and not the microwave. She ate three hot dogs spotted with black burn marks, and then she gorged on crispy marshmallows.

That night, they fixed up beds downstairs to sleep near the warmth.

Meredith passed out a couple of blankets each. "Beth, Donovan, you can sleep on the couch. Each side has leg rests that pop out. Mom, you can sleep in the recliner. I'll roll out a sleeping bag."

"No, Mom. I can sleep on the floor," Donovan offered.

"I wouldn't hear of it," Meredith objected. "You're married now. The two of you will take the couch. If I get cold or can't sleep, Grandma and I will share the recliner."

"I don't want to sleep with you," Lily said.

Meredith gaped at Lily. "Mom!"

"Oh, I'm kidding."

Beth smiled. She imagined that this would've been her and her mom, if they'd been given the opportunity. Now she prayed to have the chance to experience this with her own daughter.

Relenting, Donovan lifted the leg rests using the handles on the sides of the couch. "Sleep here, closer to the fire," he told Beth.

She stretched out, pulled the blankets up to her shoulders, and turned to her side, putting the fireplace to her back so she could face Donovan. With the candles extinguished, the room was darker. The flames in the fireplace created shadows in the corners and along the walls that expanded and shrank with their fiery dance. She reached out her hand to Donovan, and they linked fingers beneath their blankets. Eventually, she drifted off to sleep, even with Nemesis throwing an uproar outside.

Chapter Eighteen

In the morning, snow completely covered the downstairs window. A look through the peephole revealed the conditions had deteriorated more than Donovan thought. All he could see through the tiny hole in the door was darkness. Snow blocked the door. The backyard wasn't any better. Drifts had built up to his shoulders around the entire perimeter of the porch, so he wouldn't even be able to cut through the screen to escape.

After a breakfast of fruit preserves and instant coffee, the four of them played a competitive game of Monopoly. Lily schooled them and cleaned them out of money. They followed that with several card games, but boredom swooped in soon enough, killing the fun.

His mom and grandma went back to knitting, and Beth dozed with her head on Donovan's lap. He listened to the reports coming through on the wind-up radio. Apparently, Nemesis had lost steam and was now stalled overhead, giving it the perfect opportunity to dump everything it had on top of them.

Without the TV and no signal on their cell phones, the radio was their one source of information about the blizzard. He listened to it constantly. Every fifteen minutes or so, he had to re-crank the device to keep it running. The antenna on the radio was short and struggled to receive a signal through the thick layers of winter clouds.

Beth stirred. She sat up and nestled beside him. A shiver ran through her body.

He tucked a heavy afghan over her and rubbed her arm. The room had significantly dropped in degrees, as did the rest of the house. Without centralized heating running through the structure, every hour that went by, it became colder and colder inside, trying to match the below-freezing temps outside.

"I'm okay," Beth said with a yawn. "Just bored and sleepy."

Donovan glanced over at his mom and grandma. They had fallen asleep in their chairs. He shifted back to Beth. "The power is out."

"I know," she mumbled.

"Do you want to talk about baby names?"

That got her attention. She shifted to look at him. "Yeah. Absolutely."

"You go first. What name do you have in mind for a girl?"

"If I said Donna, would you totally hate it?"

Donovan scrunched up his face and nodded. "Let's not name our little girl after me."

She let out a small giggle. "Okay, deal."

"Any other girl names?"

She winced. "No."

"I have one."

"You do?"

He nodded. "I thought of Raegan for a girl, after your mom."

Beth's mouth peeled open, but she didn't say anything.

"What do you think?" He put a finger under her

chin.

"I…I love it. I can't believe I hadn't thought of it myself."

Donovan knew how not having her mom around hurt Beth beyond belief. Giving their daughter her mother's maiden name would be a nice tribute and a way to keep the name Reagan in their family. On the plus side, it wasn't a girly name, and it certainly wasn't a feminine twist to his given name.

"Okay. Now, what about a boy's name?" Beth asked.

"Honestly, I was having trouble coming up with names for a boy. Every one I thought of reminded me of some kid in school I had hated."

Beth took his hand. "Well, I thought of a boy name, and I think you'll like it." She gazed into his eyes. The glimmer of the candles made her irises sparkle with ambers and golds. "Ryan."

Hearing his brother's name struck Donovan in his heart. He hadn't thought of naming their son after his brother. It hadn't even occurred to him, but it made sense.

Ryan had been everything to Donovan—a role model, a best friend, and a voice of reason. And a part of Donovan believed Ryan had a hand in leading him to Beth.

"I'd love to name our son after Ryan, but are you sure?"

"I'm sure. Ryan is a great name, and it would be an honor to give it to our son."

Donovan leaned in and kissed Beth. "Thank you."

"Thank you for thinking of my mom's name."

"You realize we both came up with R names."

Beth smiled. "R is a great letter, and whatever name we don't get to use this time, we can use next time. They can work for either sex."

"Sounds like a plan."

They kissed on it to seal the deal.

"There's actually something I've been wanting to tell you," he said. "I planned to tell you after the holidays, but this is a better time than any...I've decided to quit monster truck driving."

Beth's jaw drop. "What?"

"It's time. I don't like how it takes me away from you, and it'll take me away from our kids. I don't want that anymore."

"But you love it."

He cupped her face with his hands. "I love you more."

She laid her hands atop his. "I know you do, but you also love Venom and the adrenaline rush. I don't want you to stop something you enjoy and are amazing at."

"I'm going to keep Venom, and I can still drive for fun, but I'm giving up competing. Instead, I want to coach young drivers, maybe find someone to take over Venom."

She smiled. "You'd be a great teacher."

"I appreciate that."

"Speaking of teaching...I've had an idea about my job."

He frowned. What did Beth mean by that? She lived and breathed her job, and it helped countless people. She couldn't possibly be thinking about giving up The Fighting Chance. Did she think Craig was going to make it dangerous to ever open the studio again?

"I want to do two weekend classes for young kids." She massaged her belly. "Being pregnant has brought out my maternal side. I'd always wanted to give women and young people what they need to defend themselves, and now I want to teach children the basics and educate them about bullying and safety."

Donovan put his hand on her belly. "That's a great idea."

"You think so?"

"I know so. And it makes sense. You teach all other ages, so why not our youth?"

"I'm really excited about this. It'll be fun to have a bunch of kids in The Fighting Chance, and I thought that maybe you could pitch in whenever you have time."

"Count me in."

A loud splintering noise suddenly echoed in the air, followed by a deep groan.

Beth sat up. "What's that?"

"A tree."

Something banged into the house.

Glass shattered.

Meredith and Lily jumped awake.

"What happened?" Lily shouted.

"A tree came down. I'll go up and check. Stay here." Donovan rushed up the stairs.

On the second floor, he opened each door and shut it quickly to keep the cold air from escaping. He found the broken window in his grandma's room. Snow and slivers of ice blew around the room in a flurry. Shielding his face, he poked his head through the opening and peered at the ground. A pine tree rested across the backyard. Directly below lay one of the broken branches, the culprit that had broken the window.

"Shit." He couldn't leave that window unprotected. Artic air would fill the house, threatening their lives.

Remembering the plywood in the garage, Donovan hurried downstairs. "The window in Grandma's room is smashed. I have to board it up."

He opened the door to the garage and stepped out into the freezing air. The cold bit his skin, so he moved with haste. He tugged on work gloves, hooked the hammer to his belt, and shoved a handful of carpenter nails into his pocket. Then he grabbed a sheet of plywood.

In Grandma's room, he set the sheet of plywood on the windowpane and pushed his shoulder into it. Nemesis rammed against the wood on the other side. He fought with it. It took all his strength to keep the plywood in place and hammer in the first few nails. Once he had several of the nails in, he was able to step back and get the rest in.

He inspected his handywork, checking to make sure snow couldn't sneak through any cracks. The board blocked the elements from getting through. Donovan breathed a sigh of relief. Before leaving his grandma's room, he mopped up the mess Nemesis had made with towels.

For the rest of the day, he tuned in to the radio, but the signal kept getting weaker and weaker. The latest update on the blizzard said it had started to move again and should be gone tomorrow morning. That sounded good to him. Except, Nemesis could do a lot more between now and then.

He fiddled with the dial on the radio when the

channel became static. Another channel came in clearer. Several minutes later, though, it also went out. He searched for another. Music played for a second before erupting into white noise. When he spun the dial back and forth, he couldn't detect anything. Not a peep, not a beat. He twisted the volume knob until the radio turned off, and he set it aside.

"We lost signal."

Chapter Nineteen

With no lights, TV, or radio, Beth had nothing to do but snack on food and listen to Nemesis. To entertain themselves, they played multiple board and card games, but after a while, they became tiresome. Sitting on the couch, wearing a sweater and one of the scarves Lily had finished, Beth munched on a stick of licorice. A pain in her lower back had her squirming. She put a hand behind her to press on the knot.

"You okay?" Meredith asked.

Beth glanced toward the kitchen where Donovan had gone. "Yeah. I've just been sitting for too long."

"I know what could take your mind off being stuck inside." Meredith got up. From the cabinets in the entertainment center, she removed a stack of photo albums. "I'll give you a visual walk down memory lane, staring Donovan Goldwyn."

Seeing pictures of Donovan as a toddler delighted Beth. She couldn't get over the fact Donovan had been little once. That he had once had a cute, bowl-cut hair style, chubby cheeks, and little bunny teeth. Her heart melted while looking at the pictures. She didn't know it could be possible, but she fell even more in love with him after viewing images of his innocent years as a child.

"He was adorable."

"You thought he'd be anything less?" Meredith

smiled. "Both of my sons were cuties when they were teeny, and they became handsome men. They were the only good things I got out of my marriage with their father."

Beth snuck a peek in Donovan's direction again. "He doesn't ever talk about his father."

"And he wouldn't. His father wasn't a good man, and he wasn't good to his sons. Or to me. If I had figured it out sooner, they wouldn't have been born. I'm sorry for what I put myself through by being with him and for what he did to my boys, but I'm not sorry for having them."

Beth touched Meredith's shoulder. "They made it worth it."

Meredith nodded. "You were smart to leave Craig when you did."

Maybe not, Beth thought. Leaving him when she did had caused him to snap. Or perhaps he had such a weak mind he would've snapped no matter what Beth would've done.

"Donovan isn't anything like his father, though. He will be a good father."

"I know he will be. He already is," Beth said.

They paged through an album of photos of Donovan from newborn to five years old. The second album showed Donovan's early school years, and a third followed his high school years. Meredith had been right. Those photos were a good distraction. Meredith shared story after story with her, passing the time and giving Beth valuable insight into Donovan's childhood. She enjoyed every minute of it.

That night, she went to sleep and replayed images of Donovan in her dreams. The stories Meredith told her came to life in her mind, but a tearing pang in her abdomen pried her awake, away from her sweet dreams. She flinched and grasped her stomach. The pain was so strong she had to bear down and grit her teeth to endure it. Donovan didn't feel her movement. Her gaze ticked from Lily to Meredith to be sure they were still sleeping.

No one suspected she was in pain.

As quickly as it came, it went. She breathed in through her nose and out through her mouth several times until the remnants of the ache disappeared. *What was that*? She smoothed her hand over her belly. *Don't do that again, okay, lil one? You're safe, and Mommy needs her sleep.*

Her eyelids grew heavy and lowered. Sleep pulled her back under. A few hours later, though, the same jab of pain returned. She inhaled sharply and held her breath. Her uterus felt as though it had transformed into a balled fist. Throbbing pain dominated her entire abdomen and back, and a tremendous pressure radiated along her pelvis. She seethed between her teeth. Her heart beat erratically, and sweat dampened her scalp.

No, no, no. Panic rushed through her, flooding her body. *This can't be happening. I can't be going into labor. It's a month too soon.*

She knew very well that early labor was an unwanted possibility and that false alarms happened all the time. *Please let it be a false alarm. Please. I can't have this baby now. Not now.*

It took her a long time to fall back asleep, and when she finally did, another contraction pried her awake. She couldn't deny it anymore; she was in full-blown labor.

This was their worst nightmare come true. She peeked at Donovan on the other side of the couch, but she didn't want to wake him. Maybe she could fend off the labor long enough for them to get freed. Some women could be in labor for days, and hers had only begun. There was no reason for her to raise the alarm so soon, especially when they had no way of getting to the hospital. So, she'd grit her teeth and bear it. For as long as she could.

Hours later, another contraction came. She used the many blankets keeping the chilly air from her skin to block a whimper from reaching Donovan's ears. The pain of the contraction was nothing like she'd ever felt before. Tears formed in her eyes as she contended with the contraction dominating her body.

Finally, it passed.

She sat up to find a comfortable position. Her movement stirred Donovan.

His eyes opened, and he gave her a groggy smile. "You're awake already?" He rubbed his eyes before checking his watch. "Well, I guess it's the morning anyway." He scooted over to her and kissed her cheek. When he leaned back, a frown pulled down the corners of his mouth. "You're sweaty." He ran his thumb across her forehead.

"I'm a little warm under all of these blankets and beside the fireplace." She peeled the blankets off her lap. "Can you help me up? I really need to relieve my bladder."

He gave her his hands and pulled her to her feet. In the bathroom, she discovered a reddish-brown discharge, another sign of what she already knew to be happening. She held her belly in her hands. "Help me out here, kiddo. Stay in there until I can get out of here. Please, do this for Mommy and Daddy."

Upstairs, it was freezing, so she hurried back downstairs to her spot by the fire. For breakfast, she ate peaches and had a cup of tea, warmed in the kettle on the bricks of the fireplace. Donovan searched for a station on the radio for them to listen to the news while they ate, but the signal couldn't break through Nemesis's wall.

"How much longer do you think the storm will be here?" she said.

Donovan shrugged. "No way to know for sure, but reports last night predicted it'd leave some time today. It could be a matter of hours."

"Good."

"Sick of us already?" His lips slanted into a smirk.

"Far from it, but I am stir crazy." She maneuvered to her feet. "Care to take me for a spin around the first floor?"

Donovan stood and held out his arm. "I'd love to."

They walked from room to room. Stretching her legs after sitting on the couch and being cooped up in the living room felt wonderful. She wouldn't be able to walk for long, though. Speeding up her labor was the last thing she wanted to do.

"I'm not sure if I'm going to want to come back here during the winter months," she said.

Donovan chuckled. "I don't blame you."

"What do you think Thorn and everyone in Florida are doing?"

"Sweating in the Florida heat and wondering if we've frozen to death."

Beth nudged him. "Not funny."

"Sorry. I'm antsy, too."

She sighed. "I don't know how Northerners can deal with this."

"They wonder the same thing about Southerners with hurricanes."

"We're all crazy."

They laughed together, but her laughter triggered a contraction that rippled her core. She bent forward and grabbed her stomach. A small sound escaped her lips.

Donovan put his arms around her, supporting her so she wouldn't fall. "Beth, what is it?"

She seethed between her teeth until the pain washed over her. The clenching of her stomach had stolen her breath. She straightened slowly, panting, to look into Donovan's concerned eyes. "Contraction."

That one word had Donovan's face turning white.

"They started last night."

Chapter Twenty

"I think the blizzard has passed." Donovan stood near the living room windows, listening. Wind no longer howled as it swirled around the house, throwing snow at the walls as if it was in a snowball fight with Michigan. Well, Nemesis won that snowball fight; all the downstairs windows were covered with snow drifts. Cold leaked in through the glass, chilling the house like a reaper's breath.

He turned to Beth, who sat in a chair near the fireplace. A thick afghan covered her lap; the edges were tucked beneath her feet and around her legs. Her belly protruded above the afghan. She rubbed her hands over it tenderly.

Fear coursed through him. Their baby was on the way. He couldn't let Beth give birth in a house buried in snow. He couldn't let their baby come into the world this way, but he didn't have a choice. The baby was dictating things now, and their baby wanted to come.

He swallowed. "Another contraction?"

She shook her head. "No. I'm just trying to soothe the baby...and myself." She gave him a small smile.

He went to her and knelt on the floor at her feet. His hands molded to either side of her belly. *Please don't come yet. Please wait. I'll get you and Mommy out of here. I promise. You can trust Daddy.*

Beth laid her hands over his. "I'm okay."

She would say that even when the baby's head was at her cervix; she was a warrior. But his mom, who had a stopwatch to monitor Beth's contractions, wouldn't lie to him. He looked to her.

"Her last one was almost ten minutes ago."

Right then, Beth leaned forward. Her hands clutched his. Beneath his palms, her stomach became as hard as a boulder. Beth's cheeks became a bright pink.

"Breathe, baby."

She took in a shaky breath and let it out slowly. In and out, he paid attention to every breath she took. God, he wished he could take some of her pain, share the hurt. But all he could do was watch, pray, and worry. He thought contractions would be fast; here one second and gone the next, but this one carried on as if it didn't want to let her go.

She eased back into an upright position. "It's going," she said, her voice soft.

Donovan rose onto his knees, put one hand on the back of her head, and pressed his lips to her forehead. He kissed her once, twice, three times. With their temples touching, he peered at his mom for the news.

"It lasted sixty-five seconds. Ten minutes apart. She still has time. Usually, it's when the contractions are two to three minutes apart when the mother is taken to the hospital. Around that time, the water breaks. This stage could last for hours. And then when she's ten centimeters dilated, it could take two hours or more before the baby is born."

He nodded and shifted back to look into Beth's eyes. "Beth, I have to dig us out."

"Donovan—"

"Paramedics can't come to you if the doors and

windows are covered with snow. And I can't get you out if the garage door is blocked. One way or another, I have to dig us out."

She nodded. "I know, but I want you to be careful."

"I will." Before getting to his feet, he caught his mom's eye.

"I'll keep an eye on Beth," she vowed.

After another kiss to Beth's forehead, he got to his feet and went to the garage. The air inside the garage was frigid. He quickly shut the door behind him to stop the cold from entering the house. Using a flashlight, he searched the garage until he found a snow shovel. His gaze landed on a two-stage snow blower, but he had no way to get it out of the house, nor would it work on the amount of snow burying the driveway. He was carrying the shovel into the kitchen when a muffled rumble met his ears. His feet froze where he stood. Could it be…?

He propped the shovel against the island and raced up the stairs, taking them two at a time. He shoved open the door to his old bedroom, made it to the window in a few strides, and yanked open a gap in the blinds, breaking several of the thin strips of plastic. His heart rapped against his chest when a truck with a plow chained to the front bumper drove down the street, clearing the road for cars to pass. Large chunks of snow piled at the foot of the driveway; just more he'd have to shovel away, but with the street cleared, he'd have a better chance of getting Beth to the hospital. Surely, workers were out there doing that right now.

The one problem now was how he'd get out of the house to shovel away the snow from the garage door and driveway. It was a two-story drop from this window. He went across the hall to Ryan's old bedroom. The window was covered with frost. Using his jacket sleeve, he scrubbed the ice away. When he stared through the glass, whiteness filled his vision. He flipped the lock at the top of the window and fought with the ice in the tracks to get the window all the way up. Then he stuck out his head. A snow drift was plastered into the side of the house, reaching up to the window. He could climb out the window and use the drift to get to the ground.

He hurried back down the stairs. "A truck plowed the street," he told the three women. "And there's a snow drift right outside Ryan's old room. I'm going to climb out the window and make my way down the drift. I'll work on clearing the snow away from the garage door first."

He went to Beth. On his knees, he bent forward to kiss her belly. "You take it easy on your mom." Then he planted a kiss on Beth's lips. "Just hold on," he said with his lips still on hers.

Her hands came up and framed his face, and she kissed him deeply. "I love you."

"I love you, too." He put a hand on the top of her belly. "I love both of you."

On his feet, he said to his mom, "Shout for me if something happens."

"I will."

Hating he had to leave Beth's side, but knowing he had to do this for her and their baby, he went into the kitchen to get the shovel and made his way up the stairs. The icy air from outside already dominated Ryan's room when he returned. He shut the door behind him. At the window, he passed the shovel through the window onto the drift on the other side. With a black knit beanie cap pulled low to cover his ears and gloves on his hands, he lifted the scarf around his neck over his mouth and nose. He made sure the scarf was tucked in and tied off so it wouldn't slip. With thoughts for Beth and their baby circulating around in his head, he glanced over his shoulder at the door. He braced his hands on the window frame and took a deep breath, preparing himself for the cold and the task at hand. Then he slipped his upper half through the opening. Instantly, the cold cocooned him. He maneuvered his legs through the opening so he sat on the windowsill. When he shifted his weight onto his feet, his legs sank in up to his knees. Moving fast, he shut the window. Then he lowered onto the snow and pulled his legs out. Gripping the shovel, he scooted down the drift. Once he made it to the bottom, he pushed to his feet and lowered a foot into the snow. Using the shovel as a support, he lifted his feet, one at a time, making one step after the other. The trek from the backyard to the front yard took a while, but he finally made it.

His heart sank; the garage door was half-buried by a snow drift. On top of that, a couple of feet of snow concealed the driveway. And the mess at the end of the driveway from the snowplow was too big for the truck to climb over. It would be a big job, but he had to do it, so he set to work.

Every time he plunged the shovel into the snow, he thought about Beth inside the house.

Was she having another contraction? How far apart were they now? How long were they lasting?

How much time did they have left?

Please, God, help me dig them out. Give me a hand.

He lunged the shovel into the snow again and hefted another heap of snow out of the way. None of it seemed to be making a difference.

The freezing air found its way through the fibers of the scarf over his face and bit into his nose and cheeks, as if his face was a snack. Around the shovel's handle, his hands were stiff with cold. Frigid tingles pricked his fingers like needles. And in his boots, his feet felt like ice sculptures. But he didn't dare stop. He could get warm after.

Another shovel-full of snow gone.

And another.

And another.

Finally, he started to see a difference. About half the drift was gone. Seeing that energized him. He dove the shovel into the snow faster, taking more and more of it away. The garage door's handle appeared. After several more shovels, he grabbed the handle and pulled up on it. The door budged by two inches.

"Come on," he said between clenched teeth and applied more muscle.

The door gradually slid up above the last couple of feet of snow. As soon as the bottom of the garage door was clear, he positioned his hands under it and shoved it up with a great heave. The door flew backward on its track. He almost fell to his knees right then and there—exhausted and relieved.

He stepped over the clumps of snow remaining and went to the garage door. Luckily, he had left it unlocked. He stomped the snow off his boots before opening the door and walking into the kitchen. At the island, he pulled the gloves off and dropped them onto the counter. His mom came into the kitchen as he worked off the scarf. Snow clumps fell from it and drifted to the floor.

"How's Beth?" He worked off his boots.

"Her last contraction lasted eighty-five seconds. They're eight minutes apart now."

His neck jerked up. "Eight?"

"Donovan, you were out there over an hour."

Shit. He hadn't known that much time had passed. He ripped the knit cap from his head and hurried to the living room. Beth still sat in the chair by the fireplace.

"Finally," she said. "I almost went out there after you."

"She's not lying," Grandma Lily said.

Donovan sank onto his knees before Beth and put a finger under her chin. "You better not," he told her and tapped his lips to hers.

"Oh my gosh." She put a hand on his cheek. "You're freezing." She pointed to the couch. "Sit down, and you're not going back out there until you're warm again."

"Beth—"

"Sit. Down."

With a sigh, he sat on the end of the couch. Beth pushed to her feet. Concern had him asking, "What are you doing? You shouldn't be moving."

"Women in labor are allowed to move."

"Yeah, when they want to speed up the labor. We don't want to do that."

She held the afghan in her arms and came to the couch. "I'm not going to drop the baby after taking two steps. Your mom says I'm in the latent phase." She joined him on the couch and draped the afghan over his legs. "Take off your socks so your feet can get warm, too."

He bent forward, peeled off his wet socks, and tossed them onto the brick hearth. Beth took his right hand, brought it to her mouth, and blew her warm breath onto his fingers. The act reminded him of how he had used his breath to warm the bruise on her shoulder when he had left the icepack on it too long. That was when they had met. Now, years later, Beth was pregnant with their baby, in labor, and in yet another disaster because of him.

"We shouldn't be here," he said.

Beth frowned. "What do you mean?"

"I never should've brought you, eight months pregnant, to Michigan for Christmas."

"Donovan." She laid a hand on his cheek and forced him to look at her. "This isn't your fault. I wanted to come before the baby was born. I wanted to spend Christmas here with Meredith and Lily. Neither of us knew a blizzard would come. Or that I'd go into early labor."

"This isn't the first time something like this has happened, and every time, I brought you to those places. I did…I do. I put you into that danger."

The earthquake—he wanted to go to San Francisco to hunt down his brother's killer.

The tsunami—they went there on their honeymoon.

And now this.

Beth blinked. What she did next surprised him; she grabbed his face, pulled him to her, and kissed him with more passion than he thought she could muster under the circumstances. Her tongue glided with his. Her lips molded to his. Her heart beat with his. She not only silenced his words but his thoughts. And she showed him with that kiss all the love she had for him, even while trapped by snow, even while in labor.

She eased back far enough to say, "*I* wanted to go to San Fran with you. *I* chose Oahu as our honeymoon destination. And *I* wanted to be here for Christmas. Me. Not you. We may have some shitty luck, but, Donovan, I don't regret any of it. You're the one I want with me in a disaster. In life. Forever. Do you understand me?"

He nodded slowly.

"Please don't ever think 'what if?' And don't blame yourself for any of it. We were made for each other, to love each other, and to endure these things together because we can survive them. You and me, Donovan." She smiled. "And now, it's you and me and this little one." She put a hand on her belly. "This baby...and our love...surmounts all, including that tsunami."

Hearing Beth say that, after what she had endured during and after that tsunami, speared him in the heart. He kissed her, thanking her with his lips for her words, her devotion, her strength. While their lips were connected, she let out a small gasp. He wrapped his arms around her as a contraction gripped her stomach.

"I've got you," he whispered in her ear.

"I know," she whispered back.

When the contraction released her, she rubbed feeling back into his fingers. The fact she was concerned with him when she was the one in labor showed him even more how strong she was, how much she cared about him.

His mom came over a moment later with a steaming cup in her hands. She handed it to him. "Thanks, Mom." He took a sip. The heat of the coffee warmed him from the inside. He savored the warmth of the coffee, of the fire, of Beth at his side. His toes no longer felt like ice cubes, and his hair was dry. He finished the last of the coffee and set the cup on the side table. When he came back to his sitting position, he watched Beth's eyes close and her hands clench. She hadn't so much as made a peep to tip him off that another contraction had her in its clutches. He set a hand on the top of her belly, felt how hard it was beneath his palm. After a moment, the muscles unclenched, and her stomach softened.

She opened her eyes.

"That one was five minutes," his mom said.

Shit.

"It can go on like this for a while yet, Donovan."

He nodded, but that didn't relieve him a bit. "I have to get back out there."

His mom held out a pair of wool socks and another knit cap. "These are dry."

Grateful, he took them and put them on.

"Don't stay out there too long," Beth said.

"I have to stay out there as long as it takes to finish this, and then I can take you to the hospital."

"You won't be able to take me to the hospital if you pass out."

"That's not going to happen." He got to his feet.

In the kitchen, he wound the scarf back around his neck and face. Determined, he snatched up the shovel in the garage and attacked the snow with vigor. Every shovelful, every snowflake was keeping him from getting Beth help. And that was unacceptable. He was a husband and a father, damn it. His family's lives were at stake.

When the snow at the garage was demolished, he scooped up large hunks of snow from the driveway. With several feet of snow on the ground, he wouldn't be able to drive the truck out of there; it'd get stuck. He had to clear the driveway and break down the large white chunks at the end of the driveway. If he lifted a good layer of it, he'd be able to use the snow blower on the rest of it. While he worked, he counted, trying to keep track of every minute. Every time he got to five minutes, he sent his thoughts to Beth. *You've got this, baby.* He lost track of how many times he made it to five minutes, but he kept on doing it. The counts became beats that worked with each plunge, each heave, each breath he took. It took his mind off how frigid it was outside, how cold he was beneath his many layers.

"Donovan!"

His head whipped around. Beth stood in the garage. He dropped the shovel and ran over. When he made it to her, he tugged the scarf below his chin and took her arms in his hands. "Are you okay?"

"Still five minutes apart."

"Then what are you doing out here?" He ushered her gently toward the door.

"Because you've been out here for an hour. You need to come in."

He inspected his progress for the first time. He'd be able to bring out the snow blower now, and then all he'd have left would be the boulders crowding the end of the driveway. "I'm almost done, Beth."

"Just come into the kitchen for a minute and have some coffee. Please."

He agreed because he wanted her out of the bitter

cold. "Okay." He opened the door and helped her inside. On the counter was a thermos. He unscrewed the cap and poured some coffee into it. If his insides could steam, he felt certain they would the moment the coffee slid down his throat and hit his stomach. That warmth felt good. He took a few swallows before replacing the cap. "I'll take this out with me."

She was about to speak, to object, so he said, "I can't stop now, Beth. I can't fail at being a father before our baby is even born."

"Donovan—"

He turned, opened the door, and took a step outside.

"Donovan, wait."

He faced her. She was up a step so he could clearly see into her eyes.

She stepped closer to him. Her belly pushed into him, and she pressed her warm cheek against his chilled one. She held it there a moment, infusing him with her body heat. "This baby is lucky to have you for a father." Then she leaned back. With a smile, she lifted the scarf back into place, hiding his face.

"Now, please, go sit down," he said. "I'll be done soon."

He waited until she turned before shutting the door. In the garage, he set the thermos on the truck's hood. The sooner he got the driveway cleared, the better.

His boots crunched on the bit of snow and ice left on the driveway. Luckily, he was able to get the snow blower to work, and he pushed it up and down the driveway to make the path for the truck easier. He had to resist the urge to run to get it done faster. Once he got it cleared as good as he could manage, he picked up the shovel again. The mountain of snow at the foot of the drive was made of solid clumps.

He drove the edge of the shovel into one of them over and over again, hoping to break it up into smaller, more manageable sizes. It took several hits. Arms straining, he lifted the pieces and tossed them out of the way. His energy was waning, and he had a lot to do. If he could at least eliminate the largest boulders on the top, he might be able to power the truck over the rest. Maybe. Hopefully.

The crunch of the shovel pounding into the snow and ice filled his ears. It was all he could hear. The rest of the street was silent beneath its wintry blanket. Breathing was difficult with the icy air clogging his lungs. His nose burned. His throat was dry and on fire. But he ignored it, focusing on his task.

Crack, crack, crack.

He jabbed the shovel into a hunk of snow. On the third hit, it shattered into several pieces. He scooped them up and flung them to the side. He surveyed what remained. There was one big ball in the middle of the path that needed to be dealt with next. He moved over to it and struck it. That one impact had it severing in two. He was about to hit it again when something crashed into the back of his head.

Explosions of white light danced over his vision. Pain enveloped his skull. The shovel slipped from his fingers. Blackness cloaked his mind, coaxing him into its depths.

Beth. Her name was a whisper in his head, as if his thoughts were being sucked into a wormhole.

His legs collapsed under his weight.

Cold. It seeped into him, consuming him. And then

his consciousness fled down that same void that ate his thoughts.

Chapter Twenty-One

Beth lay on the living room floor, with her knees pointing to the ceiling and a pillow under her back and head. The afghan covered her legs like a blue, sanitary sheet in an exam room. She focused on relaxing breathing techniques.

"You're doing good, Beth," Meredith said.

Beth couldn't even see Meredith's head while she checked Beth's progress and measured her cervix with her fingers.

"It feels like you're about six centimeters now."

"Already?"

Meredith sat up and patted Beth's knee. "You're fine. You have a whole four more centimeters to go."

Meredith helped Beth to stand and dress. Back in her chair by the fire, Beth took a sip of tea. "I'm glad you're here Meredith," she said. "This is my first time having a baby. I don't think I'd be so calm if it weren't for you."

The other woman smiled at Beth as she settled the afghan back over her. "I'm glad I can be here for you and Donovan, too. To be able to help my daughter-in-law and bring my grandchild into this world…it's a blessing. But what I love more is seeing Donovan become a father." She sat on the couch next to Beth. On the other side, Lily dozed. "I got to see him become a husband and now a father. I am so proud of the man my son has become."

Beth smiled. "He's an amazing man. Before Donovan, I couldn't envision myself with kids. Remember when Donovan brought me here for Christmas after the hurricane and you and Lily asked me if I loved him?"

Meredith laughed. "I remember."

"Well, I had panicked a little at that question. I didn't think I had it in me to be a wife or a mother. But it was when I knew I really did love Donovan that I felt I could be both."

The other woman squeezed Beth's hand. "When Donovan was young, he would swear up and down he would never get married and didn't want kids. And I kept telling him, 'just you wait. The right woman will come into your life and everything will change.' The moment I met you, for Ryan's funeral, I knew you were that woman."

Beth recalled something Meredith had said to her after Ryan's funeral that had stumped her for a long time. "Before you left, you told me you were glad Donovan found me because he had changed for the better. What did you mean by that?"

"There was a light in his eyes, a light I had never seen before. It was pure happiness that can only be conjured by love. You were healing him."

Beth swallowed. "Healing him?"

"There had been a hint of darkness…sadness…in Donovan's eyes since he was a child. I suspect it was because of his father's absence. He was a rebellious teen. And then when his knee was injured and he couldn't play basketball anymore, he spiraled down. He didn't care about much, other than me, Ryan, and his grandmother. But you changed all of that. I don't know what would've happened to him after Ryan died if you weren't there." She took Beth's hands. "I thank God for you every night."

Tears clouded Beth's eyes. "Donovan healed me, too. He healed me every day after the tsunami. I don't think I would've survived that without him."

The garage door opened. Boots stomped, the door shut, and footsteps made their way to the living room. Beth dashed away the tears lingering on her eyelashes so Donovan wouldn't see them. He had been outside for another hour, and she was glad he was back.

Donovan stood in the dim lighting a few feet from them. He reached up and removed the knit cap from his head. Dark, wet hair fell across his forehead. His other hand ripped the scarf from his face, but it wasn't Donovan's face she saw.

Meredith gasped.

"Who are you?" Lily asked.

Fear gripped Beth by the throat. She studied him from head to foot. He had dyed his blond hair dark brown and cut it to match Donovan's.

"Craig. What are you doing here?"

He smiled in a way that screamed he wasn't right in the head. "I'm here for you."

She looked at the scarf he had dropped on the floor; it was the same scarf Donovan had worn outside. If Craig had it, Donovan didn't.

"What did you do to Donovan?"

"I took care of him, like you wanted me to."

Beth's brows lowered. She spoke slowly. "I don't want you Craig. I want Donovan."

"And now you have him." He held out his hands,

indicating himself.

Nausea swam in Beth's stomach at his words. His hair, his clothes...he wanted to replace Donovan. "Craig, I broke things off with you years ago. I'm with Donovan now. I'm happily married, and I'm having his child. Wherever you came from, you need to go back there."

"I'd rather not. I've been with the neighbors' dead bodies since before the blizzard hit."

Meredith made a small sound and covered her mouth with her hand.

"And you need to stop calling me Craig. I'm not Craig anymore. To you, to everyone, I am Donovan."

Beth shook her head. "No, you're not."

Rage morphed Craig's face. He surged toward her. "I'm your husband now," he roared. "And that baby will grow up calling me Dad." He jabbed a finger at her belly.

Beth's breathing quickened. Where was Donovan? Did Craig hurt him? Kill him? She couldn't lose Donovan before she brought their baby into this world. She didn't want to lose him period. Never did she imagine Craig would become this man in front of her— a crazy stalker capable of taking life. But anyone could be pushed to the extreme.

A contraction hit her then. She gripped the chair's arms and dug her nails into the wood. Her entire body tensed against the assault.

Craig let out a laugh. "Are you having contractions?"

Her gaze flicked to him. He was coming toward her. If she could move, she'd get up and retreat far from him, but the contraction had her glued to the chair, paralyzed. He squatted in front of her, in the same place where Donovan had knelt to check on her and show her love. That wasn't Craig's place. She tried to shrink away from him, but the chair wouldn't let her move an inch. He put his hands on her belly, and her skin crawled at the contact.

"Wow. Look at that." He peered up at her, wearing the creepiest smile she'd ever seen. "I came in time to see my baby born."

She stopped breathing when she noticed his eyes. He obviously had on purple contacts, turning the eyes she loved—Donovan's eyes—into something nightmarish. He really was trying to become Donovan in every way. And that sickened her. With the contraction beating up her insides, combined with the fear Craig instilled in her, the urge to throw up washed over her. Acid swirled in her stomach and rose up her throat. She squeezed her eyes shut and inhaled through her nose.

The contraction took its time dissolving. When it did, she opened her eyes to see Craig eyeing her. She recoiled from him, not wanting to see those eyes.

His hands moved, but she didn't look down to see what they were doing. A moment later, the zipper to her jacket lowered.

He parted the sides to reveal her belly. "Wow," he said.

She jerked when his hands touched her stomach. Although her long-sleeved, cotton shirt kept his hands from contacting her skin, without the barrier of her thick winter jacket, she could feel the heat from his palms and every one of his fingers. Then his hands started to roam along the shape of her stomach, up to her breasts. He cupped them in a way that was too intimate and revolting. She grasped the armrests and clenched her jaw.

Craig's breathy sigh sent chills down her spine. "You are beautiful."

"Don't touch her." The shout came from Meredith.

Craig's jaw throbbed with anger. He surged to his feet and rounded on Meredith and Lily, who were huddled together on the couch. "What did you say to me?"

"I said, don't touch her."

"I can do whatever I want to her. And you." He towered over them. "I don't need the two of you." He reached behind him and pulled out a gun from under his jacket. The barrel came within inches of Meredith's forehead.

Beth sprang to her feet faster than she thought she could. "No!" She grabbed his arm. "Please, don't shoot them. If you hurt them in any way, I'll never forgive you." She paused. "Do you understand me? I'll *never* forgive you." She would do more than that; she'd find some way to kill him herself, even if it meant shoving the fireplace poker through his chest, through his ugly heart.

Craig angled his head toward her. "And I can't have that. Now can I?" Then he shifted so the gun pointed at her chest. "Sit back down."

She rotated stiffly, with her hands plastered to her belly and her fingers stretching as far as they could in a pathetic attempt to shield her baby. While moving back to her chair, she eyed the fireplace poker. It lay across the bricks, within an arm's reach from her chair. She contemplated grabbing it, swinging around, and plunging it into Craig's core, but he had a gun with a bullet which could travel faster than she could. That bullet could strike her in the chest, in the belly. If she knew it would hit her arm or shoulder, she'd take the risk, but there was no way of knowing, and she'd never put Donovan's baby at risk. Never. So, she sank onto the chair, heavy with fear.

Donovan. Where are you?

God, she hoped he was still alive.

Craig moved to the front of the living room and knelt down before a black duffel bag. She hadn't noticed that before. Fresh terror rolled through her. Anything could be in that bag, any type of weapon, anything that could cause her, Meredith, and Lily pain.

He unzipped it with a loud metallic ripping sound that had Beth quivering.

With his back turned, she glanced back at the poker. Her gaze met Meredith's. Meredith looked at it, too. And her eyes widened. The light from the fire danced upon her pale face.

No, she mouthed to Beth. Her finger pointed at Beth's belly. *I won't let you.*

Meredith's response was exactly what Donovan would've said to her. Now she knew where Donovan got his protective instincts.

I'll do it, Meredith mouthed.

Beth swallowed. She couldn't let Meredith risk herself, couldn't let Donovan lose his mother. But by the way Meredith stared at her, Beth got the feeling Meredith thought Donovan couldn't lose the woman he loved, the woman who brought him more happiness than anyone in the universe.

Meredith reached her arm out slowly toward the

bricks.

Holding her breath, Beth eyed Craig, who was rifling through the items in the bag. The clatter of metal had her mouth going dry. She didn't want to know what he had in there, but she'd find out. Sooner or later.

She peered back at Meredith. Her hand crept along the bricks. Her fingers touched the poker. Beth's heart skipped a beat. Meredith's fingers wrapped around the poker. Carefully, she lifted it off the bricks.

Beth swiveled her head back to Craig. His back was still to them.

Not wanting movement to attract Craig's attention, Meredith pulled the poker to her gradually. She set it across her lap and Lily's lap. Then she flung the afghan over it.

Craig stood back up.

The three of them jerked in their places.

He turned. In his hands, he held a coil of rope and a hunting knife. He went over to Meredith and Lily. With a stern face, he yanked Meredith's hands from her lap. Beth couldn't stop herself from visually searching the afghan. Did it look as if she was hiding something under there, something she planned to kill Craig with? Beth couldn't detect a telltale bulge or see a hint of the poker's shape. She exhaled with relief. But that relief was short-lived as Craig wound rope around Meredith's wrists and connected it to her ankles. After he wrapped her ankles a few times, he tied off the end with a sharp tug. He picked up the hunting knife next and sawed through the thick fibers. He did the same thing to Lily.

Seeing the two of them tied up sent a wave of queasiness through her. She inhaled and exhaled to dispel the urge to vomit. But then Craig came to her with that rope. He tied a knot around the chair's arm and her right wrist. When he tightened it, her wrist pressed roughly into the armrest.

"What are you doing?" she asked, panicked. "You can't tie me up. I'm in labor."

Craig's glare settled on her. "I don't want my pregnant wife moving around and hurting herself."

He twisted the rope around her right wrist two more times before stretching the rope across her belly to her left wrist. He looped the rope around, knotted it, and sliced through the rope with the sharp blade. The rest of the rope he snaked about her ankles.

On his knees, he leaned forward, so his face was inches from hers. "You're mine now, Beth." His voice lowered. "All mine." He plastered his mouth to hers. She wanted to pull away, but his hand caught the back of her head and pulled it forward so her lips flattened to his. His tongue came out and probed the space between her lips, but she kept them sealed tight. What he did next, though, changed the game. He pressed the tip of the hunting knife into her pelvis.

"Open your mouth," he growled.

Repulsed, terrified, she did the one thing she could do while tied up and at knife point; she peeled her lips apart.

"Wider."

Squeezing her eyelids tight, she opened her mouth a fraction more. Craig grabbed her jaw, forcing her to admit him as his tongue plunged into her mouth. She gripped the armrests with all of the anger, horror, and shame roaring through her body. His tongue probed her mouth, and she held her body still against the invasion. She considered biting him, but that could be dangerous.

He moved back. A sick smile formed on his mouth. "I want you, Beth." He peered down at her belly. His free hand inched up her shirt, and he set the blade against her skin. "But I could leave here with just the baby and live as a single father." He flipped the blade to the blunt side and dragged it across her abdomen, so she could feel the cold metal move from one hip to the other. "Remember that." He pulled her shirt back into place and got to his feet.

Beth stared straight ahead. Tears blurred her vision. She wanted to spit out the taste of Craig from her mouth. She wanted to wipe him from her lips with the back of her hand.

"Beth." Meredith's whisper came to her, but she didn't dare look at the two women sitting on the couch. She didn't want to see their shocked faces.

Chapter Twenty-Two

Craig stood in front of the fireplace, inspecting the mantel. Out of the corner of Beth's vision, she could see him, a dark figure at her side. He picked up a picture frame.

"This is a lie," he spat.

In the next instant, he whirled around and threw the picture frame on the ground. Glass shattered, and the frame broke into pieces. He went to it. Squatting on the floor, he shifted aside the backing and the filler sheet to get to the picture. He inspected it with a shaking hand. Then he grasped the top of it and tore it in half. One half, he let fall to the floor. The other half, he carried to Beth. He held it out in front of her face. It was Donovan. The picture had been the one they took together at the beach, the one that had gone missing from Donovan's apartment. They had sent it to Meredith to go into the frame Beth had gifted her during their first Christmas together. Now, it lay in shambles.

Craig tossed the torn photo of Donovan into the fireplace. She didn't look at it, didn't want to see it burn up into ashes.

"What's so special about that guy, huh?" Craig pointed at the flames. "What's so great about that man?" He bent forward to shout in her face. "What did he have that kept you from me?"

Everything, she thought.

"Answer me!"

"He was different," she whispered.

"Different how?"

She shook her head as tears built in her eyes. "I never felt for another what I felt for him."

Craig pulled himself straight. His body vibrated with rage. After an intense, quiet moment, he spun around. He flipped the coffee table. He swung at a lamp, sending it flying into the wall where it erupted. The pop of the lightbulb exploding reminded Beth of gunfire. Seething, he rushed at Beth. His hands slammed into the top of the chair, tipping the chair. Beth's head knocked backward. Her feet sought refuge with the floor. A second later, the chair's legs smacked into the floor, and Beth found herself staring right into Craig's eyes.

"That man is no more," he hissed. "I hit him in the back of the head, and he fell face-first into the snow. Do you know what hypothermia does to the body? He was already out there for a long time before I came. And now, he's getting colder and colder, lying in the snow with a concussion. His breathing will slow, his heart rate will weaken, and soon, he won't have a pulse. He'll die out there."

Beth glared out of pure hatred, even as his words terrified her.

"I am the man you want." He stroked her cheek. "I am the man you need." His gaze hardened. "Right?"

He wanted a response from her. It would be dangerous to tell him something he didn't want to hear, but all she could get out was a terse, "Yes."

A smile pulled on his lips. "That's my girl."

He walked over to the large, wooden entertainment center and opened the cabinets along the bottom. In one of them, he found the photo albums Meredith had shown Beth earlier. He pulled one out. On his feet, he flipped open the cover. Beth recognized it as Donovan's baby book with pictures of Donovan as a newborn.

"Don't burn that," Meredith shouted.

Craig cocked his head. "Why would I burn my baby pictures?"

His mind really has corrupted. He didn't just want to be Donovan, he believed himself to be Donovan. And anything or anyone who said otherwise was in danger.

He continued to flip through the pages. A laugh came from his mouth. "I was a handful for a son, wasn't I?"

"You're not—"

Beth shook her head at Meredith, stopping her from saying something fatal.

Craig's glare could cut. "I'm not what?"

Meredith swallowed. "You're not wrong about that," she muttered.

He nodded. "But you always loved me, right?"

"Right." Meredith's voice was small. Her real son was outside, possibly dying, and she had to play this sick game with Craig in order to stay alive.

He turned another page, admiring the childhood he never lived.

A contraction vised around Beth's middle. She bore down, willing the pain to stop. This was not what she needed right now. Every contraction she had was like a timer ticking down to zero, and at that zero, her baby would be coming into a dangerous situation. She didn't know what Craig would do once her baby took its first breath.

She counted to fifty before the vise released, but the ache in her back stayed. Wanting to reduce the pain, she shifted in vain. She couldn't move enough to bring relief.

Craig returned to the cabinet and pulled out another album. "Ah. Our wedding." He flashed a smile at Beth. "Do you remember what I said when I proposed?"

She swallowed, nodded.

"Say it."

She thought back to Donovan kneeling before her in the San Francisco Police Department. The moment had replayed in her thoughts many times over the years, it was the moment when everything had changed for them, when they realized they didn't want to be apart. Ever.

She cleared her throat. "Since we met, we've been through a hurricane and an earthquake together." She didn't look at him as she recited Donovan's words. "And if there are other disasters in my future, I don't want to face them without you. Beth Kennedy..." Her voice caught. "...will you marry me?"

Craig slapped the album shut. "That's not what I said. How could you forget it?" He threw the album on the floor with a thud. "I said I wanted to be the only man in your life. The man privileged to love you as you should be loved. I said I'd take that honor seriously. Until the day I take my last breath. And I asked if you'd accept me as the one man you'd ever need. And you said you would."

The realization he had conjured up memories of a

fake life with her made a cold sweat break out across her forehead and under her arms. Her palms were slicked with that fear.

"And what were my vows on our wedding day?" he prompted.

There'd be no way she'd know that. In her mind, she could hear Donovan saying, "When I first saw you, I thought you were an angel." But Craig wouldn't say that. She licked her dry lips. "You could probably tell it better than I can."

Craig knelt in front of her. "I said I had dreamt of this day for so long, when I'd make you my wife. I'd lay awake at night, trying to imagine this moment, but the reality is so much better than I could ever have thought."

Those words, she realized, were true. He probably had lain awake at night, every night, fantasizing about a wedding that never happened. And their wedding night. What had he visualized for their wedding night? She didn't want to know.

"I said that now I was in your life nothing could take me away from you."

Beth gaped at him. That was sickeningly similar to what Donovan had said. *Fate tossed us together, but nothing that fate can dish out can tear us apart. No hurricane or earthquake will ever be strong enough.*

Had Craig been there in the gardens, lurking behind a bush or tree, spying on the moment when she and Donovan had pledged their love for each other? The police had been there keeping an eye out for suspicious characters who could've been part of Jackson Storm's criminal ring, but would Craig, a seemingly normal guy, have gone unnoticed among a small crowd of onlookers on the outskirts of their wedding? She didn't doubt he could've been there, etching each detail in his mind and replacing Donovan with himself.

"Surely, you remember what I said at the end?" Craig said, bringing her back.

She had no clue, but she had no other choice but to nod.

"You'll have my love and protection forever. And my arms will be your home for all of eternity." His finger traced the infinity knot on her finger, the same symbol on her engagement ring.

Beth's chest rose and fell rapidly. *No! No, you son of a bitch. You are not Donovan. You're not him. And you'll never be him.*

The words of Donovan's vow had been a promise he swore to himself and to her. *I promise to forever love you, to forever protect you, and to forever be your home.* And he had never faltered to keep that oath, but Craig could've broken that promise for him.

She sent her thoughts to Donovan, wherever he was. *Donovan, we need you. Don't you dare give up. Don't you dare leave us.*

If he was outside in the snow, unconscious, she had to find some way to wake him up. Going outside was out of the question, even if she managed to convince Craig to untie her. She'd have to find some other way to get his attention, to pull him from the darkness keeping him from her.

"Can you get some water?" she asked. "Please. I'm thirsty."

"Anything you want."

"There are jugs of water in the kitchen."

She waited until he moved out of sight before looking to Meredith. Her voice was barely audible when she said, "Can you move?" With a jerk of her head, she indicated at the side table to Meredith's left. "Key fob. Get it."

Meredith had to shift the fire poker onto Lily's lap and pull her knees up onto the couch in order for the rope stretching from her wrists to her ankles to offer enough give to reach the fob. Her body tilted into the couch's sidearm as she strained. Her fingers inched along the table's wooden surface, inching closer and closer to the key fob. A grunt passed between her lips.

Beth glanced over her other shoulder, being sure Craig wasn't returning. A soft scraping sound had her peering back at Meredith to see the ring of the key fob balanced on the tip of Meredith's finger. If it fell, they'd all be screwed.

Meredith pulled her arms back to her body and tilted her hands up. The silver ring slid down the length of her index finger, and the black key fob landed in her palm. She pulled it from her finger and lowered her feet to the floor.

"Give it to me," Beth breathed and uncurled the fingers of her right hand.

A couple of bounces had Meredith at the edge of the couch. She extended her arms to Beth. The fob was inches from Beth's fingers. Afraid they'd get caught in the act, Beth shot a peek over her shoulder. Craig's boots thumped on the tile. He was coming back.

Beth's heart launched up to her esophagus. She faced Meredith. "Hurry." Gritting her teeth, she thrust her right arm forward as much as it would go. The rope restraining her burned her skin, but that inch was what they needed. Meredith lifted the key fob, and Beth snatched it with her fingers. Meredith leapt back onto the couch cushion and settled the afghan over her lap, as though she hadn't moved an inch.

Beth yanked her arm back into place, ignoring the fresh abrasions from the ropes rubbing against her skin, and fumbled with the fob to get her fingers securely around the small device. She had just curled her fingers around it and set her thumb on the large button when Craig returned. He came to her with a glass of water.

"Thank you."

He held it to her mouth. Trying to calm her shaking, she dipped her head to the glass. While taking a sip, she pressed the button.

A loud horn blared throughout the house. Craig jumped, sloshing water from the glass onto Beth. "What is that?" he shouted.

Beth didn't answer.

"What the hell is that?"

He slammed the glass down onto the mantel and made a full circle. His eyes were wide and wild, like an animal noticing it was trapped. He cocked his head to the side, listening. "It's coming from the garage. It's the truck." He ran out of the living room. A moment later, the door to the garage banged open. The alarm became louder. Over the blaring racket, Beth heard Craig's shouts and a few crashes.

His boots stomped on the floor. In the blink, he was back in the living room. He ripped the gun out from behind his back and pointed it at her. "Where are the fucking keys?"

"My purse. Check my purse."

He whirled around. "Where, damn it?"

"By the door."

He yanked her purse off the hook and upended it, spilling its contents onto the floor. Items rolled on the hardwood. He dropped to his knees and shifted through the contents until he found the keys. With them grasped in his hand, he launched to his feet and rushed down the hall. Seconds later, the alarm quit.

The door slammed, rattling the pictures on the walls.

"How did that alarm go off?" he demanded.

"I don't know," Beth said. "The only key I have is the one in your hand."

"Well, it wasn't Goldwyn because he's still lying out there. He's probably dead by now."

He's not dead. He can't be.

She compressed the button again. The alarm picked back up.

Craig whipped around. "What the fuck?" He rounded on her. "You're doing it."

"I'm not. I can't even move. The cold must be messing with the wiring or something."

"Could be a raccoon," Lily offered. "There's a raccoon around here that gets under hoods and ruins brake lines and sets off alarms."

"If it's a fucking raccoon, I'm going to kill it." He charged out of the living room. The garage door slammed into the wall, and the alarm filled the house with its ear-piercing cry.

A beep sounded, and the alarm died.

Beth didn't wait a beat; she jabbed the button. *Wake up, Donovan. Wake up!*

Craig's muffled curses reached them. A moment later, silence.

But Beth wasn't ready to give up yet, though. She activated the alarm again. *Come on, Donovan. Please. Wake up!*

Beep-beep.

The alarm quit.

She hit the button once more then dropped the key fob to the floor beside her feet.

Silence.

Craig's enraged yells rushed through the opened door. "Goddamn piece of shit!" Bangs followed his shout as she imagined him hitting the truck's hood with his fists.

She had to hide the key fob and fast. Bending forward, she eyed the tiny device. She lifted her boots off the floor and swept them to the side, striking the key fob with the side of a rubber sole. The fob glided over the floor and slipped beneath the couch.

And she hoped that was enough to pry Donovan into consciousness.

Chapter Twenty-Three

Donovan's head ached, as if a jackhammer was cracking into the back of his skull. Actually, he was sure a jackhammer was drilling into his head. That would explain the screeching noise in his eardrums.

Gradually, the blackness around the edges of his mind retreated. When it did, he became aware of the cold. Frigid needles pricked his face from temples to chin, numbing his nose and cheeks. He lifted his head out of the snow. A stabbing sensation at the base of his head had him lowering back down.

The racket beating against his head finally stopped. Then it started up again. He groaned. That noise agitated the pain throbbing behind his eyes, giving him a splitting headache. The blare blasting his eardrums paused before coming back, seemingly louder than before. He raised his head an inch out of the snow. Two more times the alarm went off, as if stressing urgency.

"Goddamn piece of shit!"

The man's shout penetrated the haze swooping around Donovan. It had come from behind him, from the garage…his mother's garage. That didn't make sense.

Bang. Bang. Bang.

The clash of metal prompted him to open his eyes, but his eyelids only cracked part-way.

His lashes were frozen together. And all he could

see through the clumps of eyelashes was white. He moved his right arm out from under him. A hiss escaped his lips; his arm was stiff from the cold as well as from its circulation being cut off for too long. He managed to get his hand to his face to wipe his eyes. Inside the glove, his fingers were unfeeling. Ice flaked off his lashes and onto his cheeks. Beneath the fabric, his eyes warmed. He lowered his fingers and peered groggily at his surroundings.

His vision blurred. Trying to combat the fuzzy vision, he blinked several times. Each one helped to focus his eyesight. Snow. Snow everywhere. A fog still clung to his mind. Why was he outside? What happened? Questions bounced around inside his head like a ping pong ball. Confusion danced with the questions—grab your partner, do-si-do. He laid his forehead on his arm and squeezed his eyelids shut while trying to fight through the haze.

A loud *wham* had his body jerking. He recognized that sound as a door slamming, the garage door. An image of Beth standing there at the garage door with a thermos crystalized in his mind. Suddenly, the frost on his mind thawed, and he remembered everything. Beth in labor. Shoveling snow to get her to the hospital. And getting his head bashed in. Fear iced his veins.

I have to get to her. But his muscles wouldn't move. *Get up, Goldwyn. Get the fuck out of this snow!*

Mustering his strength, he pushed up with his arms and wrestled his legs out from under him. Dizziness whirled around him, and he fell back onto his haunches. He stroked his hands over his numb face to bring warmth to his forehead and cheeks. When he could move his brows, he attempted to stand. His legs shook as if he was a newborn colt. Gritting his teeth, he managed to get to his feet, only for his legs to give out. He crumpled into the snow.

Damn it, Goldwyn! Get up now and get to your wife.

That command had him struggling to a stand, with his knees bent and his arms out to steady himself. He took a tentative step. His legs felt as though they were beyond asleep, but they held. He inched his way up the icy driveway to the garage. Once there, he grabbed onto the truck's bumper and leaned against it to give his body a moment's rest. To get more blood flowing, he rubbed his arms and smacked his legs.

Fog drifted from his mouth as he breathed. Damn, he was cold. Past cold. Colder than he'd ever been, even after growing up in Michigan. He didn't know how long he had been laid out in the snow, unconscious, but it had been long enough. Too long, in fact. And not just for him but for Beth. And his mom and grandma. And his baby.

He moved around the truck, with his feet feeling like blocks of ice. On the cement floor, he found the thermos lying on its side. Wincing, he bent down to pick it up. Warmth seeped through his glove to his hand. He held the thermos to his frozen cheeks. The contact stung. Hands shaking, he unscrewed the cap and brought the thermos to his mouth. Steam floated over his face, caressing his chilled skin. The first touch of hot coffee on his mouth startled him. He swallowed the sip down with a grimace, but that bit of coffee had warmth blooming throughout his body. His insides, anyway. He took another sip. This time, it didn't shock his system but felt good. He recapped the thermos and made a few faltering steps to the door.

The conditions inside the house were unknown and so was the intruder, the asshole who clocked him. And for what? Shelter? A fireplace to get warm by? Food? Or something more sinister? Would a burglar be so desperate or so stupid, or desperately stupid, to want to break into someone's home during a blizzard? Perhaps if the person wanted a generator or other such survival tool, but they didn't have a working generator, so what did the intruder want?

He put his hand on the doorknob and gave it a turn; it wasn't locked. Praying the chilled hinges wouldn't betray him, he eased the door open. A crack appeared between the door and the jamb, offering him a glimpse of the apple-red walls. He pushed it open more. Part of the island became visible. But Beth's voice caused him to freeze.

"Craig—"

"I'm not Craig," a man roared. "Craig wasn't good enough for you. I'm Donovan. I'm your husband."

"Okay, okay. I'm sorry, but my contractions are three minutes apart now. I have to get to the hospital."

"You're not going anywhere."

Donovan shut the door quietly. *Craig? He's the son-of-a-bitch who knocked me out?*

The man was obviously unhinged, and that put Beth in even greater danger. No matter how much Donovan wanted to charge in there and pummel Craig into the ground, he couldn't. If he came out of the kitchen, he'd be spotted instantly, and who knows what kind of weapons Craig had with him. Donovan had to be smart about this—careful, sneaky. He needed the element of surprise and a good place to hide until the opportune moment came. He knew exactly where to go.

He backed out of the garage and made his way to the side of the house. His cold and tired limbs struggled to move through the thick snow. At times, his legs sank into the snow up to his knees, and he had to dig himself out. A tingling sensation erupted in his feet as he walked. Soon, the sensation would be too great, paralyzing him from so much as lowering one of his feet to a solid surface. But he couldn't give in now. He continued to tread through the snow.

In the backyard, the tingling heightened to pricks like hundreds of electrified needles were poking his feet in a rolling, waving motion. And those pricks were crawling past his ankles to his shins. He squinted up at Ryan's bedroom window.

Crawling on his hands and knees, he worked his way up the massive snowdrift. The pricks beneath his skin reached his kneecaps, claiming the entire bottom-half of his legs. And now it was spreading. Heat washed through his hands like a flood. The first sting of his hands waking up exploded at the tips of his fingers. As a real blast would, the sensation blew outward and spread up his fingers all the way to his elbows. The pins and needles feeling consuming his limbs as his nerves regained their function set his teeth on edge.

He tucked his arms close to his chest, trying not to aggravate them and send the maddening numbness into a frenzy, and used his elbows to pull himself higher, dragging his useless legs behind him. But every slight movement activated grenades of tormented nerves. A tap against the side of his leg had sparks firing down to his toes.

Sweating from the exertion and the inner torture

attacking his every nerve ending, he slithered his way to the top. At the peak, he braced his tingling hands on the glass. When the window slid up the track without a problem, he said a silent prayer of thanks. Then he latched onto the windowpane. His grasp invited a fresh flow of pricks to rush up to his elbows.

Sitting on the outside of the windowsill, he grabbed his right leg and physically maneuvered it through the opening. Holding his leg, he set his foot carefully on the ground, to prevent anyone downstairs from hearing his footsteps and to avoid more pins and needles, but the little vibration from his boot touching the floor had him seething. He repeated the technique with his left leg. Once his feet were down on the inside, he slipped the rest of his body through the opening and sank onto his hands and knees.

Clenching his teeth, he shifted his legs, so they stretched out in front of him. With his arms draped over his lap, he sat perfectly still with his back against the wall and his head level to the opened window, where frigid air licked the back of his exposed neck. He stayed there, breathing, listening, and waiting for his nerves to settle.

After a while, the tingles dissipated. He tested out his hands by wiggling his fingers. Then he tapped the sides of his boots together, something that would've caused neural detonations, but this time, nothing happened. He rose to a standing position and took a cautious step. No pricks. No explosions. Relieved, he settled the window back into place.

Although the paresthesia had passed, he was still cold to the bone. The clothes he wore were wet from the snow he had been taking a nap on. Moving with soft steps, he went to the door, peeked out, and crept across the hall to the room he shared with Beth. He picked up his cell phone from the nightstand—no service—and shut himself into the closet where he lowered to the floor and untied his boots. The wool socks he pried off his feet were soaked. An assessment of his feet assured him he hadn't suffered any permanent damage; his toes were pink.

He stripped out of his clothes, leaving them in a pile in the corner, and put dry ones on—a black turtleneck, a navy-blue jacket, fleece-lined snow pants, and wool socks. Fortunately, he had another pair of boots, so he didn't have to get his feet wet again. He topped everything off with a knit cap and pair of gloves. Having on dry clothes felt great, but it would take longer for his body to warm. Already, his body shivered as his muscles attempted to generate heat on their own. He wouldn't be able to take on Craig when he could barely hold himself immobile, so he ventured out into the bedroom to get the blanket from the bed. Once he had it, he snuck back into the closet. With the blanket wrapped around his shoulders, he willed it to warm him fast enough so he could get to his family.

What *was* going on downstairs? He hadn't heard a shout since entering Ryan's room. Then again, that was a good thing. The three women trapped with that monster were smart; they wouldn't risk his anger and put themselves in further danger.

He had no idea how he'd overpower Craig or get the women out of there safely, but he would do whatever he had to. The first step would be drawing Craig away from them long enough to reach them. And Donovan had a plan for that, at least.

As soon as he warmed, he discarded the blanket. Out in the hall, he stepped gingerly on the ground, not wanting a single creak of a floorboard to give him away. He snuck to his mother's room. In her closet, he wormed his way through the clothes to the secret panel in the wall. It made a cracking sound as he shouldered it open. Afraid that noise could've traveled, he sprang into the tight space and nudged the panel back into place, casting himself into darkness.

Chapter Twenty-Four

In the living room, Beth watched Craig pace back and forth. Every time he came back around, she didn't know what to expect. Would he lash out? Would he come near her? She eyed him warily. She couldn't recognize the man prowling the room as the man who had been her fiancé. Back then, he had been a sleek businessman, not the usual type she'd go for. She liked athletic, adventurous men, but somehow Craig had wormed his way into her life.

At first, he had appeared confident, intellectual, and, yes, handsome. It wasn't until much later when she realized he had manipulated her, charmed her into believing he was something he wasn't. All he had really wanted from her was sex. He played the charade well, so well she thought he had genuinely cared for her. Except he never heated up a can of soup for her when she was sick, or bought her tampons, or did any of the things a man in a serious relationship would do out of love. All he had cared about was what was between her legs. He kept up his façade for a couple of years and had no problem what-so-ever in taking the relationship to the next level, probably to keep her where he could get to her anytime he wanted her.

After they were engaged, things fell apart systematically. He stopped playing his role, and she recognized him for what he was—an arrogant man who needed to be admired by all, pampered, petted, put up on a pedestal. A narcist. He didn't love her. No, he was in a lifelong love-affair with himself. And he needed women to boost his own vanity—in and out of bed. Unfortunately, his ego had trapped Beth. Unhappiness leaked into her life. A helplessness consumed her.

When she had caught him in bed with the blonde, bimbo psychic, the cloud lifted. Just like that. Yes, she had been enraged, but as soon as she had kicked them out of her home, chucked the ring at him, and slammed the door in their faces, sweet relief filled her. At that moment, she finally understood it wasn't her or anything she did or didn't do. It was Craig. And she recognized she hadn't actually loved him. How could she? The Craig she had met, who persuaded her to go out on date after date, hadn't been real.

She didn't so much as mourn the loss of him. What bothered her instead was the fact Craig had fooled her in the first place, that she had been blind to his deceit, his addiction. She spoke to a therapist for a year, fixing whatever damage her relationship with Craig had caused her mentally and to make sure no man could ever trick her like that again. As a self-defense instructor, she taught people how to be strong physically, but it was thanks to Craig that she learned mental strength was as important, not only to heal from a bad relationship but to recognize the signs of one and do everything in your power to escape it.

It was thanks to Donovan that she experienced the power of real love. Bone-deep, soul-consuming, universe-vast love.

Beth's gaze followed Craig's movements. Although he resembled a human, the man before her had transformed from a narcissist to a monster, one who she unwittingly unleashed.

A groan cried from above. Beth peered up at the ceiling. Was the roof going to cave in on them now, burying them beneath pounds and pounds of packed snow? The groan transformed into creaks that traveled from one end of the house to another. Then a thud sounded.

"What the hell is that?" Craig roared.

"It's probably sheets of snow breaking apart and sliding off the roof. It happens all the time," Meredith said.

Clomp, clomp, clomp.

Beth's heart hitched. That wasn't snow. That was footsteps.

"Someone's up there," Craig ground out.

"We have a raccoon in residence," Lily said.

"That's not a fucking raccoon." Craig cast his icy glare to Beth. "I know *who* that is." He spun around and stormed into the kitchen. The door to the garage opened. A moment later, Craig returned. He stared up at the ceiling with a maniacal smile tugging on his lips.

"Is that you, Donovan?" His insane expression settled on Beth. "If it is—" He removed the gun from behind his shirt and clasped it in his hand. Without another word, he pounded up the stairs. He didn't have to say more, though. Beth knew exactly what he intended to do; he couldn't take Donovan's place if Donovan was still alive.

The attic door's hinges squealed in protest as Craig yanked it open. The clatter of the ladder unfolding met Beth's ears. Then the pounding of boots climbing up them. After that, silence. Silence that clutched Beth's heart.

She peered at Meredith and Lily. They stared up at the ceiling, waiting for a sound that would indicate Donovan's fate. Her throat constricted. Craig was there for her, not them. It wasn't right that they suffer.

"I'm so sorry," she whispered.

The women peered at her.

"I brought Craig into your lives, and I'm so sorry." Words stopped coming from her mouth, but her thoughts continued the apology, *Donovan may die, we all may die because of me.*

"It's not your fault," Meredith said.

Beth turned her head away. She kept her voice low, soft. "Yes, it is. He's here because of me. You all are in danger because of me." She swallowed. When she had the courage to look at them again, tears blurred her vision. "I never would've thought he'd become this way. If anything, I expected him to be addicted to sex, but not this." Not a stalker. Not a killer. "I think something unhinged in him after the psychic broke up with him."

"You couldn't have known that, sweetie," Lily said. "There was clearly a chemical imbalance in his brain even while the two of you were together, and when left untreated, it progressed. If you had figured it out sooner and he had been caught, it would've been too late. He had, without a doubt, regretted cheating on you and changed things in here." She lifted her bound hands and pointed a finger to her temple.

"Mom's right," Meredith said. "He created his own fantasy, rewriting the past, and he believes in it. He has an illness, but that doesn't make him any less dangerous. More so, in fact. None of us know what he's capable of, what might make him snap."

That was exactly why she didn't want the two of them there. She didn't want him to hurt them—Donovan's last remaining family members. And she didn't want them to see whatever he may do to her, or the baby.

Bang.

Beth gasped.

"That was a gunshot," Meredith said.

Bang. Bang.

Horror gripped Beth. Those gunshots could mean one thing—Craig found Donovan.

Tears spilled down Beth's cheeks, and a pressure jabbed her uterus, causing her to clench her body. A pop, like a knuckle cracking, tapped against her eardrums, and a bursting sensation inside her preceded a gush of warm water between her legs. The fluid soaked through her pants and trickled down her legs.

Wide-eyed, she looked to Meredith. "My water broke."

Chapter Twenty-Five

Donovan stepped out of the hidden passageway into the attic. He scanned the dark surroundings. A pair of gleaming eyes in the corner caused him to jump. He dug out his cell phone from his pocket and activated the flashlight. In the small beam, he found a raccoon curled up on a cushion on a worn rocker. "Hey there, Rodney," he said. "Don't mind me."

Rodney lowered his head onto his paws.

Donovan stomped his feet on the attic's floorboards, while moving from one end to the other. Craig had to leave Beth's side, and the farthest place Donovan could draw Craig was the attic. He shoved aside a dresser, wanting to make as much racket as he could.

A shout reached him. "Is that you, Donovan?"

"Yeah, it's me, you son-of-a-bitch," he seethed. "Come and get me."

He hurried back to the secret doorway. With his hand on the tiny knob on the other side of the door, he glanced back at Rodney. "You might want to hide." And he ducked inside, shutting himself in. He didn't wait to make sure Craig was coming, though, as he snaked his way down the rickety steps to the panel in his mother's closet. He pushed it open.

Just outside the door, the attic's ladder hit the floor, and heavy boots marched up them.

Donovan squirmed out of the closet. At the door, he paused. Risking a peek around the doorframe, he saw Craig's boots disappear up the attic opening. Holding his breath, he slipped out into the hallway. Keeping to the wall, he took one step after the other. He wouldn't have much time before Craig realized he wasn't in the attic, but he couldn't hurry and tip the bastard off that he was below him on the second floor. Would he have enough time to get to Beth and his mother and grandma? He didn't know, but he had to try.

He kept glancing over his shoulder at the attic's opening, searching for any sign of Craig returning. With every step he took, he felt like running. He inched past Ryan's bedroom. A few more strides remained between him and the staircase. Gunshots made him freeze. They sounded close. Too close. He turned, and his breath fled from his lungs. Thankfully, Craig wasn't standing behind him with a gun.

It was now or never.

He rushed to the stairs. His feet touched the first step and then the second.

"Damn, raccoon."

Donovan whipped around. A shadow appeared at the attic's entrance. He peered down the stairs. He was so close to them and yet too far. Mouthing curses, he peered back at the attic. A boot descended onto the top rung of the ladder.

Shit.

Donovan hurried back down the hall. Craig's boots lowered onto the third rung, and Donovan dove into his mother's bedroom. He pressed his back to the wall on the other side of the door. Heart thundering inside his chest, he clenched his hands into fists and held his breath hostage. Would Craig check each room to be sure Donovan wasn't there? It was what Donovan would do. If Craig did, they'd come face to face. And Craig had a gun.

The attic's ladder rattled and slammed into place.

Heavy footsteps prowled down the hallway and punched the stairs.

Feeling like a failure, Donovan closed his eyes and leaned his head back against the wall. How would he get to them now? What other opportunity would he have? He needed a good head-start and a way to disarm Craig. If only. Needing a safe place to think and plot, he went back into the hidden passageway and dropped to his knees. Hoping. Praying.

Chapter Twenty-Six

Water slithered down Beth's calves to her ankles. More dropped off the sides of her chair. *No, no, no, you can't come yet.* Although labor could last for another couple of hours, the fact she had progressed this quickly wasn't a good sign. Her fear could have this baby arriving in a matter of moments. The thought of giving birth with Craig looking on sent chills down her spine. And who knew what he'd do once the baby was here. She imagined a tiny, wailing bundle in Craig's arms and his twisted laughter, having gotten what he came for.

Craig returned. His presence was menacing, sinister, instantly darkening the room and making it feel colder. "It was a raccoon, after all."

Beth barely stopped the sob of relief from coming out of her mouth.

"The rodent won't be bugging us again, though, because I killed it."

"You killed Rodney?" Lily's voice was small.

Craig sneered. "Maybe I'll go back up and get it. We can have fire-roasted raccoon for dinner." He faced Beth. "How does that sound?"

She couldn't help the visual that came to her of Craig skinning the poor animal and roasting it in the fireplace—the tuffs of fur, the smell of cooking meat, the blood coating his hands. She gagged. Acid rose up her throat, but she swallowed it down. Tied to the chair, she had nowhere to turn to if vomit did come out of her mouth, and she did not want to throw up all over herself. It was one thing to be drenched in amniotic fluid and another to be covered in amniotic fluid *and* rancid vomit.

"Beth's water broke," Meredith said, mercifully drawing Craig's attention to her while Beth fought to get her stomach muscles under control.

"So, my baby is coming soon, huh?" Craig took a step toward her.

"She needs to change into something dry," Meredith interjected. Her words cut off Craig's approach. "It's not good for her to stay in wet, cold clothes. I can go upstairs, get her something dry to wear, and help her put it on. She'll feel more comfortable."

Craig studied Beth. "She does look pale."

She didn't meet his eye, but inside she screamed. *I'm pale because I thought you had killed my husband. I'm pale because you make me sick.*

"Fine. I'll let you go." Craig untied Meredith. Holding her shoulders, he tugged her to her feet. The afghan tumbled off Meredith's lap, and the fire poker along with it. The bundle landed between their feet. Beth stared at it with wide eyes. If the afghan had unraveled and the fire poker had clattered onto the floor, they would've been caught red-handed.

Meredith swept the heap to the side with her boot, away from Craig.

Twisting her arm, he shoved her forward. "Be quick about it, or I'll come up there after you." He waved the gun, letting her know he'd be armed when he did.

Meredith's gaze connected with Beth's a fraction of a second before she scurried up the stairs. With her gone, Craig slunk up to Beth. She refused to look at him, though, so he grasped her chin with his fingers and yanked her head up. He bent down real low so his nose came within an inch of hers. "Looks like Donovan ran with his tail between his knees. He left you," he hissed. "Now I can slide right into place."

Beth clenched her jaw.

His fingers tightened on her. "Do you have something to say about that?" He jerked her chin. "Huh? Do you?"

"No," she growled between clenched teeth.

"Good." He moved his hand to her face and stroked her cheek. "My dear Beth. The two of us will have a better life together." He laid a hand on her belly. "The three of us will."

As if her baby wanted his hand off her, a contraction rolled through her uterus. Her fingernails bit into her palms. Now, the contractions were two minutes apart. Sixty seconds of pain every two minutes while being held hostage.

This was not the way she had wanted labor to go. She wanted Donovan at her side, comforting her. She wanted Donovan to be there the moment their baby took its first breath. Even if those things couldn't happen in a hospital and she had to have a home birth, she wanted Donovan there.

And she wanted Craig dead.

Yes, dead.

He had put a knife to her abdomen. No way did she want the bastard to live after that. The love she had for her unborn child was limitless. And, damn it, she was one fierce mama bear. If anyone had the nerve to cause her child harm, they'd regret it.

Craig let out an eerie laugh. He stared at her belly as the contraction moved through her core like a wave. "Look at that. Our baby knows who his daddy is. He's excited to see me." He stroked her belly. "It is a boy, right? Or is it a girl?" His stared at her, expecting a response.

"We…we didn't want to know."

"How could I forget that? We wanted the baby's gender to be a surprise. And are you ready to be surprised, Mommy?" How he said it made it sound as though he meant something entirely different, not just about the sex of the baby.

Her chest heaved. She didn't answer, but she didn't look away, either. What she really wanted to do was gouge out his eyes. And so much more.

Meredith rushed back into the living room. She paused a few feet away. In her arms she had clothes, a couple of towels, and a black, folded bed sheet. "Beth will need to be untied."

"Of course," Craig said. He set aside the gun to his right and got to work undoing the knots at her ankles.

Beth eyed the gun, which was on the side of Craig where Meredith stood. Her attention shifted to Meredith, who looked down at the gun, too, understanding the significance of this. Craig had made a mistake. A big one.

The rope fell away from Beth's legs.

Craig's hands came to the rope at her left wrist. She thought about kicking him in the chest at that instant, sending him onto his back, giving Meredith time to snatch up the gun and shoot him. But his right hand suddenly went down, out of sight, and came back up with the hunting knife. Beth's breath caught in her chest as he positioned the blunt edge of the blade against her belly and started to saw at the rope that stretched across her. Her mouth went dry. She couldn't kick him now. Not with the blade dangerously close to her stomach. Kicking him at the wrong moment could cause his arm to jerk at an odd angle, cutting her or piercing her with the tip of the blade.

Craig eyed her. The corner of his mouth quirked, as if he knew what she had been thinking and this was his warning.

The blade sliced through the fibers of the rope with a jerk. Before he put it away, he shifted closer, pinning her feet beneath his knees. With the knife tucked away, he picked the gun up again and hid that weapon from her, too.

The opportunity passed.

He finished untying her. Taking her arms, he pulled her to her feet.

"I can handle it from here," Meredith said and stepped up to Beth's elbow. "But can you untie my mom, too?"

"What for?"

"So, she can hold up this sheet."

"I've seen my wife naked before."

The fact he had seen her naked, had engaged in intercourse with her once upon a time, disgusted Beth. She cringed back from him when his lustful gaze settled on her.

"But this will be different," Meredith insisted. "Some women bleed. It's called the bloody show, and it isn't a pretty sight. Do you want to see that?" She lifted a brow.

Craig relented. "Fine, but the two of you need to stand back while I untie her."

Beth toddled to the far side of the room with Meredith supporting her. While Craig unknotted the ropes, Meredith leaned toward Beth's ear. "Donovan is in the house somewhere. I saw a pile of his wet clothes in the closet. He might be in the hidden passageway."

Hope fluttered through Beth. She wanted to ask, *what hidden passageway*? But it didn't matter. Donovan was okay.

Meredith squeezed Beth's hand. "He'll come for you."

"Us," Beth whispered back. *He'll come for us.*

Craig got to his feet. Smirking, he looped the length of rope around and around his hand. The slow, deliberate movement told Beth he did it on purpose, so she could think of all the ways he could use that rope. He tossed it onto the couch and replaced it with the gun, which he leveled at them. "Hurry up."

Meredith and Beth joined Lily on the rug. Lily took the sheet off the top of the pile in Meredith's arms and shook it out promptly. Stretching her arms as far as she could, she held the sheet in the air. On the other side of it, Beth clutched Meredith's hand. "Thank you," she mouthed.

Meredith gave her a quick hug. With her help, Beth slipped out of her boots, pants, and underwear. The cold touched her damp thighs. Her skin broke out in goosebumps. Meredith wiped the amniotic fluid clean from Beth's skin with one of the towels. She spread out that same towel on the floor for Beth to lay down on, and the other towel she draped over Beth's legs.

"What the hell is taking so long?" Craig demanded from the other side of the sheet.

Meredith put her hands on Beth's knees when she started to level herself up, afraid that Craig would come around the sheet and witness this intimate moment of which he shouldn't be a part. "I'm checking on Beth and the baby to see far she is."

Beth closed her eyes while Meredith examined her. *Please, God, don't let this baby come yet. Please.*

"You're ten centimeters."

Oh no.

"But I don't feel the head." Meredith gave her a reassuring pat on the foot. "That's a good thing. You still have time."

With a heave, she got Beth to a standing position. One foot at a time, Beth stepped into a fresh pair of lined snow pants.

"What's going on?" Craig asked.

Meredith shook her head, showing the first signs of annoyance. "We're not doing a disappearing act. She's almost dressed." She took the zipper on Beth's jacket and pulled it up, hiding her belly. That one act made Beth realize how much Meredith hated seeing Craig touching her daughter-in-law.

Tears bloomed in Beth's eyes.

Meredith noticed them and gathered Beth close. "Stay strong," she whispered.

"I'll try."

"Okay. Times up." Craig ripped the sheet from Lily's fingers. When he found Beth and Meredith embracing, he clamped a hand on Meredith's shoulder and wrenched her away. "That's enough of that."

Meredith stumbled but caught her footing and stood her ground. "I need to help her put her boots back on." She pushed past him. From the floor, she plucked up Beth's boots.

Beth perched on the edge of the chair. She didn't have to hear Meredith's thoughts to know she intended not to let Craig touch Beth again, and that increased the chances of Craig wanting to hurt her. Keeping him from Beth would anger him more. But also, Meredith wanted Beth to have her boots on in case things took a turn for the worse; in case Craig dragged her outside into the cold.

As soon as Meredith finished tying her boots, Craig yanked her up and shoved her onto the couch. "The next time you touch my wife, you'll be delivering our baby, is that understood?" He towered over Meredith, who nodded. "Good." He snatched up a coil of rope.

"Don't!" Beth pushed to her feet. "Don't tie them up. Please."

Craig was already getting physical with Meredith and brandishing blades before Beth's belly. She didn't want Craig to harm Meredith or Lily, and she definitely didn't want them to see Craig inflict any pain on her. She wanted to spare them at all costs.

"Take them upstairs, and then we can be alone."

"Beth, no," Meredith exclaimed and gaped at her in horror, unbelieving of what she was hearing.

"You came for me and the baby," she told Craig, "so you can leave them out of it."

"Beth, don't do this," Meredith begged.

"Beth." That came from Lily.

But Beth didn't dare look at either of them or else she'd fall apart. And she couldn't afford to do that. Not now.

Craig smiled. "I knew you'd come around to me, but I'm still going to tie them up." He forced the three of them to sit on the couch where he could see them as he bound Meredith's and Lily's wrists together. Then he directed Beth into the chair where he used the severed rope to tie her wrists individually to the chair's arms. When he bent down to do the same to her ankles, she crossed her feet and hid them under the chair. Craig's hands latched onto her legs with a bruising grip. He pulled her feet back out, forcefully uncrossed her ankles, and pressed the bottoms of her boots to the floor.

"You can't tie up my feet," she blurted out.

He glared. "I can't?"

She swallowed. "I'm in labor. My legs shouldn't be tied together."

Craig took a moment to consider that. "Okay, but *their feet* will be tied." His smile was wolfish. "Say goodbye to his family." He extracted the gun and pointed it at Meredith and Lily.

Beth's heart sank into her uterus, which summoned another contraction.

"Get up," Craig ordered. The two women, sticking as close to each other as they could, got off the couch. With Craig pointing the gun at their backs, they had no other choice but to leave Beth alone in the living room, where she'd be alone with a monster.

Beth listened to their footsteps on the staircase. Once she felt it was safe, she scooted her bottom to the edge of the chair and extended her right leg, reaching for the afghan on the floor. The toe of her boot touched a colorful corner. She pulled on it, hoping it was enough to bring the entire afghan and the fire poker it hid within reach. The threads stretched. Biting her bottom lip, she tried harder, but the tip of her boot slipped off. The corner sling-shot from her, folding over backward. Fighting with her restraints, she made another attempt. She caught the folded corner with the toe of her boot. Sliding her foot along the floor, she managed to get the corner to lay out flat.

Taking a breath, she reached again. Half her boot stepped on the corner. She lifted as much as she could with her arms to put more weight on her foot. Her biceps quivered, but she didn't lower herself down, didn't give her muscles relief.

She needed that fire poker to be closer, so the next time Craig untied her and she got onto the floor, she could grab it and impale him with it.

The afghan crawled along the floor. She repositioned her foot, now stepping the entire sole of her boot onto the afghan. Heart racing, she dragged it a few inches; the fire poker weighed it down, making it harder to move. The entire afghan spread out longer the more she drew her intended weapon closer.

Footsteps tramped onto the stairs.

Gasping, she straightened back up in her chair. She eyed the afghan. Would he notice it had moved?

Craig strode into the living room. He smiled as he came up to her, and she felt like a helpless, injured animal being stalked by a large predator. "I'm glad we can be alone." He knelt in front of her, with his left knee mere inches from coming in contact with the afghan. "This is as it should be, as it always should've been." He took her hands. "Don't you agree?"

No, she did not fucking agree!

But she nodded to appease him.

"You're mine now. Forever and always, isn't that what you vowed to me?"

She didn't. Nor would she ever. But to Donovan she had. On their wedding day, she had revealed parts to him she hadn't had the courage to voice before. *You've made me stronger than I could ever imagine. With you by my side, I can handle anything. Your love is like my armor. I wear it proudly. And I vow to return that strength to you. To be your warrior. To fight for us and our love every day of my life. To be your forever and always.*

In this moment, she wore his love like armor, which not only shielded her but their unborn child. She would do whatever it took to be strong for him, for their baby. She would do whatever it took to fight for their small family, their life, their forever.

Hearing Craig say things she and Donovan had told each other on the best day of their lives infuriated her. Those memories weren't for him. Those promises weren't his. And the words she had spoken were for Donovan only.

A contraction battered her insides for another sixty seconds. She seethed from the pain and from rage. Every contraction brought the baby closer and closer to the birth canal. Soon, she'd have to push, and she didn't want Craig to be the first man to hold her newborn. She didn't want him to touch her baby at all.

The contraction faded. Sweat bloomed along her brow. She panted, "My labor is progressing too fast, because I'm stressed and scared."

Craig tilted his head. "You're scared of me?"

"Yes."

He stroked her cheek. "You don't have to be scared of me."

Wanting to cringe, but holding her spine stiff, she said, "You've pointed a gun at me and held a knife to my stomach."

A sinister smile flashed on his face. "Well…if you do something stupid, you do have something to fear. I want *you*, Beth. We can't have a baby without you, but we can always create another. We don't need this one."

The meaning behind his words punched her in the gut. She couldn't stop the wrath his statement caused from bubbling up her neck.

Every warning bell inside her that told her to tread carefully went silent as she imploded. "You're not going to touch my baby!"

Fury morphed Craig's face into hard, sharp lines. His eyes bulged, and he shot to his feet. "Your baby?" He reached behind her and sent objects on the mantel flying. Glass and ceramic shattered on the floor and against the wall.

"That's *my* baby!" He stood over her. His body vibrated. "Our baby. *I'm* the father." He dropped onto his knees and jabbed the gun's muzzle into the side of her stomach. "And I can do whatever I want to it," he growled.

Tears seared Beth's eyes. She desperately wanted to shield her baby, but she couldn't.

Craig leaned forward. His voice lowered. "Whose baby is this?"

"Yours." Beth's voice was so small, so weak.

"What's my name?"

"Donovan."

"And who am I to you?"

Her answer came out on a wisp of a breath. "Husband."

Chapter Twenty-Seven

Donovan crept through the attic, hoping to find something he could use for a weapon, but all he found were boxes of school mementos from when he and Ryan were little, holiday decorations, and old clothes. He was opening a box marked "camping" when a skittering noise sounded behind him. He found the raccoon poking its head out from behind the trunk. The critter scurried out into the open and climbed onto the rocker. It lifted a tiny paw into the air and made a little chattering sound as if to say, "Hey, man, I'm okay."

"So, he didn't get you after all? Good boy."

The raccoon raised its chin.

"It's not over yet," Donovan told Rodney. "You wouldn't happen to know where to find a weapon up here, would you?"

Rodney picked up the molding apple core and held it out to Donovan.

Donovan sighed. "That's what I thought." He shook his head. "You keep it."

Rodney sniffed the apple core and must've decided he didn't even want it because he let it fall to the ground. Donovan stifled a chuckle and turned back to the box of camping supplies.

Inside it he discovered titanium cups, three-piece ring utensil sets, a pot scrubber, a can opener, a grill rack, and, at the very bottom, a cast iron skillet. He pulled the pan out and hefted it in his hand. It was about twelve inches and weighed a good seven pounds. If he could sneak up behind Craig and wail this into the back of his head, he could do a lot more damage than merely knocking the man unconscious. He wouldn't feel bad if he did.

Carrying the iron skillet, he went back to the secret passageway. On the other side of the wall panel, he listened for any movement, for any sign Craig could be close. He couldn't hear a thing, so he risked pushing the panel open. The clothes swayed on their hangers. He slipped through them and stepped out into the open. What he saw made him freeze—his mom and grandma sitting side by side on the bed.

Meredith gasped. "Donovan, oh thank God."

Donovan got to them in two strides. "Are you okay? Is Beth okay?" He started to untie the ropes restraining Lily.

"We're fine," Meredith said. "But Beth's water broke. She's ten centimeters."

Hearing that made it clear Donovan had to make his move now. He tugged the ropes from his grandma's hands and feet and then shifted to his mom.

"Donovan, Beth had him bring us up here." Meredith looked him straight in the eye. "I think she wanted to spare us."

He clenched his jaw. Beth would do that, especially if she thought there was no hope of her getting out safely. Even now, even while in labor, she thought of everyone else's safety and well-being ahead of hers. But more than anything, she wouldn't let him hurt their baby. She'd sacrifice herself instead.

A crash down below made them jump.

"That's *my* baby!"

Donovan shoved to his feet. Craig's words shot a cold blade of fear through his heart.

"Our baby. *I'm* the father." The shouts continued.

His right hand tightened around the skillet's handle, whitening his knuckles. His other hand balled into a fist. The urge to rush down the stairs, tackle Craig to the floor, and pummel his head with the skillet flashed through him. It was almost too strong to ignore. His body revved to go.

But he didn't give in. Not yet.

Pulse hammering, he knelt back down to finish freeing his mom.

"Donovan, that man is sick," Meredith whispered. "And I don't just mean he belongs in a psychiatric hospital. He killed the neighbors and rode out the blizzard with their dead bodies. He's volatile."

"He held a knife to Beth's stomach," Lily added.

Donovan's head whipped around. "What?"

Lily nodded. "He forced her to kiss him at knife-point. Not a closed-mouth kiss, either." Her body shivered as tears coursed down her wrinkled cheeks. "You have to save her."

"I will." And that was an oath he swore with every fiber of his being.

The ropes loosened around Meredith's feet, and she kicked out of them. Donovan got to his feet with the skillet in his hand, but he no longer felt confident in its seven pounds or his swing. "If I'm going to get Beth, I'll need your help."

Meredith clutched his hand. "We'll do anything."

He glanced at the door. Downstairs, all was quiet. He didn't know if that was a good thing or a bad thing, but it didn't matter. The silence could be sinister or a reprieve. Either way, Beth was still in Craig's grasp and so was their baby.

"Do either of you know where I can find a weapon?"

Meredith shook her head helplessly.

"Yep," Grandma Lily said. "I've got a 9mm under the pillow where Grandpa used to sleep."

Donovan blinked at his grandma.

Meredith gaped at her mom.

"What? We're two old women living alone. Of course, I've got a gun."

Donovan kissed her on the cheek, thankful for his grandma's spunkiness. "I'm going to get the gun, and the two of you are going into the secret passageway. Give me a minute and then stomp around. We need to draw Craig into the attic. But make sure you're hidden before he gets up there. I'm going to get Beth out. Stay in the passageway until I come back for you."

They nodded wordlessly.

By the closet, he held the clothes to the side while Grandma ducked inside. His mom paused at the closet door and threw her arms around his shoulders. "Please be careful."

He rubbed her back. The words she wanted to hear—I will—got stuck in the back of his throat. No matter how careful he was, with Craig, there was no guarantee he wouldn't get hurt.

Meredith sighed, as if knowing his thoughts. She squeezed him a second longer before releasing him and following Grandma into the passageway.

"Remember," he whispered, "give me a minute, and don't let him find you."

His mom took the tiny knob on the inside of the panel. "You don't worry about us. Just get Beth." And she pulled the panel shut.

Donovan crept to the door. A peek toward the end of the hallway showed it to be empty. With light footsteps, he shot across the way into Grandma's room. In the middle of the room stood a bed decked out with a dust ruffle, a flower print comforter, and half a dozen lacey throw pillows. He didn't remember which side his granddad used to claim for his slumber, so Donovan went to the closest side to the door. Except, nothing was there.

Damn it.

He made his way around to the other side of the bed. A floorboard beneath his right foot let out a high-pitched scream. He froze and held his breath. Grimacing, he placed his left foot well away from the squeaky floorboard, but when he lifted his other foot off it, the wood let out a groan. Afraid Craig had heard it, he hurried on tiptoe to the head of the bed. He slid his hand underneath the stack of pillows, but he didn't feel anything,

It has to be here.

He moved his hand from side to side over the smooth bed sheet.

Where is it?

Reaching deeper beneath the pillow, his pulse escalated. The gun was his one form of protection. Considering Craig had one, too, he needed to fight bullet for bullet. He couldn't bring a skillet to a gun fight, unless he could use it to deflect a speeding bullet, which was highly unlikely. Then his fingers brushed cold metal. He pulled it out and held it as though it was a lost treasure. With a click, he checked the magazine; it was full. Apparently, his luck was improving.

A bang reverberated through the house. Seconds later, a series of clomping shook the ceiling above his head. It sounded as though his mom and grandma were jumping up and down in place. Then there was a crash. He cocked a brow. *Did they throw something?*

"You've got to be kidding me," Craig shouted.

Donovan raced to take cover behind the bedroom door.

Boots punched the stairs.

"You wanna play a game, Goldwyn?" Craig roared.

From his hiding place, Donovan caught a glimpse of Craig through the crack between the door and jamb when he ran to the end of the hall. The attic door creaked as Craig pulled the cord, and the ladder clattered as it tumbled to the floor.

"Let's play," Craig mumbled while clambering up the ladder.

Donovan slithered out from behind the door. He risked a glance to see the bottom half of Craig's legs; the top of his body was lost in the mouth of the attic's opening. Another step up and even more of him disappeared. Donovan crept into the hall, sticking close to the wall so Craig wouldn't be able to look down through the opening and see him. He moved backward, eyeing Craig's boots and holding his breath. Craig lifted his right boot into the attic. The moment his left boot joined it, Donovan spun around.

Craig's voice called out, "Where are you, you son-of-a-bitch?" Something broke when Craig sent it sailing across the attic.

Trying not to make a lot of noise, Donovan hurried down the stairs. He estimated he had a few minutes to free Beth and get her the hell out of there. To do that, he'd need to get the keys to the truck. The only way they'd get far from Craig fast enough was if they had wheels. And that was how he'd be able to get Beth to the hospital.

He jumped off the second-to-last step and raced around the corner to the living room. Beth sat in the chair by the fireplace, with rope looped into fat knots around her wrists. She was pulling an afghan closer to her with her feet. When he ran into the living room, she froze. Then recognition dawned in her eyes, and she gasped.

"Donovan?"

He shot across the room and dropped to his knees in front of Beth. "It's okay," he whispered. "I'm here."

Tears streamed down Beth's cheeks.

"Don't cry." He set the gun at her feet before dashing her tears away with his thumbs. "Do you have the keys to the truck?"

She nodded eagerly. "Under the couch. I kicked them there."

He bent down to peer under the couch. Fortunately, he didn't have to look hard because the keys were right in front of his nose. He snatched them up. "I'm getting you out of here."

"Where's Meredith and Lily?"

"Safe. Don't worry." He began untying the knot at her right wrist. His fingers trembled. Seeing her tied up had made his heart plummet to his stomach. At the same time, it sent his blood roaring like lava through his veins. That bastard tied up his pregnant wife...his pregnant wife who was in labor.

Beth crunched forward. A whimper escaped her lips. "The baby is coming," she huffed.

Donovan's heart pounded even faster at those words. The rope uncurled from Beth's wrist and fell like a dead snake to the floor. He shifted to the other bundle of knots. The sooner he got these ropes off her, the better. Their time was running out. Already, he couldn't hear Craig up in the attic, taking out his rage on the boxes and furniture up there, trashing the place. He hoped that didn't mean he'd found the hidden door, which Craig could've accidentally discovered by throwing something heavy at the right part of the right wall.

The final rope came undone.

"Let's go." He grabbed the gun with one hand, took Beth's hand with the other, and got to a partial stand.

A whistle pierced the air.

They turned at the same time.

Craig stood a few paces away. His eyes glittered with madness, and his hand held a gun at chest-level. Donovan froze. Before he could form a thought, Craig fired the gun. A force plowed into Donovan, launching him backward. A searing sensation ripped through him, and blackness descended.

Chapter Twenty-Eight

The gunshot echoed in Beth's ears. When Donovan flew back onto the couch, she screamed. He lay sprawled on his back, unmoving, with his eyes closed. She shoved to her feet, wanting to go to him, to make sure he was still alive. She couldn't even tell if he was breathing or not. A bullet had burned a hole through the fabric of Donovan's jacket, near his left shoulder. The jacket was so thick and the turtleneck he wore underneath it so dark she couldn't see any blood. But there had to be blood. Unlike back on Oahu, Donovan wasn't wearing a bullet proof vest. That bullet had hit him. Somewhere. And she prayed to God the bullet hadn't hit anything vital. She wanted to check him herself, search for the wound with her own hands, but Craig was at her side before she could reach him.

He jabbed the gun's muzzle into her belly. "Don't you dare touch him," he growled in her ear. "I think it's time we left." He yanked Beth to him and dragged her away from Donovan. She tripped over the afghan she had been hauling closer to her chair. The fire poker tumbled out of the afghan with a thud. The moment that gun had gone off, she had forgotten all about the fire poker, her one weapon. And the gun Donovan had was in his limp hand. She had no way to defend herself or her baby.

She did all she could. "Donovan! Donovan, wake

up."

"Shut up!" Craig shook her by her arm.

"Donovan, I need you. Wake up!"

"Shut the fuck up." Craig tugged her along. At the kitchen's island, he picked up the truck's spare keys. Then he shoved open the garage door and pushed Beth outside.

Frozen air circled around Beth as if it were a boa constrictor. Her breath came out in white clouds. The cold cut straight through her layers. Even her eyes were cold. "Where are we going?" Beth asked.

"Where do you think?" He wrestled her around the truck to the passenger's side. "I'm taking you to the hospital to have my baby." He wrenched open the door. "Get in."

With the gun pressed to her back, she had no other choice but to get in the truck. Holding her belly, she climbed into the seat. While Craig went around to the other side, she popped open the glove compartment, but only found an instruction manual for the truck. She was hoping for emergency supplies—a road flare, a wrench, a screwdriver. Heck, she'd settle for an ice scraper for the windshield. She closed it before Craig opened the driver's door. He got in and inserted the key into the ignition.

Beth held her breath, hoping the engine wouldn't turn, but it did. And she couldn't help but feel her fate was sealed.

Craig backed the truck out of the garage. On the driveway, the tires spun on the ice, causing the truck to veer sharply from side to side. Beth grabbed the handle on the door as Craig fought with the steering wheel. The truck slid this way and that way on the slippery, frozen driveway. Curses flew from Craig's mouth. He managed to straighten the wheels, but when the truck reached the snow piled at the end of the driveway, it lurched to a stop. The engine revved as Craig pushed harder and harder on the gas pedal.

After a few halting attempts, the back tires finally made it over the mound. Craig drove the gas pedal to the floor, and the truck rocked violently, tossing Beth back and forth. The front tires climbed over the clumps of ice, and the truck bounced onto the road.

Craig shoved the stick shift into drive. "When we get to the hospital, you're going to tell everyone I am your husband, that I am the baby's father. And when the name Donovan Goldwyn is put on the baby's birth certificate, it will be referring to me. Do you got it?"

She nodded.

Craig maneuvered the truck down a snowy road. Although a plow had cleared most of the snow, a lot of it still covered the asphalt. White dust flew into the air from behind the tires, obscuring the view from out the passenger's window. Beth could barely make out the neighbor's house across the street as they passed. It signified the growing distance between her and Donovan. She couldn't let him take her farther away, couldn't let him win.

Through the windshield, she eyed a snow drift piled in front of a tree, and that drift was her way out. When the truck got closer, she grabbed the steering wheel and jerked it to the right. Craig attempted to force it back, but she held on tight, using all her strength.

They zeroed in on the drift. A moment before the impact, Beth released the wheel and braced with her hands on the dash. She'd rather risk broken wrists than a blunt force trauma to her stomach. The truck hit the drift, and the hood sank into the snow. Her neck snapped forward. Beside her, Craig's upper body slammed into the steering wheel. The gun fell from his hand and bounced onto the seat between them. Beth snatched it up and jabbed the muzzle into Craig's temple. Her index finger rested on the trigger.

"Don't move," she growled. "Let me see your fucking hands."

He raised his hands slowly to either side of his head. "Don't shoot," he whimpered.

That voice, that fear, those words…they did nothing to her. Absolutely nothing.

"You threatened my baby, you piece of shit." Her finger flinched on the trigger, almost squeezing it. A part of her, a huge part of her, the fierce mama bear part of her, wanted to pull that trigger, but a sliver of her conscience didn't want another person's blood on her hands, especially if she'd be holding her newborn baby with those same bloody hands. She didn't want to taint her baby's precious, new, innocent life.

Before she could do anything murderous, she bashed the butt of the gun into Craig's temple. Then she compressed a pressure point in his neck. When he became lax and collapsed into the door, she kept the gun poised, not ready to believe that her menace, the monster who threatened her unborn baby's life, was really knocked out. She didn't want to chance it. After counting to ten, she inched the gun down.

A contraction ravaged her core, reminding her of her dire need to get to safety, to warmth, to Donovan, who could be bleeding out or dead.

Dear God, please don't let him be dead.

With that prayer, she reached for the handle on the passenger's door. She opened it a few inches before the door hit a wall of snow that blocked her escape. Her way out would be through the door Craig's unconscious body leaned against. She reached across him and grabbed hold of the door handle. The moment she pulled on it, the weight of Craig's body shoved the door open, and he toppled out into the snow.

She scrutinized him. He appeared to be passed out cold. She shifted her body sideways, brought her legs onto the seat, and scooted across to the driver's side. Turning her bulk around, her belly bumped against the steering wheel, causing the horn to beep. She laid her hand on her navel and took a peek at Craig.

"Oops," she said.

Luckily, the horn didn't rouse Craig, but he wouldn't be unconscious that much longer. Her time was dwindling. More importantly, her baby's time was running low. Each contraction made her feel as though her abdomen and womb were going to crack open like an egg. Just shatter into a million pieces.

Not wanting to leave the gun behind, she put it on safety and slipped it into her pants pocket. Then she slid out of the truck. Her boots sank into the snow. With careful footing, she moved around Craig and stepped over the clumps of snow along the side of the road. Thankfully, with the road clear, she didn't have to struggle through each step, but the road was slick with snow-crusted ice, making walking precarious.

She took a few steps and then doubled over when a contraction ravaged her insides. A searing pain bloomed between her legs. "Not yet, baby. Not yet," she panted between her teeth, with her hands cupping her pumpkin-sized belly. "We have to get back to Daddy…" She stared at Meredith's house, a couple of houses away. A cinch for anyone if it weren't freezing with post-blizzard temperatures or they weren't in heavy labor.

"…back to Donovan," she murmured and took one step. And then another and another. She counted ten steps before another wave hit her, but she clenched her teeth. Breathing sharply, she continued to walk. She wouldn't stop again, not until she saw Donovan…saw he was still alive.

The cold swooped around her, seeped through the many layers of fabric meant to keep her warm. Her teeth chattered uncontrollably. She clenched her hands into fists and shoved them into the pockets of her jacket. It didn't make a difference.

Not much farther, not much farther, she repeated to herself. *Not much farther, not much farther.* The mantra helped her to push through.

A contraction gripped her, but she gripped her fists tighter and dragged her feet onward. At the foot of the driveway, she let out a frosty breath. "Almost there," she panted. Trekking up the driveway was tougher with the slight incline and the icy surface. Her left boot slipped on the slickness. She gasped and held her entire body still. Falling was the last thing she needed to do. Using smaller footsteps, she picked her way up the driveway. Inside the garage, she paused where the truck had sat. Her legs wanted to give out. Breathing hurt. Her body shook. She was too close to give up now, so she forced her feet to move, but she was exhausted. When she reached the door, she collapsed into it. Her hands groped for the knob. The metal bit her skin. Her hands shook as she twisted it.

The door opened.

Sounds came to her through the opening.

"Here are the scissors." It was Lily.

"Hold still." That order came from Meredith.

"Beth is out there." And that pained hiss belonged to Donovan.

"You were shot Donovan."

Beth's mouth was dry from the cold weather. Her tongue stuck to the roof of her mouth, so she couldn't speak. Heaving her bulk up the step into the house, relief hit her along with another contraction. Donovan was alive, and she was home. She pulled the door shut behind her, blocking the cold from stalking her inside.

"Do you think that's him? Do you think he's back?" Lily asked.

"Ssh."

Beth made her way to the living room. Once she passed the wall, she saw the women bent over Donovan, tending to his wound. She put a hand on a stand to keep her balance.

"You're…alive," she breathed.

Meredith and Lily whirled around.

Donovan's shirt and sweater were cut down the middle of his chest. Blood coursed from a hole in his shoulder. "Beth!" He made to get up, but Meredith and Lily prevented him from moving.

Beth tugged the gun out of her pants pocket and set it on the stand. "Is he…okay?" Breathing hard, she held her belly. Between her legs, a fire burned as her skin stretched. An immense pressure formed. She shifted her feet farther apart, as if something was there, pushing, pulling, tearing.

"The bullet passed straight through," Meredith told her. "How are you doing?"

Beth bent forward. "I…I feel something down there. I think it's the baby's head."

"That's not possible."

Beth winced. "I need to push."

"No, Beth, don't push. Mom, grab one of the couch cushions and put it on the floor in front of the fireplace and cover the area with a blanket. Beth, can you move?"

She straightened her back and took a step, but the pressure was too great. "I can't."

"Mom, help Beth over to the fireplace. I have to cauterize Donovan's gunshot wound or he'll keep on bleeding."

Lily took Beth's arm and led her, tiny step by tiny step, toward the fireplace. Using the couch's arm rest, Beth eased down to her knees onto the couch cushion and then shifted until she was sitting on it, with her legs bent in front of her and her upper back against the couch. Beside the fireplace, it was warm, reassuring. Until Meredith removed the fire poker from the flames and used it to cauterize Donovan's wound. His throaty shout of pain had Beth flinching from eyelids to toes. His yells transformed to seething.

"Donovan, you okay?" she said.

"Fine." His voice was deep.

He pushed himself off the couch as Meredith set the fire poker aside. "How'd you get away?" he asked Beth.

"I'll tell ya later," she said, breathlessly.

"Donovan, get behind Beth, let her lean against

you." Meredith draped the afghan over her. "I'm going to need you to lift up, Beth, so I can remove your pants."

Donovan did as Meredith instructed and put his right arm around her. Beth mustered the dregs of her strength to lift up her rear end. Without the warmth and protection of her pants, she couldn't stop from shivering. Donovan's body heat penetrated her clothes and comforted her.

"Okay, Beth, I'm going to take a look." She pulled the afghan up to Beth's knees and ducked down. A second later, her head popped back up. "I see a head of dark hair." She peered back down with wide eyes, in shock, and not prepared. "Mom, get a bunch of towels and my medical kit. I prepped it with baby stuff."

"On it." Lily shuffled away in her slippers.

Meredith laid her hands on Beth's knees. "Okay, sweetie. When I tell you to push, bear down as hard as you can. If I tell you to stop, stop immediately. You can do this. We have to get this baby out. Donovan, hold her."

"I can do that."

Beth put her hands over his, squeezing them for strength and stability, and he kissed her on the top of her head. Having him there with her was exactly how she wanted it, but she had imagined herself at the hospital for this part.

Meredith checked again. "We don't know if the baby is low on oxygen or what's going on, so we need to deliver this baby now."

"No, you're not."

Beth's pounding heart palpitated in her chest. She looked toward the kitchen, and Craig came out in the open, brandishing a knife.

"I'll take over from here. Sorry, Beth, but you're going to lose your mother-in-law, your husband, your baby, and then your own life." He walked closer, and his voice rose to a shout. "We could've lived happily together." Then he spoke in a whisper. "But. You. Ruined. Everything." He waved his knife in the air. "Now I have no choice but to kill you, too." He took another step.

Beth held her breath. Meredith couldn't hold him off, and neither Beth nor Donovan were in fighting shape. This was the end. For all of them.

A loud whistle cut through the air.

Craig spun around.

A gunshot exploded.

Craig stumbled backward.

A second gunshot.

And Craig slammed into the ground. The back of his head bashed into the floor. He didn't move. His chest didn't rise or fall. A puddle of blood formed around him, stretching out from beneath him.

Lily stepped forward with a gun in her hands, the one Beth had left on the stand. "That's what you get for messing with my family," she spat.

Beth's eyes widened.

"Holy shit, Grandma," Donovan said.

Lily faced them. "What? I didn't forget the supplies." She showed them her stash of towels and a medical kit tucked under her arm.

"Bring that over here, Mom," Meredith said. "And you're on psycho duty. Make sure he doesn't come back to life. They always do in the movies."

Lily pointed the gun at Craig. "I'd be happy to."

Meredith situated the towels around Beth. "Okay, sweetie. Push!"

Beth bore down and pushed with all her might. She felt as though her blood vessels would break from straining too much. Her face warmed. A pressure built in her temples. She pushed and pushed, but for all she knew, it wasn't doing a thing.

"Relax, Beth. Breathe."

She dropped back against Donovan, forgetting about his wound, and panted. He stroked her hair. "You've got this, baby. You're doing great."

All she could do was nod.

"It's your turn again, Beth. Push."

Beth incorporated all her abdominal muscles into the effort.

"Push, push, push, push," Meredith chanted.

She pushed so hard that a low growl tore through her vocal cords.

"Breathe."

She inhaled and exhaled rapidly. Sweat dotted her forehead and dampened her hair around her face. Could a woman pass out from pushing too hard? She was sure it had happened before, and she didn't want it to happen to her, but there was no time to catch her breath and calm her heart rate.

"Okay, Beth, give it all you've got."

And she did, depleting her energy stores. Her leg muscles shook. Her flesh stretched. An immense pain ripped her flesh.

"I've got two shoulders."

Beth panted.

"Come on, sweetie. One more push. One more."

Even though she didn't think she had it in her, Beth

pushed. Relief flooded through her when the baby came out, into Meredith's waiting hands. Beth leaned against Donovan. Even so, she strained to see over her knees at what was happening. Meredith worked quickly and carefully to take care of the baby. She suctioned out the mucous from the baby's mouth and nose. A cry pierced the air that relieved Beth and filled her with the strongest sense of love. Meredith unwound a length of yarn and picked up the scissors. Then she bundled the baby in two towels and lifted the baby over Beth's knees.

"Beth, Donovan, you have a baby boy."

Beth gasped when she had her little boy in her arms, and the moment he was where he belonged, he stopped crying. His forehead, nose, and cheeks had been wiped clean. His eyes were so incredibly dark, and he had the cutest porcelain-baby doll lips and round cheeks. Her heart swelled to bursting. His sweet face, his tiny hands. Love couldn't even begin to explain it.

Donovan's arms came around the two of them. His hand cradled the baby's head, and he stroked the baby's soft, damp hair with his thumb.

Beth gazed over her shoulder. "We have our Ryan," she whispered.

He pressed his lips to her temple.

When Beth gazed at Meredith, she saw her wiping tears from her eyes. Neither of them had told Meredith about their choice for a boy's name, because they had wanted to surprise her when the time came. And for all they knew, it could've been years before they had a boy.

Beth bent down and kissed Ryan's forehead. His eyes were already closed—content and happy. He looked like Donovan but with dark eyes—her eyes.

"Happy Birthday, Ryan," she whispered.

While the two of them admired their baby, Beth felt the undeniable urge to push again. She knew all about afterbirth, though, so she put it out of her mind. Until a pain had her wincing and catching her breath.

"Beth, what is it?" Donovan asked.

Her eyes widened. "Call our doctor. Ask him if we're having twins."

"What?"

While putting away her supplies, Meredith's neck snapped up. "What?"

Lily lowered the gun. "What?"

Beth started to pant.

Meredith scrambled back onto her hands and knees and peered beneath the blanket covering Beth. "She's right. You're having twins!"

"WHAT?" Donovan repeated.

"Mom, you're off gun duty. Come take baby Ryan."

Lily set the gun on the coffee table and hurried over to take Ryan from Beth's arms. Meredith stroked Beth's legs. "Okay. Same thing as before, Beth. You can do this. Ready?"

Beth nodded.

"Push."

Beth scrunched down and pushed.

"Oh, the baby is almost out. Keep pushing."

Beth took a deep breath and, gritting her teeth, sent her mustered strength to her abdomen and womb. Her body gave way to a tiny form, almost like exhaling. A second later, a wail touched her eardrums.

"Your little girl wanted to make things easy on

you," Meredith said.

Beth blinked. "A girl?" She settled her head on Donovan's shoulder and took his hand. "We have a girl, too?"

Meredith lifted the towel-wrapped baby. "You have a boy *and* a girl." Beaming, she put the new baby in Beth's arms. Then she got to her feet and transferred Ryan from Lily's arms to her own. Kneeling on the ground, she settled Ryan's head in the crook of Beth's other arm, so she held both babies.

Beth stared at them in wonder. Twins. How could she carry them for eight months and not know there were two in her belly, not one?

"Hi, Reagan," she said to the bundle on her right. "Happy Birthday." The bluest of blue eyes stared back at her, as calm as her brother.

"Next time, don't tell your doctor to keep *everything* a secret," Meredith said and swiped the back of her hand across her forehead.

Beth and Donovan laughed. Lesson learned. But at least this secret was a wonderful one.

Heavy footsteps pounded the kitchen tile. In the next second, uniformed men flooded inside the living room. They took one look at Craig's dead body and reacted immediately.

"Police!"

"Police!"

"Everybody, freeze!"

Beth stared at five police officers, pointing their weapons from one of them to the next. Meredith and Lily lifted their hands in the air. Beth couldn't. Not with the babies in her arms.

And Donovan didn't, either.

"Don't you dare point your guns at my wife or my newborn babies," Donovan snapped.

"Besides, you guys are late," Lily told them. "The bad guy is dead."

From the line of police officers, a uniformed man stepped forward after putting his gun back into its holster. "Lower your weapons."

The other four officers put their weapons away.

"We got a phone call from a Detective Thorn from the Orlando Police Department. He told us about the danger you guys were in. That a man named Craig Mitchell could be here, threatening your lives."

"That's him right there." Lily pointed. "I shot him."

Donovan groaned. "Grandma."

She planted her hands on her hips. "Well, I did. He shot my grandson, kidnapped my grand-daughter-in-law, and wanted to kill us."

The officers exchanged looks with raised brows. The man who had addressed them nodded. "An ambulance is right behind us." He compressed the button on his shoulder mike. "We have a gunshot victim and a woman who gave birth to twins. What's the ETA on the bus?"

After a moment, a woman's voice came through. "The bus is pulling up now."

When the ambulance came, medics loaded on Beth, Donovan, and the twins. Meredith and Lily rode to the hospital in the back of a cop car, much to Lily's delight.

On the stretcher, holding her bundled up twins, with a thermal blanket covering her, Beth gazed at Donovan as a medic patched gauze over his gunshot wound. He reached out his other hand to Beth and laid it on both of hers, which held their twins.

"I love you," he said.

"And I love you."

Chapter Twenty-Nine

Donovan sat in a cushioned rocking chair beside Beth's hospital bed. He held Ryan, and Beth held Reagan. They each had a tiny bottle of milk. For every feeding, they took turns holding one baby then the other so they could bond equally. He enjoyed this part. Listening to their milk-guzzling sounds, their sighs and deep breaths, and seeing their tiny lips suckle, it made him smile.

Staring down at his son, and seeing Beth holding their daughter, Donovan couldn't believe it. He had always been blessed having Beth in his life. Now he was triple blessed, thanks to their twins. Such new lives. Such great love.

After the milk lured the twins into a peaceful sleep, they set them side-by-side in their single hospital bassinette. Donovan, wearing a sling on his left arm, stretched out on the hospital bed beside Beth. She turned on her side and reached across him to set her hand on his left shoulder. "We have matching scars now." With her other hand, she tapped her own left shoulder where she had a round scar from a bullet.

"And twins," Donovan said.

She chuckled and looked toward the bassinette. "We definitely have twins."

Lying side by side, Donovan played with Beth's fingers, interlocking them and sliding his fingers between hers. "I thank God for the three of you. This day could be very different." He could be mourning the three of them. Or his mom and grandma could be grieving the four of them. Thankfully, they survived. They had each other, and they had their love.

"I have a feeling…" Beth paused.

He peered at her. "A good feeling or a bad feeling?"

"Good. Great, in fact." She shifted so she could gaze into his eyes. "I have a feeling that everything we've gone through up until now has finally come to an end. Like…with the birth of our babies, the tide has turned in our favor. Anyone who has ever threatened us is officially gone. The part of our lives plagued by disasters and crimes has come to an end. Now we're starting another."

"That sounds good to me." He pressed a kiss to her lips.

Donovan's cell phone buzzed on the bedside table. He picked it up with his good arm. "It's a video call from Thorn. Do you want to answer it?"

"Yeah. He spent several days being frantic down in Florida. Besides, we have some news for him." She gave him a wink.

Donovan answered the call and held his phone up to his face. "Hey, Thorn."

On the screen, Thorn nodded. "Hey, Goldwyn. I'm glad you're okay."

"Thanks. And thank you for everything you did."

Without words, with a mere glance, Thorn knew what he meant. Thanks for working through the holidays. Thanks for not giving up. Thanks for tracking Craig and discovering the flight he booked to Michigan under the name Craig Goldwyn. Thanks for sending cops and medics. Thanks for always having their backs.

"You're welcome."

"Do you want to talk to Beth?"

Thorn squirmed. "Uh. Is she sleeping?"

"No."

"Breastfeeding?"

Donovan squinted his eyes. "No."

Relief flashed across Thorn's face. "Okay. Good. Yeah."

Donovan passed his phone to Beth. She smiled. "Hey, Thorn."

"Hey, Beth. Motherhood looks good on you."

"Thank you. Donovan and I want to ask you something."

"Shoot."

"We'd like you to be godfather."

Thorn stared at her a moment, not saying a word. He blinked. "Really?"

"Who else?" Her smile grew. "You've been there for us all these years. You're the person we would trust to take care of our children if we're not here anymore. Not that we're planning on not being here." She peered at Donovan over the top of the cell phone. "All you have to do is be an uncle. Pass on your wisdom. Bond."

Thorn nodded. "I can do that."

"That's great. And I have someone to introduce you to." She got out of bed and went to the bassinette. Donovan joined her. He didn't want to miss this.

Standing before the bassinette, she hovered the phone over Ryan, wrapped up in a pale blue blanket, with a blue cap on his head and little mittens on his hands to keep him from scratching his face. She switched the camera view, so instead of showing her, it showed Ryan.

"Thorn, meet Ryan."

"Wow," Thorn said. "You had a boy. That's cool." He paused. "Although it would've been cool if you've had a girl. Don't get me wrong."

Beth peeked over her shoulder at Donovan. She was holding back a laugh. Donovan put his arms around her waist and put his chin on her shoulder.

When Beth moved the camera to the side to show Reagan, Thorn blinked a few times. "Wait. Hold on." He scratched his head. "A second ago, the baby was in blue. Then I blinked. And now the baby is in pink. Did you name a girl Ryan? I mean, you could, but…I'm really confused."

Beth giggled. "Thorn, this is Reagan."

"Huh?" Thorn's face went blank.

Beth raised the phone so the camera caught the twins sleeping side by side.

"Holy shit." Thorn covered his mouth. "Sorry," he whispered. And then he went on staring, with wide eyes and his hand over his mouth.

Donovan chuckled. "You okay there, Thorn?"

"You…you…you had twins?"

"Yup." Beth flipped the camera and held up the phone to show her and Donovan's faces. "We had twins."

Although Thorn still appeared shocked, inklings of happiness were beginning to show. "And I repeat…holy shit." He gave a little laugh and a smile. "Congratulations."

"Thank you," they said together.

Donovan leaned closer to the screen. "Do you still

want to be their godfather?"

"Hell yeah."

Epilogue

The flight home took hours, but Beth didn't mind. She had her man at her side, and at least one of her twins in her arms at all times. Looking back on her life, while staring at the sweet faces of her twins, she couldn't believe there was a time when she doubted her motherhood, when she didn't think she had the mothering gene.

After getting married to Donovan, she ended up wanting to have kids, to have a little piece of her and a little piece of Donovan forming as one in a way that neither of them could physically do. She dreamt about what their children would look like, be like, and she had wondered what it would feel like to see her children and know their love created that, know that their children carried parts of them, know that, even when they were gone from this world, they would continue to live on in their children, and in their children's children. Forever. And ever.

These thoughts had scared her at first. How could they not? They were so much bigger than her. So much bigger than her and Donovan.

During their struggle to get pregnant, Beth started to doubt that dream. It wasn't in her cards. That tsunami had guaranteed it. Those bad guys had made sure of it.

Thankfully, she had been wrong. The universe granted her wish in a way that she had never deemed possible. Twins. A boy and a girl. Ryan and Reagan.

Two precious gifts, more than she ever thought she'd be given.

She bent her neck to press a kiss to Ryan's forehead. Then she leaned over to kiss Reagan's forehead, who snoozed in Donovan's arms. She couldn't believe the miracles they held—miracles of a lifetime. Her heart was fuller than she ever thought possible. She didn't know if it could handle anymore happiness, anymore love.

The twins slept through most of the flight and the car ride home, the perfect babies, which most likely meant they'd be rambunctious toddlers, but she and Donovan could handle it. If they could handle all the disasters that had come their way, they could take on the Terrible Twos and Horrible Threes like bosses.

When they pulled on to the driveway, Beth sighed in relief upon seeing their house. It was good to be home. She didn't want to leave it for a long time. She planned to nest with her babies, in her happiness, for as long as she could.

Beth picked up Ryan from the car seat, and Donovan picked up Reagan. They carried the bundles in their arms and into the house where they would raise them. In the center of their home, they faced each other. Everything they ever wanted was inside that house at that moment—one another, their babies, and their love. Beth's heart was full to the brim, and part of her heart was in her arms. The other parts were in front of her.

She gazed into Donovan's eyes. "I love you."

"I love you," he said back.

In his arms, Reagan squirmed. He chuckled and peered down at their daughter.

Beth stepped up to him, so the twins were next to

each other.

"Welcome home, Reagan," Donovan said.

Beth stared lovingly at her daughter's precious face. Then she smiled at their baby boy.

"Welcome home, Ryan."

A word about the author...

Chrys Fey is the award-winning author of *Hurricane Crimes,* Book One of the Disaster Crimes series, a unique concept blending romance, crimes, and disasters. She's partnered with the Insecure Writer's Support Group, running their Goodreads book club. She's also an editor for Dancing Lemur Press.

Fey lives in Florida and is always on the lookout for hurricanes.

Get *The Crime Before the Storm*, Donovan's FREE short story and prequel to *Hurricane Crimes*, by signing up for Chrys Fey's newsletter at:

http://bit.ly/2UlZjU0

Thank you for purchasing
this publication of The Wild Rose Press, Inc.

For questions or more information
contact us at
info@thewildrosepress.com.

The Wild Rose Press, Inc.
www.thewildrosepress.com